**Albert Edwa**

# A Man's World

# Albert Edwards

# A Man's World

1st Edition | ISBN: 978-3-75233-949-9

Place of Publication: Frankfurt am Main, Germany

Year of Publication: 2020

Outlook Verlag GmbH, Germany.

# A MAN'S WORLD

BY

ALBERT EDWARDS

# BOOK I

## I

All books should have a preface, to tell what they are about and why they were written.

This one is about myself—Arnold Whitman.

I have sought in vain for a title which would be truly descriptive of the subject and form of my book. It is not a "Journal" nor a "Diary" for these words signify a daily noting down of events. Neither "Memoirs" nor "Recollections" meet the case, for much which I have written might better be called "Meditations." It certainly is not a "Novel," for that term implies a traditional "literary form," a beginning, development and end. I am quite sure that my beginning goes back to the primordial day when dead matter first organized itself—or was organized—into a living cell. And whether or not I will ever "end" is an open question. There is no "unity" in the form of my narrative except the frame of mind which led me to write it, which has held me to task till now.

It is the story of how I, born at the close of The Great War, lived and of the things—common-place and unusual—which happened to me, how they felt at the time and how I feel about them now.

"Autobiography" is the term which most truly describes what I have tried to do. But that word is associated with the idea of great men. The fact that I am not "great" has been my main incentive in writing. We have text books a plenty on how to become Emperor, at least they tell how a man named Napoleon did it. There are endless volumes to which you may refer if you wish to become President of these United States—or rival the career of Captain Kidd. But such ambitions are rare among boys over eighteen.

Even before that age I began to wish for a book like the one I have tried to write. I wanted to know how ordinary people lived. It was no help in those days to read how this Cæsar or that came and saw and conquered. I shared the ambitions of the boys about me. To be sure there were day-dreaming moments when we planned to explore Central Africa or found dynasties. But this was pure make-believe. We knew that not one man in thousands wins fame. For each moment we dreamed of greatness there were days on end when we looked out questioningly on the real world. We got no answers from our teachers. Most of the boys who were in school with me are today running a store, practicing law or medicine. They were prepared for it by reading Plutarch in class and Nick Carter on the sly.

As a youth I wanted of course to gain a comfortable living. I wanted mildly to win some measure of distinction, but all this was subordinate to a more definite desire to be a man, and not to be ashamed. A book about the ordinary life I was to enter, would have been a God-send to me.

This then is to be the story of my life as it appears to me now, and how, in the face of the things which happened to me, I tried to be decent.

I have only two apologies to offer. All the rest of my writing has been scientific—on the subject of criminology. I am unpracticed in narration. And I have been enough in courts to realize the difference between "evidence" and "truth." At best I can only give "evidence." Others who knew me would tell of my life differently, perhaps more truly. But it will be as near truth as I can make it.

And now to my story.

## II

My earliest distinct memory is of an undeserved flogging. But from this grew my conception of Justice. It was, I think, my first abstract idea.

My parents died long before I can remember and I was brought up in the home of the Rev. Josiah Drake, a Cumberland Presbyterian minister of the Tennessee Mountains. He was my uncle, but I always called him "the Father." He was the big fact of my childhood and my memory holds a more vivid picture of him than of any person I have known since.

He was very tall, but stooped heavily. If he had shaved he would have resembled Lincoln, and this, I suppose, is why he wore so long and full a beard. For he was a Southerner and hated the Northern leader with all the bitterness of the defeated. And yet he was a Christian. I have never known one who served his God more earnestly, more devotedly. He was a scholar of the old type. He knew his Latin and Greek and Hebrew. And as those were rare accomplishments among the mountain clergy of Tennessee it gave him a great prestige. In all but name he was the Bishop of the country-side. His faith was that of Pym and Knox and Jonathan Edwards, a militant Puritan, fearless before the world, abject in humility before his God.

Of his wife, my aunt Martha, I have scarcely a memory. When I was very young she must have been important to me, but as I grew to boyhood she faded into indistinct haziness. I recall most clearly how she looked at church, not so much her face as her clothes. In all those years she must have had some new ones, but if so, they were always of the same stuff and pattern as the old. Sharpest of all I remember the ridges the bones of her corset made in the back of her dress as she leaned forward, resting her forehead on the pew in front of us, during the "long prayer." There was always a flush on her face when it was over. I think her clothing cramped her somehow.

I have also a picture of her heated, flurried look over the kitchen stove when she was engaged in the annual ordeal of "putting up" preserves. Even when making apple-butter she maintained a certain formality. The one time when she would lapse from her dignity was when one of the negroes would rush into the kitchen with the news that a buggy was turning into our yard. The sudden scurry, the dash into her bedroom, the speed with which the hot

4

faced woman of the kitchen would transform herself into a composed minister's wife in black silk, was the chief wonder of my childhood. It was very rarely that the guests reached the parlor before her.

All of her children had died in infancy except Oliver. As the Father's religion frowned on earthly love, she idealized him in secret. I think she tried to do her Christian duty towards me, but it was decidedly perfunctory. She was very busy with the big house to keep in order, endless church work and the burden of preserving the appearances her husband's position demanded.

There was a large lawn before the house down to a picket fence. Mowing the grass and whitewashing that fence were the bitterest chores of my childhood. The main street of the village was so little used for traffic that once or twice every summer it was necessary to cut down the tall grass and weeds. Next to our house was the church, it was an unattractive box. I remember that once in a long while it was painted, but the spire was never completed above the belfry. There was a straggling line of houses on each side of the street and two stores. Beyond the Episcopal Church, the road turned sharply to the right and slipped precipitously down into the valley. Far below us was the county seat. About five hundred people lived there, and the place boasted of six stores and a railroad station.

That was its greatest charm to my schoolmates. From any of the fields, on the hill-side beyond the village, we could look down and watch the two daily trains as they made a wide sweep up into this forgotten country. There was one lad whom I remember with envy. His father was carter for our community and sometimes he took his son down with him. They slept in the great covered wagon in the square before the county court house, and came back the next day. The boy's name was Stonewall Jackson Clarke. He lorded it over the rest of us because he had seen a locomotive at close quarters. And he used to tell us that the court house was bigger than our two churches "with Blake's store on top."

I think that as a boy I knew the names of one or two stations on each side of the county seat. But it never occurred to me that the trains down there could take you to the cities and countries I studied about in my geography. Beyond the valley were Missionary Ridge and Lookout Mountain. But none of the boys I played with realized that the world beyond the mountains was anything like the country we could see. It would have surprised us if the teacher had pointed out to us on the school map the spot where our village stood. The land over which Cinderella's Prince ruled was just as real to us as New York State or the countries of Europe, the names of whose capitals we learned by rote.

My cousin Oliver I disliked. As a youngster I did not know why. But now I can see that he had a craven streak in him, a taint of sneakiness, an inability to be bravely sincere. It was through him that I got my lesson in justice.

He was then about sixteen and I eight. His hobby at the time was carpentry and, as I was supposed to dull his tools if I touched them, I was forbidden to play in the part of the barn where he had his bench. He was going to make an overnight visit to some friends in a neighboring township and at breakfast—he was to start about noon—he asked the Father to reiterate the prohibition. A few hours later I found Oliver smoking a corn-silk cigarette behind the barn. He begged me not "to tell on him." Nothing had been further from my mind. As a bribe for my silence he said I might play with his tools. The spirit of his offer angered me—but I accepted it.

After he had left the Father found me at his bench.

"Ollie said I could," I explained.

"At breakfast," the Father replied, "he distinctly said you could not."

But I stuck to it. The Father had every reason to believe I was lying. It was not in Oliver's nature to be kind to me without reason. And I could not, in honor, explain the reason. The Father was not the kind to spoil his children by sparing the rod, and there was no crime in his code more heinous than falsehood. He tried to flog me into a confession.

There was nothing very tragic to me in being whipped. All the boys I

6

knew were punished so. I had never given the matter any thought. As I would not admit that I had lied, this was the worst beating I ever received. He stopped at last from lack of breath and sent me to bed.

"Oliver will be back to-morrow," he said. "It is no use persisting in your lie. You will be found out. And if you have not confessed...." The threat was left open.

I remember tossing about in bed and wishing that I had lied and taken a whipping for disobedience. It would not have been so bad and would have been over at once. The next morning I sat sullenly in my room waiting for Oliver's return, wondering if he would tell the truth. I was not at all confident. Towards noon, the blackboard turned in at the gate, one of the negroes took the horse and I heard the Father call Oliver into his study.

Then suddenly a door slammed and I heard the Father's step on the stair. He was running. He burst into my room and before I knew what was happening, he had picked me up in his arms. And, wonder of wonders, he was crying. I had never before seen a grown man cry. He was asking me, I could not understand what he meant, but he was asking me to forgive him. Then I heard the Mother's voice at the door.

"What is the matter, Josiah?"

"Oh, Martha. It's horrible! I caned the lad for a lie and he was telling the Truth! Oh, my son, my son, forgive me."

At first all I realized was that I was not to be whipped any more. But all day long the Father kept me close to him and gradually from his talk I began vaguely to understand that there was such a thing as justice. I had always supposed that punishments were a matter of the parents' good pleasure. That it had any relation to cause and effect, that sometimes a father might be right and sometimes wrong in beating a child, had never occurred to me.

It is interesting how such things take form in a child's mind. The Father bought me a set of tools like Oliver's as a peace offering, and of course I was much more interested in them than in any abstract conception of justice. Yet

7

in some gradual, subconscious way, the idea arranged itself in my mind. I began to judge everything by it. I suppose it marked the end of babyhood, the first faint beginning of manhood.

## III

It Is not surprising that, in that austere home, my first fundamental idea should have been of justice rather than of love.

There may have been a time when the affection between the Father and Mother had an outward showing. I would like to think that they had tasted gayer, honey-mooning days. I doubt it. They were helpmates rather than lovers. The Mother was well named Martha, busy with much serving. Her work had dovetailed into his. It would be juster to say her work was his. Their all-absorbing business was the winning of souls to Christ, and anything of only human interest seemed to them of the earth, earthy. I never saw anything like a quarrel between them, nor any passage of affection—except that the Father kissed her when going on a journey or returning.

It is hard for me to understand such people. Everything which has given me solace in life, all the pleasures of literature and art, all the real as well as the written poems, they had rigorously cut off.

Oliver and I kissed the Mother when we went to bed. I never remember kissing the Father. Yet he loved me. Sometimes I think he loved me more than his own son. I doubt if I was often separated from his thoughts, ever from his prayers.

But all I knew as a boy about the affections, which expresses itself openly, was from Mary Button, my Sunday school teacher. She was brimming over with the joy of living and in every way the opposite of the austerity I knew at home. She was altogether wonderful to me. When the Mother was away at Synodical meetings, Mary used often to come for a whole day to keep the house in order. It was strange and typical to hear her sing rollicking college songs at our parlor organ—a wheezy contraption which seemed entirely dedicated to Moody and Sankey.

All through my childhood Mary passed as a celestial dream, a princess from some beautiful land of laughter and kisses.

When I was about nine, and she I suppose near nineteen, Prof. Everett, who had been with her brother in college, began to visit the village. I disliked him at once with an instinctive jealousy. He has since won a large renown as a geologist, and was no doubt an estimable man, but if I should meet him now, after all these years, I am sure the old grudge would come to life and make me hate him. After a few months he married her and took her away to a nearby college town.

About a year later, when the ache of her absence was beginning to heal, and, boy-like, I was in danger of forgetting her, a photograph came of her and the baby. It was such a loving picture! She looked so radiantly happy! It was set up on the mantel-piece in the parlor, and seemed to illuminate that sombre room. I remember exactly how it leaned up against the bronze clock, between the plaster busts of Milton and Homer. In those days I supposed one had to be blind to be a poet. The picture kept her memory alive for me.

Some months later Mary wrote that her husband was going away to attend a convention and she asked that I might come to bear her company for the week.

The excitement of that first sortie out into the world is the most vivid thing which comes to me from my childhood. The Father drove me down the mountain-side to the county seat and so at last I saw a train at close quarters. Even when I had watched them through the Father's campaign glasses I had not realized how large they were. He gave me in charge of the conductor, a man with an armless sleeve and drooping moustaches, who had been a corporal in his regiment.

There was a rattle and jerk—we had no air-brakes on the Tennessee trains in those days—and the railroad station and the Father slipped out of sight. Such an amazing number of things went by the car window! I counted all the fields to the next station. There were thirty-seven. The conductor told me I was not to get off till the eighteenth stop. I started in valiantly to count them all, but my attention was distracted by the fact that things near the track went by so much faster than things far away. In "physics A" at college I learned an explanation of this phenomena which seemed all right on paper but even today it is entirely inadequate when I am in a train and actually watching the earth revolve about distant points in either horizon. Trying to find a reason for it on that first railroad trip put me to sleep. At last the conductor woke me up and handed me over to Mary.

I can recall only vaguely the details of that delectable week, the strangeness of the entire experience is what sticks in my memory. There was the baby, so soft and round and contented. There was the German nurse, the first white servant I had ever seen. And there were the armchairs in the living-room, curved and comfortable and very different from the chairs in the parlor at home. After supper, instead of sending me off to bed, Mary read to me before the open fire, read me the wonderful stories of King Arthur. When at last I was sleepy, she came with me to my room. It embarrassed me to undress before her, but it was very sweet to have her tuck me in and kiss me "goodnight."

Mary "spoiled" me, to use the Father's expression, systematically, she let me eat between meals and gorged me with sweets. One night it made me sick. I have forgotten whether "dough-nuts" or "pop-overs" were to blame. When the doctor had gone away, laughing—for it was not serious—Mary took me into her own bed. I would gladly have suffered ten times the pain for the warm comfort of her arms about me.

It was during this visit that all the side of life we call Art began to appeal to me. The King Arthur legends were my introduction to literature, Malory and Tennyson's "Idylls" were the first written stories or poems I ever enjoyed.

And I think my first impression of Beauty, was the sight of Mary nursing the baby. I am sure she did not realize with what wondering eyes I watched her. I was only a little shaver and she could not have guessed what a novel sight it was for me. At home, everything human, which could not be suppressed, was studiously hidden. I think some of the old Madonnas in which the Mother is suckling the Child would have seemed blasphemous to the Father. Art has always seemed to me at its highest when occupied with some such simple human thing.

# IV

I had two playmates in those days, Margaret and Albert Jennings. Their father had been on "Stonewall" Jackson's staff. "Al" was my own age, but seemed older and Margot was a year younger. Until I went away to school we were almost inseparable. Only in affairs of the church were we apart, for they were Episcopalians.

Our biggest common interest was a "Chicken Company." We had built an elaborate run in the back yard of the parsonage and sometimes had as many as thirty hens. This enterprise led us into the great sin of our childhood —stealing.

Why I stole I cannot explain. I never pretended to justify it. We would sell a dozen eggs to my household and then take as many out of the pantry as were necessary to complete a dozen for Mrs. Jennings. We did this off and on for four or five years. When the hens laid freely we did not have to. But if there were not eggs to satisfy the demands of the two families, we stole. I think we blamed it on the chickens. Al and I were always full of great projects for improving the stock or the run and so needed money. There was little danger of discovery, because housekeeping was a very unexact science in our southern homes. And just because the chickens refused to lay as they should, seemed a very trivial reason for sacrificing our plans. But we did not like to do it. We always searched the nests two or three times in the hope of finding the eggs we needed.

Al was a queer chap. I remember one time we were two eggs short.

"We'll have to steal them from your mother," I said.

"You may be a thief," he retorted angrily, as we started after the spoils. "But I intend to pay it back. It's just a loan."

There was a weak subterfuge to the effect that Margot knew nothing of our dishonesty. The three of us had decided upon this in open council, to protect her in case we were caught. If there were to be any whippings, it was for the masculine members of the firm to take them. But Margot knew, just as well as we did, how many eggs were laid and how far our sales exceeded that number. But the candy she bought did not seem to trouble her conscience any more than it did her digestion. I have met no end of older women, in perfectly good church standing, who are no more squeamish about how their men folk gain their income.

There was another very feminine trait about Margot. We divided our profits equally, in three parts. Al and I always put most of our share back into the business. Margot spent hers on candy. Al used to object to this arrangement sometimes, but I always stood up for her.

This was because I expected to marry her. I do not remember when it was first suggested, but it was an accepted thing between us. Col. Jennings used laughingly to encourage us in it. I spoke of it once at home, but the Father shook his head and said it would grieve him if I married outside of our denomination. The Baptists were his special aversion, but next to them he objected to Episcopalians, whom he felt to be tainted with popery.

This led to a quarrel with Margot. I told her flatly that I would not marry her, unless she became a Presbyterian. She was a little snob and, as the most considerable people of the county belonged to her church, she preferred to give me up rather than slip down in the social scale. For several days we did not speak to each other. I refused to let any misguided Episcopalians in my yard. As the chicken run was in my domain, Al, who was smaller than I, became an apostate. But Margot held out stubbornly, until her mother intervened and told us, with great good sense, that we were much too young to know the difference between one sect and another, that we had best suspend hostilities until we knew what we were fighting about. So peace was restored.

This calf-love of mine was strangely cold. Some of the boys and girls in school used to "spoon." But "holding hands" and so forth seemed utterly inane to me. I do not know what Margot felt about it, but I no more thought of kissing her than her brother. The best thing about her was that she also loved King Arthur. Mary had given me a copy of Malory. Up in our hay-loft, Margot and I used to take turns reading it aloud and acting it. Only once in a long while could we persuade Al to join us in these childish dramatics. I was generally Launcelot. Sometimes she would be Elaine, but I think she loved best to be the Queen.

At fourteen I discovered Froissart's Chronicles in the Father's library. It had a forbidding cover and I might never have unearthed it, if he had not set me to work dusting his books in punishment for some minor delinquency. On the bottom shelf there were three big lexicons, Latin, Greek, and Hebrew. Next to them was the great family Bible. Then came Cruden's Concordance, a geography of Palestine, "The Decline and Fall of the Roman Empire," Motley's "Dutch Republic"—and Froissart! As I was dusting it gloomily, it slipped from my hands and fell open to an old engraving of the Murder of Richard II. There were twenty-four plates in that volume. Never did boy enter into such a paradise.

I can only guess what the Father would have thought of my filling my mind with such lore. I took no chances in the matter. With great pains, I arranged the books so that the absence of Froissart would not be noticed. Until I went East to school at sixteen, it reposed in the bottom of the bran bin in the loft, and when at last I went, I gave it to Margot as my choicest treasure.

When I saw her ten years ago, she showed me the old book. The sight of it threw us both under constraint, bringing back those old days when we had planned to marry. The funeral of a dream always seem sadder to me than the death of a person.

Permanent camp meetings, the things which grew into the Chautauqua movement, were just beginning their popularity. One had been started a few score miles from our village and the year I went away to school, the Father had been made director. We left home early in the summer, and I was to go East without coming back.

On the eve of my departure, I went to see Margot. It was my first formal call and, in my new long trousers, I was much embarrassed. For an hour or so we sat stiffly, repeating every ten minutes a promise to write to each other. I remember we figured out that it would take me ten years to finish the Theological Seminary and be ready to marry her. It was ordained that I was to study for the ministry. No other career had ever been suggested to me.

The constraint wore off when I asked her for a photograph to take with me to school. From some instinct of coquetry she pretended not to want me to have one. Boys at school, she said, had their walls covered with pictures of girls, she would not think of letting hers be put up with a hundred others. When I solemnly promised not to have any picture but hers, she said she had no good one. There was one on the mantel, and I grabbed it in spite of her protest.

She was a bit of a tomboy and a hoydenish scuffle followed. In the scramble my hand fell accidentally on her breast. It sent a dazzling thrill through me. The vision came to me of Mary nursing the baby and the beauty of her white breast. The idea connected itself with Margot, struggling in my arms. I knew nothing of the mystery of life. I cannot tell what I felt—it was very vague—but I knew some new thing had come to me.

Margot noticed the change. I suppose I stopped the struggle with her.

"What's the matter?" she asked.

"Nothing."

But I went off and sat down apart.

"What's the matter?" she insisted, coming over and standing in front of me. "Did I hurt you?"

"No," I said. "But we mustn't wrestle like that. We aren't children any more."

She threw up her head and began to make fun of me and my new long trousers. But I interrupted her.

"Margot! Margot! Don't you understand?"

I took hold of her hands and pulled her down beside me and kissed her. It was the first time. I am sure she did not understand what I meant—I was not clear about it myself. But she fell suddenly silent. And while I sat there with my arm about her, I saw a vision of Mary's home and the warm joy of it. Margot and I would have a home like that; not like the Father's.

I was under the spell of some dizzying emotion which none of our grown up words will fit. The emotion, I suppose, comes but once, and is too fleeting to have won a place in adult dictionaries. It was painful and awesome, but as I walked home I was very happy.

# V

Of course I never questioned the Father's religious dogmas. I did not even know that they might be questioned. But two things troubled me persistently.

I had been taught that our Saviour was the Prince of Peace, that His chief commandment was the law of love. But when adults got together there was always talk of the war. I do not think there was any elder or deacon in our church who had not served. How often I listened to stories of the wave of murder and rapine that had swept through our mountains only a few years before!

I remember especially the placing of a battle monument just outside our village and the horde of strangers who came from various parts of the state for the ceremony. The heroes were five men in gray uniforms, all who were left of the company which had stood there and had been shot to pieces. One was an old man, three were middle aged, and one was so young that he could not have been more than sixteen on the day of the fight. The man who had been their captain stayed at the parsonage. After supper the principal men of the village gathered in our parlor. I stood by the Father's chair and listened wide-eyed as, in his cracked voice, the Captain told us all the details of that slaughter. I remember that in the excitement of his story-telling the old soldier became profane, and the Father did not rebuke him.

Somehow I could not feel any romance in modern warfare, there seemed no similarity between these men and the chivalric heroes of The Round Table. Perhaps if Launcelot had been a real person, there in the parsonage parlor, and had told me face to face and vividly how he had slain the false knight Gawaine, had made me see the smear of blood on his sword blade, the cloven headed corpse of his enemy, that also they might have seemed abhorrent.

As a little boy I could not understand how a follower of Jesus could be a soldier. I did not know that grown men were also asking the same question. Years afterwards I remember coming across Rossetti's biting sonnet—"Vox ecclesiæ, vox Christi"—

"O'er weapons blessed for carnage, to fierce youth

From evil age, the word has hissed along:—

Ye are the Lord's: go forth, destroy, be strong:

Christ's Church absolves ye from Christ's law of ruth."

I do not know what the Father would have thought of those words, for, like some of the Roundhead leaders of Cromwell's time, he had been Chaplain as well as Captain of his company. If the war had broken out again, as the "Irreconcilables" believed it surely would, and if Oliver had refused to enlist on the ground that he was studying for Christ's ministry, I think the Father would have cursed him.

The other thing which worried me was a "gospel hymn," which we sang almost every Sunday. It had a swinging tune, but the words were horrible.

> There is a fountain filled with blood,
>
> Drawn from Emanuel's veins;
>
> And sinners plunged beneath that flood
>
> Lose all their guilty stains.

Such a gory means of salvation seemed much more frightful to my childish imagination than the most sulphurous hell.

These things I was told I would understand when I grew up. This was the answer to so many questions, that I got out of the habit of asking them. I believed that the Father was very wise and was willing to take his word for everything.

At eleven he persuaded me "to make a profession of faith" and join the church. It is only within these latter, mellower years that I can look back on this incident without bitterness. It was so utterly unfair. The only thing I was made to understand was that I was taking very serious and irrevocable vows. This was impressed on me in every way. I was given a brand new outfit of clothes. I had never had new underwear and new shoes simultaneously with a new suit and hat before. Such things catch a child's imagination. I had to stand up before the whole congregation and reply to un-understandable questions with answers I had learned by rote. Then for the first time I was given a share of the communion bread and wine. The solemnity of the occasion was emphasized. But there was no effort—at least no successful one —to make me understand what it was all about. When I became old enough to begin to think of such things, I found that I had already sworn to believe the same things as long as I lived. Try as hard as I can to remember the many kindnesses of my adoptive parents, realizing, as I surely do, how earnestly and prayerfully they strove to do the best for me, this folly remains my sharpest recollection of them. It was horribly unfair to a youngster who took his word seriously.

But I never had what is called a "religious experience" until that summer in camp meeting when I was sixteen.

In after years, I have learned that the older and richer sects have developed more elaborate and artistic stage-settings for their mysteries. I cannot nowadays attend a service of the Paulist Fathers, or at Saint Mary the Virgin's without feeling the intoxication of the heavy incense and the wonderful beauty of the music. But for a boy, and for the simple mountain folk who gathered there, that camp was sufficiently impressive.

It stood on the edge of a mirror lake, under the shadow of Lookout Mountain, in one of the most beautiful corners of Tennessee. Stately pines crowded close about the clearing and beyond the lake the hill dropped away, leaving a sweeping view out across the valley. Man seemed a very small creature beneath those giant trees, in the face of the great distances to the range of mountains beyond the valley. There was nothing about the camp to recall one's daily life. The thousand and one things which insistently distract one's attention from religion had been excluded.

Every care had been taken to make the camp contrast with, and win people from, "The Springs,"—a fashionable and worldly resort nearby. There was no card playing nor dancing, as such things were supposed to offend the Deity. The stage to the railroad station did not run on Sunday.

After breakfast every day the great family—a hundred people or more—gathered by the lake-side and the Father led in prayer. During the morning there were study courses, most of which were Bible classes. I only remember two which were secular. One was on Literature and the King James Version was taken as a model of English prose. No mention was made of the fact that much of the original had been poetry. There was also a course on "Science." A professor of Exigesis from a neighboring Theological Seminary delivered a venomous polemic against Darwin. The "Nebular Hypothesis" was demolished with many convincing gestures.

My little love affair with Margot had put me in a state of exaltation. Other things conspired to make me especially susceptible to religious suggestion. Oliver was back from his second year in the seminary. My dislike for him was forgotten. He seemed very eloquent to me in the young people's meetings, which he conducted.

Mary was there with her three children and had taken for the summer the cottage at one end of the semi-circle overlooking the lake. Her husband, Prof. Everett, had been away for several months on the geological expedition to Alaska, which was, I believe, the foundation of the eminence he now holds in that science. Mary also had been caught up in the religious fervor of the place. To me she seemed wonderfully spiritualized and beautiful beyond words. Oliver and I used often to walk home with her after the evening meetings and, sitting out on her porch over the water, talk of religion.

Sundays were continuous revival meetings. Famous fishers-of-souls came every week. All methods from the most spiritual to the coarsest were used to wean us from our sins. It was "Salvation" Milton, who landed me.

He was the star attraction of the summer's program. He stayed in the camp two weeks, fourteen days of tense emotion, bordering on hysteria. To many people "Salvation" Milton has seemed a very Apostle. His message has come to them as holy words from the oracle of the Most High. To such it may, I fear, seem blasphemous for me—a criminologist—to write of him as a specimen of pathology. But I have met many who were very like him in our criminal courts.

I have no doubt of his sincerity—up to the limit of his poor distorted brain. He had moments of exaltation when he thought that he talked face to face with God. He believed intensely in his mission. He had lesser moments, which he regretted as bitterly as did his friends who, like the sons of Noah, covered him with a sheet that his drunken nakedness might not be seen by men. He was pitifully unbalanced. But I think that if he had been given the strength of will to choose, he would have always been the ardent servant of God we saw in him at the camp meeting.

He was a master of his craft. By meditation and fasting and prayer he could whip himself into an emotional state when passionate eloquence flowed from his lips with almost irresistible conviction. He was also adept at the less venerable tricks of his trade.

It was his custom in the afternoon about four to walk apart in the woods and spend an hour or more on his knees. Once he took me with him. I remember the awe of sitting there on the pine needles, in the silence of the forest and watching him "wrestle with the Spirit." I tried to pray also, but I could not keep my mind on it so long. Suddenly he began to speak, asking Christ's intercession on my behalf. And walking home, he talked to me about my soul. For the first time I was "overtaken by a conviction of sin." That night he preached on the Wages of Sin.

I will never forget the horror of fear which held me through that service. Milton was in the habit of dealing with and overcoming men of mature mind. Such a lad as I was putty in his hands. When, out of the shivering terror of it, came the loud-shouted promise of salvation, immunity from all he had made me feel my just deserts, I stumbled abjectly up the aisle and took my place among the "Seekers." I must say he had comfort ready for us. I remember he put his arm over my shoulder and told me not to tremble, not to be afraid. God was mighty to save. Long before the world was made He had builded a mansion for me in the skies. He would wash away all my sins in the blood of the Lamb. Milton had scared me into a willingness to wade through an ocean filled with blood if safety lay beyond.

The next morning brought me peace. I suppose my overstrained nerves had come to the limit of endurance. I thought it was the promised "peace which passeth all understanding." I was sure of my salvation. Several weeks of spiritual exaltation followed. I read the Bible passionately, sometimes alone, more often with Oliver or Mary, for it was the fashion to worship in common. Whenever the opportunity offered in the meetings, I made "public testimony."

But I would have found it hard to define my faith. I had been badly frightened and had recovered. This, I thought, came from God. I had only a crude idea of the Deity. In general, I thought of Him as very like the Father, with white hair and a great beard. I thought of Him as intimately interested in all I did and thought, jotting it all down in the tablets of judgment—a bookkeeper who never slumbered. I was not at all clear on the Trinity. These mountain Presbyterians were Old Testament Christians. The Christ had a minor role in their Passion Play. They talked a good deal of the Holy Ghost, but God, the Father, the King of Kings, the jealous Jehovah of Israel was their principal deity. We were supposed to love Him, but in reality we all feared Him. However, I was very proud in the conviction that I was one of His elect.

Advancing years bring me a desire for a more subtle judgment on things than the crude verdict of "right" or "wrong." I look back on my religious training, try to restrain the tears and sneers and think of it calmly. I doubt if any children are irreligious. Some adults claim to be, but I think it means that they are thoughtless—or woefully discouraged. We live in the midst of mystery. We are born from it and when we die we enter it again. Anyone who thinks must have some attitude towards the Un-understandable—must have a religion. And loving parents inevitably will try to help their children to a clean and sweet emotional relation towards the unknown. Evidently it is not an easy undertaking. For the adults who surrounded me in my childhood, in spite of their earnest efforts, in spite of their prayers for guidance, instead of developing my religious life, distorted it horribly. They were sincerely anxious to lead me towards Heaven. I do not think it is putting it too strongly to say they were hounding me down the road which is paved with good intentions.

I can think of no more important task, than the development of a sane and healthy "course of religious education for children." The one supplied in our Sunday schools seems to me very far below the mark. It is a work which will require not only piety, but a deep knowledge of pedagogics.

Certainly the new and better regime will discourage precocious "professions of faith." I do not think it will insist that we are born in sin and born sinful. Above all it will take care not to make religion appear ugly or fearsome to childish imagination. Even the most orthodox Calvinists will learn—let us hope—to reserve "the fountain filled with blood" and the fires of Hell for adults. The Sunday school of the future will be held out in the fields, among the flowers, and the wonder of the child before this marvelous universe of ours will be cherished and led into devotion—into natural gratitude for the gift of the earth and the fulness thereof. Surely this is wiser than keeping the children indoors to learn the catechism. I can think of nothing which seems to me less of a religious ceremony than those occasions, when Bibles are given to all the Sunday school scholars who can recite the entire catechism. What have youngsters to do with such finespun metaphysics? Oh! the barren hours I wasted trying to get straight the differences between "Justification," "Sanctification," and "Adoption"—or was it "Redemption." One would suppose that Jesus had said "Suffer the little children, who know the catechism, to come unto me."

But, of course, at sixteen, I had no such ideas as these. I knew of no religious life except such as I saw about me. I had been carefully taught to believe that a retentive memory and a glib tongue were pleasing to the Most High. I was very contemptuous towards the children of my age who were less proficient.

# VI

In the midst of this peace a bolt fell which ended my religious life. Its lurid flame momentarily illumined the great world beyond my knowing. And the visioning of things for which I was unprepared was too much for me. I may not be scientifically correct, but it has always seemed to me that what I saw that July night stunned the section of my brain which has to do with "Acts of faith." Never since have I been able to believe, religiously, in anything.

It was a Sunday. At the vesper service, all of us seated on the grass at the edge of the lake, the Father had preached about our bodies being the temples of God. As usual, Oliver led the young people's meeting after supper. These more intimate gatherings meant more to me than the larger assemblies. Our text was "Blessed are the pure in heart." I remember clearly how Oliver looked, tall and stalwart and wonderful in his young manhood. He has a great metropolitan church now and he has won his way by oratory. The eloquence on which he was to build his career had already begun to show itself.

Mary sang. I have also a sharp picture of her. She wore a light lawn dress, which the brilliant moon-light turned almost white. Her years seemed to have fallen from her and she looked as she had done on her wedding night. In her rich, mellow contralto she sang the saddest of all church music: "He was despised."

Something delayed me after the service and when I looked about for Oliver and Mary they were gone. I went to her house but the maid said they had not come. The mystery of religious fervor and the glory of the night kept me from waiting on the verandah, called me out to wander down by the water's edge. But I wearied quickly of walking and, coming back towards the house, lay down on the grass under a great tree. The full moon splashed the country round with sketches of ghostly white and dense black shadows.

Two ideas were struggling in my mind. There was an insistent longing that Margot might be with me to share this wonder of religious experience. Conflicting with this desire, compelled, I suppose, by the evening's texts, was a strong push towards extreme asceticism. I was impatient for Oliver's return. I wanted to ask him why our church had abandoned monasticism.

How long I pondered over this I do not know. Perhaps I fell asleep, but at last I heard them coming back through the woods. There was something in Oliver's voice, which checked my impulse to jump up and greet them. It was something hot and hurried, something fierce and ominous. But as they came out into a patch of moonlight, although they fell suddenly silent, I knew they were not quarreling. Mary cautioned him with a gesture and went into the house. Through the open windows I heard her tell the negro maid that she might go home. I heard her say "Good night" and lock the back door. The girl hummed a lullaby as she walked away. All the while Oliver sat on the steps.

I do not know what held me silent, crouching there in the shadow. I had no idea of what was to come. But the paralyzing hand of premonition was laid upon me. I knew some evil was approaching, and I could not have spoken or moved.

"Oliver," she said, in a voice I did not know, as she came out on the porch, "you must go away. It is wrong. Dreadfully wrong."

But he jumped up and threw his arms about her.

"It's sin, Oliver," she said, "you're a minister."

"I'm a man," he said, fiercely.

Then they went into the house. It was not till years afterwards, when I read Ebber's book—"Homo Sum" that I realized, in the story of that priest struggling with his manhood, what the moment must have meant to Oliver.

I tiptoed across the grass to the shade of the house. A blind had been hurriedly pulled down—too hurriedly. A thin ribbon of light streamed out below it.

I could not now write down what I saw through that window, if I tried. But in the frame of mind of those days, with my ignorance of life, it meant the utter desecration of all holiness. Oliver and Mary had stood on my highest pedestal, a god and goddess. I saw them in the dust. No. It seemed the veriest mire.

I turned away at last to drown myself. It was near the water's edge that they picked me up unconscious some hours later. The doctors called it brain fever. Almost a month passed before I became rational again. I was amazed to find that in my delirium I had not babbled of what I had seen. Neither Oliver nor Mary suspected their part in my sickness. More revolting to me than what they had done was the hypocrisy with which they hid it.

Above all things I dreaded any kind of an explanation and I developed an hypocrisy as gross as theirs. I smothered my repugnance to Mary's kisses and pretended to like to have Oliver read the Bible to me. And when I was able to get about again, I attended meetings as before. There was black hatred in my heart and the communion bread nauseated me. What was left of the summer was only a longing for the day when I should leave for school. Nothing mattered except to escape from these associations.

I am not sure what caused it—the weeks of religious hysteria which accompanied my conversion, what I saw through the crack below the window curtain, or the fever—but some time between the coming of "Salvation" Milton and my recovery, that little speck of gray matter, that minute ganglia of nerve-cells, with which we *believe*, ceased to function.

# BOOK II

# I

Early in September Oliver took me East to school. It was not one of our widely advertised educational institutions. The Father had chosen it, I think, because it was called a Presbyterial Academy and the name assured its orthodoxy.

I remember standing on the railroad platform, after Oliver had made all the arrangements with the principal, waiting for the train to come which was to carry him out of my sight. How long the minutes lasted! It is a distressing thing for a boy of sixteen to hate anyone the way I hated my cousin. I was glad that he was not really my brother.

It is strange how life changes our standards. Now, when I think back over those days, I am profoundly sorry for him. It was, I think, his one love. It could have brought him very little joy for it must have seemed to him as heinous a sin as it did to me.

Five years later he married. I am sure he has been scrupulously faithful to his wife. She is a woman to be respected and her ambition has been a great stimulus to his upclimbing. But I doubt if he has really loved her as he must have loved Mary to break, as he did, all his morality for her. To him love must have seemed a thing of tragedy. But boyhood is stern. I had no pity for him.

His going lifted a great weight from me. As I walked back alone to the school, I wanted to shout. I was beginning a new life—my own. I had no very clear idea of what I was going to do with this new freedom of mine. I can only recall one plank in my platform—I was going to fight.

The one time I can remember fighting at home, I had been thrashed by the boy, caned by the school teacher and whipped by the Father, when he noticed my black eye. Fighting was strictly forbidden. After this triple beating I fell into the habit of being bullied. As even the smallest boy in our village knew I was afraid to defend myself, I was the victim of endless tyrannies. The first use I wanted to make of my new freedom was to change this. I resolved to resent the first encroachment.

It came that very day from one of the boys in the fourth class. I remember that his name was Blake. Just before supper we had it out on the tennis-court. It was hardly fair to him. He fought without much enthusiasm. It was to him part of the routine of keeping the new boys in order. To me it was the Great Emancipation. I threw into it all the bitterness of all the humiliations and indignities of my childhood. The ceremonial of "seconds" and "rounds" and "referee" was new to me. At home the boys just jumped at each other and punched and bit, and pulled hair and kicked until one said he had enough. As soon as they gave the word to begin, I shut my eyes and hammered away. We battered each other for several rounds and then Blake was pronounced victor on account of some technicality.

They told me, pityingly, that I did not know how to fight. But all I had wanted was to demonstrate that I was not afraid. I had won that. It was the only fight I had in school. Even the bullies did not care to try conclusions with me, and I had no desire to force trouble. I had won a respect in the little community which I had never enjoyed before.

In a way it was a small matter, but it was portentous for me. It was the first time I had done the forbidden thing and found it good. The Father had been wrong in prohibiting self-defense. It was an entering wedge to realize that his wisdom had been at fault here. In time his whole elaborate structure of morals fell to the ground.

The school was a religious one, of course. But the teachers, with eminent good sense, realized that other things were more important for growing boys than professions of faith. It seemed that, after my illness, my mind woke up in sections. The part which was to ponder over Mary and Oliver, which was to think out my relation to God, for a long time lay dormant. I puttered along at my Latin and Greek and Algebra, played football and skated and, with the warm weather, went in for baseball.

In the spring a shadow came over me—the idea of returning home. The more I thought of another summer in the camp, the more fearsome it seemed. At last I went to the doctor.

He was the first, as he was one of the most important, of the many people whose kindness and influence have illumined my life. He was physical director of the school and also had a small practice in the village. There were rumors that he drank and he never came to church. If there had been another doctor available, he would not have been employed by the school.

I never knew a man of more variable moods. Some days on the football field he would throw himself into the sport with amazing vim for an adult, would laugh and joke and call us by our first names. Again he would sit on the bench by the side-line scowling fiercely, taking no interest in us, muttering incoherently to himself. One day another boy and I were far "out of bounds" looking for chestnuts. We saw him coming through the trees and hid under some brush-wood. He had a gun under one arm, but was making too much noise for a hunter. He gesticulated wildly with his free arm and swore appallingly. We were paralyzed with fear. I do not think either of us told anyone about it. For in spite of his queer ways, all the boys, who were not sneaky nor boastful, liked him immensely.

One Saturday afternoon I found courage to go to his office. There were several farmers ahead of me. I had a long wait, and when at last my turn came I was mightily frightened.

"If I go home this summer," I blurted out, "I'll be sick again."

Oliver had told him about my illness. At first he laughed at me, but I insisted so doggedly that he began to take me seriously. He tried to make me tell him my troubles but I could not. Then he examined me carefully, tapping my knee for reflexes and doing other incomprehensible things which are now commonplace psychological tests. But for a country doctor in those days they were very progressive.

"Why are you so excited?" he asked suddenly, "Are you afraid I'll hurt you?"

"No," I said, "I'm afraid I'll have to go home."

"You're a rum chap."

He sat down and wrote to the Father. I do not know what argument he used, but it was successful. A letter came in due course giving me permission to accept an invitation to pass the summer with one of my schoolmates.

It was a wonderful vacation for me—my first taste of the sea. The boy's family had a cottage on the south shore of Long Island. The father who was a lawyer went often to the city. But the week ends he spent with us were treats. He played with us! He really enjoyed teaching me to swim and sail. I remember my pride when he would trust me with the main-sheet or the tiller. The mother also loved sailing. That she should enjoy playing with us was even a greater surprise to me than that my friend's father should. Whatever their winter religion was, they had none in the summer—unless being happy is a religion. I gathered some new ideals from that family for the home which Margot and I were to build.

In the spring-term of my second and last year in the school, we were given a course on the "Evidences of Christianity." It was a formal affair, administered by an old Congregationalist preacher from the village, whom we called "Holy Sam." He owed the nickname to his habit of pronouncing "psalm" to rhyme with "jam." He always opened the Sunday Vesper service by saying: "We will begin our worship with a holy sam." I think he took no more interest in the course than most of the boys did. It was assumed that we were all Christians and it was his rather thankless task to give us "reasonable grounds" for what we already believed.

It had the opposite effect on me. The book we used for a text was principally directed against atheists. I had never heard of an atheist before, it was a great idea to me that there were people who did not believe in God. I had not doubted His existence. I had hated Him. The faith and love I had given Mary and Oliver had turned to disgust and loathing. Their existence I could not doubt, and God was only the least of this trinity.

It would be an immense relief if I could get rid of my belief in God. The necessity of hate would be lifted from me. And so—with my eighteen-year-old intellect—I began to reason about Deity.

The pendulum of philosophy has swung a long way since I was a youth in school. To-day we are more interested in the subjective processes of devotion—what Tolstoi called the kingdom of God within us—than in definitions of an external, objective concept. The fine spun scholastic distinctions of the old denominational theologies are losing their interest. Almost all of us would with reverence agree with Rossetti:

> To God at best, to Chance at worst,
>
> Give thanks for good things last as first.
>
> But windstrown blossom is that good
>
> Whose apple is not gratitude.
>
> Even if no prayer uplift thy face
>
> Let the sweet right to render grace
>
> As thy soul's cherished child be nurs'd.

The Father's generation held that a belief in God, as defined by the Westminster confession was more important than any amount of rendering grace. I thought I was at war with God. Of course I was only fighting against the Father's formal definition. Our text book, in replying to them, quoted the arguments of Thomas Paine. The logic employed against him was weak and unconvincing. It was wholly based on the Bible. This was manifestly begging the question for if God was a myth, the scriptures were fiction. Nowadays, the tirades of Paine hold for me no more than historic interest. The final appeal in matters of religion is not to pure reason. The sanction for "faith" escapes the formalism of logic. But at eighteen the "Appeal to Reason" seemed unanswerable to me.

I began to lose sleep. As the spring advanced, I found my room too small for my thoughts and I fell into the habit of slipping down the fire-escape and walking through the night. There was an old mill-race near the school and I used to pace up and down the dyke for hours. Just as with egg-stealing something pushed me into this and I worried very little about what would happen if I were found out.

After many nights of meditation I put my conclusions down on paper. I have kept the soiled and wrinkled sheet, written over in a scragly boyish hand, ever since. First of all there were the two propositions "There is a God," "There is no God." If there is a God, He might be either a personal Jehovah, such as the Father believed in, or an impersonal Deity like that of the theists. These were all the possibilities I could think of. And in regard to these propositions, I wrote the following:

"I cannot find any proof of a personal God. It would take strong evidence to make me believe in such a cruel being. How could an all-powerful God, who cared, leave His children in ignorance? There are many grown-up men who think they know what the Bible means. They have burned each other at the stake—Catholics and Protestants—they would kill each other still, if there were not laws against it. A personal God would not let his followers fight about his meaning. He would speak clearly. If he could and did not, he would be a scoundrel. I would hate such a God. But there are no good arguments for a personal God.

"An impersonal God would be no better than no God. He would not care about men. Such a God could not give us any law. Every person would have to find out for himself what was right.

"If there is no God, it is the same as if there was an impersonal God.

"Therefore man has no divine rule about what is good and bad. He must find out for himself. This experiment must be the aim of life—to find out what is good. I think that the best way to live would be so that the biggest number of people would be glad you did live."

Such was my credo at eighteen. It has changed very little. I do not believe—in many things. My philosophy is still negative. And life seems to me now, as it did then, an experiment in ethics.

My midnight walks by the mill-race were brought to an abrupt end. My speculations were interrupted by the doctor's heavy hand falling on my shoulder.

"What are you doing out of bed at this hour? Smoking?"

I was utterly confused, seeing no outlet but disgrace. My very fright saved me. I could not collect my wits to lie.

"Thinking about God," I said.

The doctor let out a long whistle and sat down beside me.

"Was that what gave you brain fever?"

"Yes."

"Well—tell me about it."

No good thing which has come to me since can compare with what the doctor did for me that night. For the first time in my life an adult talked with me seriously, let me talk. Grown-ups had talked to and at me without end. I had been told what I ought to believe. He was the first to ask me what I believed. It was perhaps the great love for him, which sprang up in my heart that night, which has made me in later life especially interested in such as he.

I began at the beginning, and when I got to "Salvation" Milton, he interrupted me.

"We're smashing rules so badly to-night, we might as well do more. I'm going to smoke. Want a cigar?"

I did not smoke in those days. But the offer of that cigar, his treating me like an adult and equal, gave me a new pride in life, gave me courage to go through with my story, to tell about Oliver and Mary, to tell him of my credo.

He sat there smoking silently and heard me through.

"What do you think?" I asked at last, "Do you believe in God?"

"I don't know. I never happened to meet him in any laboratory. It sounds to me like a fairy story."

"Then you're an atheist," I said eagerly.

"No. A skeptic." And he explained the difference.

"How do you know what's good and what's bad?"

"I don't know," he replied. "I only know that some things are comfortable and some aren't. It is uncomfortable to have people think you are a liar, especially so when you happen to be telling the truth. It is uncomfortable to be caught stealing. But I know some thieves who are uncaught and who seem quite comfortable. Above all it's uncomfortable to know you are a failure."

His voice trailed off wearily. It was several minutes before he began again.

"I couldn't tell you what's right and what's wrong—even if I knew. You don't believe in God, why should you believe in me? If you don't believe the Bible you mustn't believe any book. No—that's not what I mean. A lot of the Bible is true. Some of it we don't believe, you and I. So with the other books —part true, part false. Don't trust all of any book or any man."

"How can I know which part to believe?"

"You'd be the wisest man in all the world, my boy, if you knew that," he laughed.

Then after a long silence, he spoke in a cold hard voice.

"Listen to me. I'm not a good man to trust. I'm a failure."

He told me the pitiful story of his life, told it in an even, impersonal tone as though it were the history of someone else. He had studied in Germany, had come back to New York, a brilliant surgeon, the head of a large hospital.

"I was close to the top. There wasn't a man anywhere near my age above me. Then the smash. It was a woman. You can't tell what's right and wrong in these things. Don't blame that cousin of yours or the girl. If anybody ought to know it's a doctor. I didn't. It's the hardest problem there is in ethics. The theological seminaries don't help. It's stupid just to tell men to keep away from it—sooner or later they don't. And nobody can tell them what's right. You wouldn't understand my case if I told you about it. It finished me. I began to drink. Watch out for the drink. That's sure to be uncomfortable. I was a drunkard—on the bottom. At last I heard about her again. She was coming down fast—towards the bottom. Well, I knew what the bottom was like—and I did not want her to know."

He smoked his cigar furiously for a moment before he went on. He had crawled out and sobered up. This school work and the village practice gave him enough to keep her in a private hospital. She had consumption.

"And sometime—before very long," he ended, "she will die and—well —I can go back to Forgetting-Land."

Of course I did not understand half what it meant. How I racked my heart for some word of comfort! I wanted to ask him to stay in the school and help other boys as he was helping me. But I could not find phrases. At last his cigar burned out and he snapped the stub into the mill-race. There was a sharp hiss, which sounded like a protest, before it sank under the water. He jumped up.

"You ought to be in bed. A youngster needs sleep. Don't worry your head about God. It's more important for you to make the baseball team. Run along."

I had only gone a few steps when he called me back.

"You know—if you should tell anyone, I might lose my position. I don't care for myself—but be careful on her account. Goodnight."

He turned away before I could protest. His calling me back is the one cloud on my memory of him. His secret was safe.

For the rest of the school year I gave my undivided attention to baseball. The doctor was uniformly gruff to me. We did not have another talk.

Two weeks before the school closed he disappeared. I knew that she had died, he would not have deserted his post while her need lasted. On Commencement Day, John, the apple-man, handed me a letter from him. I tore it up carefully after reading it, as he asked—threw the fragments out of the window of the train which was carrying me homeward. There was much to help me to clear thinking in that letter, but the most important part was advice about how to act towards the Father. "Don't tell him your doubts now. It would only distress him. Wait till you're grown up before you quarrel with him."

# II

Nothing of moment happened in the weeks I spent in camp meeting that summer. Luckily Mary was not there and Oliver, having finished the Seminary, was passing some months in Europe. I bore in mind the Doctor's advice, avoided all arguments and mechanically observed the forms of that religious community. No one suspected my godlessness, but I suspected everyone of hypocrisy. It was a barren time of deceit.

Even my correspondence with Margot gave me no pleasure. I could not write to her about my doubts, but I wanted very much to talk them over with her. While I could not put down on paper what was uppermost in my heart, I found it very hard to fill letters with less important things. Whenever I have been less than frank, I have always found it dolefully unsatisfactory.

I imagine that most thoughtful boys of my generation were horribly alone. It is getting more the custom nowadays for adults to be friends with children. The Doctor at school was the only man in whom I had ever confided. And in my loneliness I looked forward eagerly to long talks with Margot. I supposed that love meant understanding.

The serious sickness of the Mother took us home before the summer was ended. I had not been especially unhappy there during my childhood, but now that I had seen other pleasanter homes, my own seemed cruelly cheerless. Its gloom was intensified because the Mother was dying. I had had no special love for her but the thing was made harder for me by my lack of sympathy with their religious conventions. It was imperative that they should not question God's will. The Mother did not want to die. The Father was, I am sure, broken-hearted at the thought of losing her. They kept up a brave attitude—to me it seemed a hollow pretense—that God was being very good to them, that he was releasing her from the bondage of life, calling her to joy unspeakable. However much she was attached to things known—the Father, her absent son, the graves of her other children, the homely things of the parsonage, the few pieces of inherited silver, the familiar chairs—it was incumbent on her to appear glad to go out into the unknown.

It was my first encounter with death. How strange it is that the greatest of all commonplaces should always surprise us! What twist in our brains is it, that makes us try so desperately to ignore death? The doctors of philosophy juggle words over their *Erkenntnis Theorie*—trying to discover the confines of human knowledge, trying to decide for us what things are knowable and what we may not know—but above all their prattle, the fact of death stands out as one thing we all do know. Whether our temperaments incline us to reverence pure reason or to accept empirical knowledge, we know, beyond cavil, that we must surely die. Yet what an amazing amount of mental energy we expend in trying to forget it. The result? We are all surprised and unnerved when this commonplace occurs.

Christianity claims to have conquered death. For the elect, the Father taught, it is a joyous awakening. The people of the church scrupulously went through the forms which their creed imposed. Who can tell the reality of their thoughts? There is some validity in the theory of psychology which says that if you strike a man, you become angry; that if you laugh, it makes you glad. I would not now deny that they got some comfort from their attitude. But at the time, tossing about in my stormy sea of doubts, it seemed to me that they were all afraid. Just as well disciplined troops will wheel and mark time and ground arms, go through all the familiar manoeuvres of the parade ground, while the shells of the enemy sweep their ranks with cold fear, so it seemed to me that these soldiers of Christ were performing rites for which they had lost all heart in an effort to convince themselves that they were not afraid.

A great tenderness and pity came to me for the Mother. As I have said there had been little affection between us. All her love had gone out to Oliver. Yet in those last days, when she was so helpless, it seemed to comfort her if I sat by her bed-side and stroked her hand. Some mystic sympathy sprang up between us and she felt no need of pretense before me. I sat there and watched sorrow on her face, hopeless grief, yes, and sometimes rebellion and fear. But with brave loyalty she hid it all when the Father came into the room, dried her tears and talked of the joy that was set before her.

There was also a sorrow of my own. Disillusionment had come to me from Margot. Why I had expected that she would sympathize with and understand my doubts, I do not know. It was a wild enough dream.

The first night at home I went to see her. The family crowded about with many questions. Al was attending a southern military academy and there were endless comparisons to be made between his school and mine. But at last Margot and I got free of them and off by ourselves in an arbor. She seemed older than I, the maturity which had come to her in these two years startled me. But I blurted out my troubles without preface.

"Margot," I said, "Do you believe everything in the Bible?"

I suppose she was expecting some word of love. Two years before, when I had left her, I had kissed her. And now——

"Of course," she said, in surprise.

If she had doubted one jot or tittle of it, I might have been content. Her unthinking acceptation of it all angered me.

"I don't," I growled.

"What do you mean?"

"I mean what I say. I don't believe in the Bible."

I remember so well how she looked—there in the arbor, where she had led me—her eyes wide with surprise and fear. I thought she looked stupid.

"I don't believe in God," I went on.

I expected her to take this announcement quietly. But two years before I had never heard of men who doubted the existence of God, except, of course, the benighted heathen. Margot's hair is almost white now, but I suppose that in all her life, I am the only person she has heard question the teachings of the church.

Now I realize the extent of my folly in expecting that she would understand. The two years I had been away had changed everything for me, even the meaning of the words I used. I had been out in a wider world than hers, had begun to meet the minds of men who thought. In that little mountain village, a second rate, rather mushy-brained rector had been her intellectual guide. It was insane for me to think she would sympathize with me. And yet, because I loved her, I did. I was only eighteen.

How the fright grew in her eyes as I went on declaiming my unbeliefs!

"It's wicked—what you are saying."

"It's true. Is truth wicked?"

"I won't listen to you any more."

She got up. Suddenly I realized that I was losing her.

"Margot," I pleaded, "you mustn't go. We're going to get married. I've got to tell you what I think."

"I'll never marry a man who doesn't believe in God."

We were both very heroic. There was no older, wiser person there to laugh at us. So we stood and glared at each other. She waited some minutes for me to recant. I could not. Then two tears started down her cheeks. I wanted desperately to say something, but there were tears in my eyes also and no words would come. She turned and walked away. I could not believe it. I do not know how long I waited for her to come back. At last I went home.

Sullen, bitter days followed. I suppose she hoped, as I did, that some way would be found to restore peace. But neither of us knew how.

If I might have my way, I would first of all arrange life so that boys should escape such crises. Sooner or later, I suppose, every human being comes to a point where to compromise means utter damnation. But if I could remould this "sorry scheme of things," I would see that this portentous moment did not come till maturity. A Frenchman has said that after thirty we all become cynics. It is a vicious saying, but holds a tiny grain of truth. As we get older we become indifferent, cynical, in regard to phrases. The tragedy of youth is that it rarely sees beyond words. And of all futilities, it seems to me that quarrels over the terms with which we strive to express our mysticism— our religion, if you will—are the most futile. At eighteen I let a tangle of words crash into, smash, my love. Youth is cruel—above all to itself.

The mother's funeral seemed to me strangely unreal. It was hard to find the expected tears, and the black mourning clothes were abhorrent. I felt that I was imprisoned in some foul dungeon and was stifling for lack of air.

Release came with time for me to start to College. There was a lump in my throat as I climbed into the buckboard, beside the negro boy who was to drive me down to the county seat for the midnight train. The Father reached up and shook my hand and hoped that the Lord would have me in His keeping and then we turned out through the gate into the main street. I saw the Father standing alone in the doorway and I knew he was praying for me. I felt that I would never come back. I was sorry for the Father in the big empty house, but I had no personal regret, except Margot. The memory of the former leave-taking, how with her I had found the first realization of love, the first vague sensing of the mystic forces of life, came back to me sharply. All through the two years she had been a constant point in my thinking. I had not mooned about her sentimentally, more often than not, in the rush of work or play, I had not thought of her at all. But the vision of her had always been there, back in the holy of holies of my brain, a thing which was not to change nor fade.

The Episcopal Church was lit up, as we drove by I could hear some laughter. I knew they were decorating it for a wedding. Margot would be there, for she was one of the bride's maids. As soon as we were out of the village I told the negro boy I had forgotten something and jumping out, I walked back into the woods and circled round to the side of the church. I put a board up under a window and looked in. There were other people there, but I saw only Margot. She was sitting apart from the laughter, weaving a wreath of ground-pine for the lectern. Her face was very sad. Of course she knew I was going away, everyone knows such things in a little village. But she held her head high. If I had called her out onto the steps, she would have asked me once more to recant. I knew it was irrevocable. The fates had made us too proud.

I slipped down from my perch and made my way back to the buckboard. There was a wild west wind blowing, it howled and shrieked through the pines and I caught some of its fierce exultation. The summer had been bitter beyond words. The full life before me called, the life without need of hypocrisy.

When at last I was on the train, and felt the jar as it started, I walked forward into the smoking car. As a symbol of my new liberty, as reverently as if it had been a sacrament to the Goddess of Reason, I lit a cigarette. The tears were very close to my eyes as I sat there and smoked. But the pride of martyrdom held them back. Was I not giving up even Margot for the Cause of Truth?

# III

The College was set on a hill top, overlooking a broad fair valley. There was none of the rugged grandeur of our Tennessee Mountains, it was a softer landscape than my home country offered. But the greatest difference lay in the close packed, well tilled fields. Here and there were patches of woods, but no forest. It was an agricultural country.

If I should set out to construct a heaven, I would build it on the lines of that old campus. Whenever nowadays I am utterly tired and long for rest, the vision comes to me of those ivy grown buildings and the rows of scrawny poplars. It is my symbol for light-hearted joy and contentment. The doleful shadow of my home did not reach so far, and I was more carefree there than I have ever been elsewhere.

I joined heartily in the student life, played a fair game of football and excelled in the new game of tennis. There is a period at the end of adolescence when if ever, you feel an exuberance of animal well-being, when it is a pride to be able to lift a heavier weight than your neighbor, when it is a joy to feel your muscles ache with fatigue, when your whole being is opening up to a new sensation for which you know no name. I remember glorious tramps in the deep winter snow, as I look back on them I know that the thrilling zest, which then seemed to me intimately connected with the muscles of my thighs and back, was the dawning realization of the sheer beauty of the world. I spent this period at college. I suppose that is why I love the place.

From the first only one subject of study interested me. It was not on the freshman year's curriculum. By some twist of fate "Anglo-Saxon" appealed to me vividly. I suppose it was an outgrowth from my boyish fondness for Malory's "Morte d'Arthur." In the library I found many books in the crabbed Old English of the earliest chronicles. They still seem to me the most fascinating which have ever been written. I deciphered some of them with ease. Before I could get the meat out of the others I had to master a grammar of Anglo-Saxon. All my spare moments were spent among the shelves. My classroom work was poorly done. But among the books I came into close contact with Professor Meer, the librarian and head of the English Literature Department. His specialty was Chaucer, but my interest ran back to an even earlier date. He was my second adult friend and many an evening I spent in his home. But our talk was always of literature rather than of life, of the very early days, when there were no traditions nor conventions and each writer was also a discoverer.

A phase of life which had never before troubled me began to occupy considerable of my thought. My attention was drawn to the women question by the talk of the football men. There were two very distinct groups among the athletes; the Y.M.C.A. men and the others. It was inevitable that I should feel hostile to the former. They used the phrases, spoke the language of the Camp Meeting. With great pain and travail I had fought my way free from all that. Many of them were perhaps estimable fellows, I do not know. I did not get well acquainted with any of them. But I was surprised to find myself often ill at ease with the others. Their talk was full of vague hints which I seldom understood. They had come to college very much more sophisticated than I. In the quest for manly wisdom, I read a book on sex-matters, which I found in my fraternity house.

It taught me very little. I have seen dozens of such books since and I cannot understand the spirit in which they are written. In the effort to be clean spirited and scientific the authors have fallen over backwards and have told their readers almost nothing at all. It was like a book which described the mechanism of a printing press without one word about its use or place in life. A printing press is a very lifeless thing unless one has some comprehension that not so much in itself but in its vast utility it is the most wonderful thing which man has made. The book which fell into my hands, described in detail, in cold blooded and rather revolting phraseology, the physiology of sex, but it gave no hint of its psychologic or social significance, it did not even remotely suggest that sooner or later everyone who read it would have to deal with sex as a problem of personal ethics. It was a poor manual for one just entering manhood.

I had never been told anything about sex. I judged from the witticisms of the gymnasium that the others had discussed these matters a great deal in their preparatory schools. And with the added knowledge of later years, I am persuaded that my school had been unusually clean spirited. I never heard the boys talking of such things, and if any of them were getting into bad habits, they did it privately.

These college men boasted. Of course I hid my ignorance with shame. As the football season wore on the talk became more explicit. Some of the team, after the Thanksgiving Day game, with our rival college, which ended the season, were "going into town to raise hell." The Y.M.C.A. men expected to "come right home." A week or so before the last game, Bainbridge, our captain and a senior, showed some of us a letter which a girl in town had written him. The other fellows who saw the letter thought it hilariously funny. To me it seemed strange and curious. A woman, who could have written it was something entirely foreign to my experience.

Thanksgiving night—we had won the game—all of us, but the Y.M.C.A. men, went into town for a dinner and celebration. I happened to be the only man from my fraternity on the football team, and, when the dinner broke up, I found myself alone. My head was swimming a bit and I remember walking down the main street, trying to recall whether or not I had decided to launch out on this woman adventure. I was sure I had not expected to be left to my own resources. I was making my way towards the station to catch a train back to college, when I fell in with some of the fellows. They annexed me at once. Down the street we went, roaring out the Battle Cry of Freedom. They had an objective but every barroom we passed distracted their attention. It was the first time I had ever approached the frontier of sobriety—that night I went far over the line. Out of the muddle of it all, I remember being persuaded to climb some dark stairs and being suddenly sobered by the sight of a roomful of women. I may have been so befuddled that I am doing them an injustice,

43

but no women ever seemed to me so nauseatingly ugly. Despite the protest of my friends, I bolted.

It is not a pleasant experience to relate, but it kept me from what might easily have been worse. I had missed the last train. Not wanting to spend the night in a hotel, nor to meet my fellows on the morning train, I walked the ten miles out to college. Somehow the sight of those abhorrent women had driven all the fumes of alcohol from my brain. In the cold, crisp night, under the low hanging lights of heaven, I felt myself more clear minded than usual. As sharply as the stars shone overhead, I realized that I had no business with such debauch. It was not that I took any resolution, only I understood beyond question that such things had no attraction to me.

It is something I do not understand. The Father had taught me that many things were sinful. But I do not think there was anything in my training to lead me to feel that drunkenness and debauch were any worse than card-playing. Yet I learned to play poker with a light heart. It was the same with theatre going and dancing. He had very much oftener warned me against these things than against drunkenness. The best explanation I can find, although it does not entirely satisfy me, is that vulgar debauch shocked some æsthetic, rather than moral instinct. It was not the thought of sin which had driven me to run away from those women, but their appalling ugliness.

Towards the end of the spring term, the long-delayed quarrel with the Father came to a head. I forget the exact cause of the smash-up, perhaps it was smoking. I am sure it commenced over some such lesser thing. But once the breach was open there was no chance of patching it up. In the half dozen letters which passed between us, I professed my heresies with voluminous underlinings. I had only one idea, to finish forever with pretense and hypocrisy.

I was foolish—and cruel. I did not appreciate the Father's love for me, nor realize his limitations. He was sure he was right. His whole intellectual system was based on an abiding faith. From the viewpoint of the new Pragmatic philosophy, he had tested his "truth" by a long life and had found it good. Perhaps in his earlier days he had encountered skepticism, but since early manhood, since he had taken up his pastorate, all his association had been with people who were mentally his inferiors. He was more than a "parson," he was the wise-man, not only of our little village, but of the country side. All through the mountains his word carried conclusive weight. Inevitably he had become cock-sure and dogmatic. It was humanly impossible for him to argue with a youth like me.

In my narrow, bitter youth, I could not see this. I might have granted his sincerity, if he had granted mine. But for him to assume that I loved vice because I doubted certain dogma, looked to me like cant. But the men he knew, who were not "professing Christians," were drunkards or worse. He really believed that Robert Ingersoll was a man of unspeakable depravity. He could not conceive of a man leading an upright life without the aid of Christ. Peace between us was impossible. His ultimatum was an effort to starve me into repentance. "My income," he wrote, "comes from believers who contribute their mites for the carrying on of the work of Christ. It would be a sin to allow you to squander it on riotous living."

So my college course came to an end.

# IV

In one regard the fairies who attended my christening were marvelously kind to me. They gave me the gift of friends. It is the thing above all others which makes me reverent, makes me wish for a god to thank. There is no equity in the matter. I am convinced that it is what the Father would have called "an act of grace." Always, in every crisis, whenever the need has arisen, a friend has stepped beside me to help me through.

So it was when the Father cut off my allowance. Utterly ignorant of the life outside, I was not so frightened by my sudden pennilessness as I should have been, as I would be to-day. Work was found for me. My friend, Prof. Meers discovered that he needed an assistant to help him on a bibliography which he was preparing. He offered me a modest salary—enough to live comfortably. So I stayed on in the college town, living in the fraternity house.

The library work interested me more than my study had done. Even the routine detail of it was not bad and I had much time to spend on the Old English which fascinated me. I was not ambitious and would have been content to spend my life in that peaceful, pleasant town. But Prof. Meers had other plans for me. Back of my indolent interest in old books, he was optimistic enough to see a promise of great scholarship. He was better as a critic of literature than as a judge of men. He continually made plans for me. I paid scant attention to them until almost a year had passed and we were beginning to see the end of the work he could offer me. I began to speculate with more interest about what I would do next.

Without telling me about it, Prof. Meers wrote to the head of a New York Library, whom he knew and secured a position for me. When he received the news he came to me with a more definite plan than I would ever have been able to work out for myself. He knew that a certain publishing house wanted to bring out a text book edition of "Ralph Roister Doister." He had given them my name and I was to prepare the manuscript during my free hours. This he told me would not bring me much money, but some reputation and would make it easier for him to find other openings for me, where I could develop my taste for Old English. I caught some of his enthusiasm and set out for my new work with high hopes.

Of my first weeks in the city there is little memory left except of a disheartening search for a place to live. After much tramping about I took a forlorn hall bedroom in a not over peaceful family. The quest for an eating place was equally unsatisfactory.

In the library I was put to uninteresting work in the Juvenile Department. But there, handling books in words of one syllable, I found a new and disturbing outlook on life. There was more jealousy than friendship among my fellow employees. The chances of advancement were few, the competition keen—and new to me. I did not understand the hostility, which underlies the struggle for a living. Once I remember I found a carefully compiled sheet of figures, which I had prepared for my monthly report, torn to bits in my waste paper basket. Another time some advice, which I afterwards discovered to have been intentionally misleading, sent me off on a wild goose chase, wasted half a day and brought me a reprimand from the chief. Such things were incomprehensible to me at first. It took some time to realize that the people about me were afraid of me, afraid that I might win favor and be advanced over their heads. I resented their attitude, but gradually, by a word dropped here and there, I learned how a dollar a week more or less was a very vital matter to most of them. One girl in my department had a mother to support and was trying desperately to keep a brother in school. There was a man whose wife was sick, the doctor's and druggist's bills were a constant terror to him. Very likely if I had been in their place, I would have done the little, mean things they did. Life began to wear a new aspect of sombreness to me. I could not hope for advancement without trampling on someone.

By temperament I was utterly unfitted for this struggle. My desire for life was so weak that such shameful, petty hostilities seemed an exorbitant price to pay for it. I would much rather not have been born than struggle in this manner to live. I began to look about eagerly for some other employment. But I could find none which did not bear the same taint.

However it was there in that library that I encountered Norman Benson. He was near ten years older than I, tall and loose jointed. His face, very heavily lined, reminded me of our Tennessee mountaineers. But the resemblance went no farther. He was a city product, bred in luxury and wealth. He was variously described by the people of the library as "a saint," "a freak," "a philanthropist," "a crank." The chief called him "a bore." He was the idol of the small boys who ran errands for us and put the books back on the shelves. He gave them fat Egyptian cigarettes out of his silver case, to their immense delight and to the immense horror of Miss Dilly, who had the boys in charge.

His hobby, as he soon explained to me, was "a circulating library that really circulates." He had a strange language, a background of Harvard English, a foreground of picturesque slang—all illumined by flashes of weird profanity. Of course I cannot recall his words, but his manner of speaking I shall never forget.

"They call this a circulating library," he would shout. "Hell! It never moves an inch. It's stationary! Instead of going out around the town, it sits here and waits for people to come. And the people don't come. Not on your life! Only a few have the nerve to face out all this imposing architecture and red-tape. If there is anything to discourage readers, they don't do it because they've been too stupid to think of it. If a stranger comes in and asks for a book they treat him like a crook. Ask him impertinent questions about his father's occupation. Won't let him take a book unless he can get some tax-payer to promise to pay for it if he steals it! What in thunder has that got to do with it? Someone wants to read. They ought to send up an Hosanna! They ought to go out like postmen, and leave a book at each door every morning.

Circulating? Rot!"

He had given his time and money for a year or two to bring about this reform. At first he had met with cold indifference. But he stuck to his point. He had put up his money as guarantees for any books which might be lost. He had persuaded half a dozen or more school teachers to distribute books among their scholars and the parents, paying them out of his own pocket for the extra work. He had established branches in several mission churches and in one or two saloons.

"That corpse of a librarian," he explained to me, "had the fool idea that his job was to preserve books—to pickle them! I've been trying to show him that every book he has on his shelves gathering dust, is money wasted, that his job is to keep them moving. The city's books ought to be in the homes of the tax-payers—not locked up in a library. The very idea horrified him at first. He was afraid the books would get dirty. Good Lord! What's the best end that can come to a book, I'd like to know? It ought to fall to pieces from much reading. For a book to be eaten by worms is a sin. I've been hammering at him, until he's beginning to see the light. He don't cry any more if a book has to be rebound."

Indeed, the "hammering" process had been effective. That year the chief read a paper at the National Congress on "Library Extension." Of course he took all the credit; boasted how the idea had come from his library and so forth. But Benson cared not at all for that. His plan had been accepted and he was content.

He interested me immensely. Why did a man with a large income spend his time, rushing about trying to make people read books they did not care enough for to come after? I could get no answer from him. He would switch away from the question into a panegyric on reading. It was a frequent expression of his that "reading is an invention of the last half century."

"Of course," he would qualify, "the aristocracy has enjoyed reading much longer. But the people? They've just learned how. The democratization of books is the most momentous social event in the history of the world. Think of it! More people read an editorial in the newspaper within twenty-four hours than could possibly have read Shakespeare during his entire life. There are dozens of single books which have had a larger edition than all the imprints of Elizabethan literature put together. Don't you see the immensity of it? It means that people all over the world will be able to think of the same thing at the same time. It means a social mind. Plato lived in his little corner of the world and his teachings lived by word of mouth and manuscripts. Only a few people could read them, fewer still could afford to buy them. 'Uncle Tom's Cabin' swept across the country in a couple of years. Think how long it took Christianity to spread—a couple of hundred miles a century. And then think of the theory of evolution! It has captured the world in less than a generation! That's what books mean. We're just entering the epoch of human knowledge as compared to the old learning of individuals. It's gigantic! Wonderful!"

Benson, like many another, took a liking to me. I was lonely enough in that library. And finding no sympathy elsewhere, I improved every opportunity to talk with him.

One evening he asked me to come home with him to dinner. I accepted gladly, being more than tired of my pallid little room, and the sloppy restaurant where I ate. An evening with this rich young man, seemed attractive indeed. To my surprise he led the way to a downtown Bowery car. I did not know the city well and I thought perhaps this dismal street led to some fairer quarter. But the further we went the grimmer became the neighborhood. It was my first visit to the slums.

We got off at Stanton Street. It is so familiar to me now—with its dingy unloveliness, the squalor of its tenements, its crowding humanity, and the wonder that people can laugh in such a place—that it is hard to recall how it looked that first time. I think the thing which impressed me most was the multitude of children. Clearest of all I remember stepping over a filthy baby. It lay flat on its back, sucking an apple core and stared up at me with a strange disinterestedness. It did not seem to be afraid I would step on it. I wanted to stop and set the youngster to one side, out of the way. But I felt that I would look foolish. I did not know where to take hold of it. And Benson strode on down the street without noticing it.

A couple of blocks further, we came to a dwelling house with flower boxes in the windows. A brass-plate on the door bore the inscription, "The Children's House." So I was introduced to the Social Settlement. They were novelties in those days.

A tumult of youngsters swarmed about us as we entered. A sweet faced young woman was trying to drive them out, explaining with good natured vexation that they had over-stayed their time and would not go. They clambered all over Benson, but somehow he was more successful than the young woman in persuading them to go home. Her name, when Benson introduced me, gave me a start. It recalled a fantastic newspaper story of a millionaire's daughter who had left her diamonds and yachts to live among the poor. I had supposed her some sallow-faced, nun-like creature. I found her to be vibrantly alive, not at all a recluse.

The Settlement consisted of a front and rear tenement. The court between had been turned into a pleasant garden. With the hollyhocks along the walls and the brilliant beds of geraniums it was a strangely beautiful place for that crowded district. The men's quarters were in the back building. Benson had two rooms on the top floor, a small monastic bedroom and a larger study. It surprised me more than the courtyard. It was startling to find the atmosphere of a college dormitory in the center of the slums. The books, the fencing foils, the sofa-pillows in the window-seat—after my months in a furnished room—made me homesick for my fraternity house.

Downstairs in the cheery dining room, I met the staff of "Residents." The Rev. James Dawn, an Englishman, was the Head Worker. He was a graduate of Oxford and had been associated with Arthur Toynbee in the first London Settlement. His wife, also English, sat at the foot of the table. Benson introduced me rapidly to the others. "Miss Blake—District Nurse," "Miss

Thompson—Kindergartner," "Long, Instructor in Sociology in the University," "Dr. Platt—of the Health Department." I did not begin to get the labels straight.

It was a very much better dinner than I could get in any restaurant, better than the food I had had at College and school. But the thing which impressed me most was the whizz of sharp, intellectual—often witty—conversation. The discussion centered on one of the innumerable municipal problems. I was ashamed of my inability to contribute to it.

It was to me a wonderfully attractive group of people. They enjoyed all which seemed most desirable in college life and added to this was a strange magnetic earnestness, I did not understand. I saw them relaxed. But even in their after-dinner conversation, over their coffee cups and cigarettes, there was an undercurrent of seriousness which hinted at some vital contact with an unknown reality. I was like an Eskimo looking at a watch, I could not comprehend what made the hands go round. I could see their actions, but not the stimuli from which they reacted. I knew nothing of misery.

That evening set my mind in a whirl. It was an utterly new world I had seen. I had never thought of the slums except as a distressful place to live. Stanton Street was revolting. I did not want to see it again. And yet I could not shake myself free from the thought of it—of it and of the strange group I had met in the Children's House. There seemed to be something fateful about it, something I must look at without flinching and try to understand.

On the other hand some self-defensive instinct made me try to forget it. The distaste for the struggle for life which had come to me from experiencing the petty jealousies of the library was turned into a dumb, vague fear by the sight of the slum. I turned to "Ralph Roister Doister"—on which I had made only listless progress—with a new ardor. The only escape which I could see from perplexing problems of life lay in a career of scholarship.

The Old English which had formerly been an amusement for me, now seemed a means of salvation. When Benson next suggested that I spend the evening with him, I excused myself on the ground of work.

But very often as I sat at my table, burning the midnight oil over that century old farce, the vision of that baby of Stanton Street, sucking the piece of garbage, came between me and my page. And I felt some shame in trying to drive him away. It was as though a challenging gauntlet had been thrown at my feet which I must needs pick up and face out the fight, or commit some gross surrender. I tried to escape the issue, with books.

# BOOK III

# I

Not long after this visit to the slums, when I had been in the city a little more than a year, I received a new offer of employment, through the kindness of Professor Meer. The work was to catalogue, and edit a descriptive bibliography of a large collection of early English manuscripts and pamphlets. A rich manufacturer of tin cans had bought them and intended to give them to some college library.

It offered just the escape I was looking for. I wrote at once, in high spirits, to accept it. However some cold water was thrown on my glee by Norman Benson. He was my one friend in the library and I hastened to tell him the good news. But when he read the letter he was far from enthusiastic.

"Are you going to accept it?" he asked coldly.

"Of course," I replied, surprised at his tone. "I hardly hoped for such luck, at least not for many years. It's a great chance."

"This really interests me," he said, laying down the books he was carrying and sitting on my desk. "What earthly good," he went on, "do you think it's going to do anyone to have you diddle about with these old parchments?"

"Why. It——" I began glibly enough, but I was not prepared for the question. And, realizing suddenly that I had not considered this aspect of the case, I left my response unfinished.

"I haven't a bit of the scholastic temperament," he said, after having waited long enough to let me try to find an answer. "It's just one of the many things I don't understand. I wouldn't deny that any bit of scholarship, however 'dry-as-dust,' may be of some use. I don't doubt that a good case of this kind could be made for the study of medieval literature. I don't say it's *absolutely* useless. But *relatively* it seems—well—uninteresting to me. It's in the same class as astronomy. You could study the stars till you were black in the face and you wouldn't find anything wrong with them, and if you did you couldn't make it right. Astronomy has been of some practical use to us, at least it helps us regulate our watches. But how in the devil do you expect to wring any usefulness out of Anglo-Saxon? Don't you want to be useful?"

His scorn for my specialty ruffled my temper.

"What would you suggest for me to do? Social-Settlement-ology?" I replied with elaborate irony.

But if he caught the note of anger in my retort, he was too busy with his own ideas to pay any attention to it. He got off the table and paced up and down like a caged beast, as he always did when he was wrestling with a problem. In a moment he came back and sat down.

"You don't answer my question," he said sharply. "You can stand on your dignity and say I have no right to ask it. But that's rot! I'm serious and I give you the credit of thinking you are. Now you propose to turn your back on the world and go into a sort of monastery. This job is just a beginning. You're making your choice between men and books, between human thought that is alive and the kind that's been preserved like mummies. Why? I ask. What is there in these old books which can compare in interest to the life about us. Truth is not only stranger than fiction, it is more dramatic, more comic, more tragic, more beautiful. Even Shelley never wrote a lyric like some you can see with your own eyes, perhaps feel. I like to know what makes people do things. I'd like to know what makes you accept this offer. I assume that you want to be useful to your day and generation. What utility do you hope to serve in tabulating these old books, which nobody but a few savants will ever read?"

I was entirely unprepared to answer his question. And I felt myself sink in his estimation. Why was I reaching out for the life of a bookworm with such eagerness? I understand now. I was a coward. I was still sore from the wounds of my childish endeavor to comprehend God. I was afraid of life. I was afraid of the little child sucking the apple core on Stanton Street. The life about me, of which Benson spoke so enthusiastically, seemed to me threatening. It evidently laid an obligation of warfare on the people who entered it actively. I wanted peace. Books seemed to me a sort of city of refuge.

My new employer, Mr. Perry, the tin-can man, was a strange type. He had grown up in a fruit preserving industry and at thirty-odd he had invented a method of crimping the tops onto cans, without the use of solder. Good luck had given him an honest business partner and the patent had made a fortune for both of them. When the first instalment of royalties had come in, Perry had stopped stirring the kettle of raspberry preserves and had not done a stroke of work since. At forty he had built a "mansion" in the city and had gone in for politics. He bought his way to a seat in the State Senate, only to find that it bored him to extinction. After several other fads had proved uninteresting, he had set his heart on a LL.D. A friend had advised him to donate a valuable collection of books to some college.

He had sent a large check to a London dealer and this heterogeneous mass had been the result. As his interest in the matter had been only momentary he was decidedly penurious about it after the first outlay. That, I suppose, is why I, instead of a recognized authority, was chosen for the work. He had no idea what the catalogue should be like, and his one instruction to me, was to make it "something scholarly."

There was in his monstrous mansion an apartment originally designed for the children's tutor. But there had never been any children. These quarters were given to me. There was a private entrance, a bedroom, bath and study, where my meals were served, and there was a stairway down to the library.

In the three years I worked for him I did not see him ten times. His wife was dead, he lived away a good deal and, to my great satisfaction, he never invited me to his bachelor parties—the reverberations of which sometimes shook me out of sleep. Once every six months or so he would bring an expert to look over my work. As they found no fault and he could not understand it, he was convinced that it was scholarly.

It was a period of great content for me. The rut into which I fell was deep indeed. I saw no one. Almost my only contact with others was by mail. And my letters all related to my specialty. Eight full hours I worked in the library. The architect had not expected Mr. Perry to do much reading and, the windows being few, the room was gloomy. I had often to use artificial light. At five I went for an hour's walk in the park. At least this was my theory. But the least inclemency was an excuse to take some manuscript up to my room, to my shaded lamp and open fire. The daily eight hours on the catalogue was only a beginning. As soon as I had finished my edition of "Ralph Roister-Doister," I began a monograph on Anglo-Saxon Roots. My ambition was to win a fellowship in an English University. By the time my catalogue was finished, I would have enough money put by for a year or more of study in Oxford. My life was mapped out.

## II

The darkness came unexpectedly.

Sometimes my eyes had been tired, but I had not taken it seriously. One afternoon, as I laid out a sheet of paper on the desk, the page was suddenly obscured by a dancing spider-web—a dizzying contortion of black and white —growing denser and denser. I clapped my hands over my eyes and felt so sudden a relief I was afraid to take them away again.

I got up slowly and felt my way with my foot to an easy chair. How long I sat there, my hands pressed hard against my eyes, I do not know. I had read somewhere of a man going blind with just such symptoms. It was fear unspeakable, fear that made me laugh. When one feels that the gods are witty it is a bad sign.

I was suddenly calm. It was accepted. I thought for a few minutes, my eyes still shut, and then felt my way to the telephone.

"Central," I said, and I remember that my voice was calm and commonplace. "Will you give me the Eye and Ear Hospital? I can't look up the number. I'm blind."

"Sure," came back the answer. "It must be hard to be blind."

A clutch came to my throat. It comes to me now as I write about it, comes every time I hear people complaining that modern industry has robbed our life of all humanity, has turned us into mechanisms. Such talk makes me think of the sudden sympathy which came to me out of the machine. Whenever I am utterly blue and discouraged, I go into a telephone booth.

"Hello, Central," I say, "tell me something cheerful. I'm down on my luck."

It has never failed. Always some joking sympathy has come out of the machine and helped me to get right again.

When the doctor came, he looked a minute at my desk, at the whole eye-straining mass of faded print and notes. He snapped on the electric light.

"I suppose you work a lot in this fiendish glare?"

"I need a strong light," I said.

He grunted in disgust.

"This will hurt," he said, as he made me sit down near the electric light, "but you've got to bear it."

He fixed a little mirror on his forehead and flashed the cruel ray into my eye. Back somewhere in the brain it focussed and burned. The sweat broke out all over me.

"Now the other eye."

I flinched for a moment, holding my hand before it.

"Come, come," he said gruffly, and I took my hand away.

When the ordeal was over, he tied a black bandage over my eyes, laid me down on the lounge and lectured me. When he stopped for breath, I interrupted.

"What hope is there?"

He hesitated.

"Oh! Tell me the truth."

"Well—I guess the chances are even—of your seeing enough for ordinary work. But they will never be strong. You'll have to give up books. You must keep your eyes bandaged—complete rest—six weeks—then we can tell how much damage you've done. It is only a guess now."

We talked business. I had enough money saved for a private room and good treatment, so he put me into a cab and told the driver to deliver me at the hospital.

It was an appalling experience, that ride. Try it yourself. Ride through the streets with your eyes darkened: you will hear a thousand sounds you never heard before, even familiar sounds will be fearsome. Every jolt, every stoppage will seem momentous. I was glad the doctor did not come with me, glad that no one saw me so afraid.

At last we stopped and I heard the cabby call.

"Hey! there. Come out and take this man."

I revolted at my helplessness, pushed the door open and stumbled as I stepped out. I would have fallen heavily, if an orderly had not been there to catch me.

"You must be careful at first, Mister," he said. "You'll get used to it in time."

That was just what I was afraid of—getting used to the darkness!

However, his words jogged my pride. The ways of the gods seemed funny to me again, and I joked with him as he led me up some stairs and into a receiving room. The house surgeon, to me only a voice, was nervously cheerful. He kept saying, "It'll be all right." "It'll be all right." He seemed to be dancing about in all directions. My ears had not become accustomed to locating sounds. I suppose he moved about normally, but he seemed to talk from a different angle every time.

"This is Miss Barton," he said at last. "She is day nurse in your ward. She'll make you comfortable."

Mechanically I thrust my hand out into the darkness. It was met and grasped by something I knew to be a hand, but it did not feel like any hand I had ever seen.

"I'm glad to meet you," I said.

With some jest about people not usually being glad to meet nurses, she led me off to the elevator and my room.

"You've quite a job before you—exploring this place," she said with real cheer in her voice. "There are all sorts of adventures in this *terra incognita*. Everything is cushioned so you can't bang your shins, but watch out for your toes. At first you'd better stay in bed for a few days and rest. Have you all you need in your valise?"

"I don't know. A servant packed it."

"Well then. That's the first bit of exploring to do. I'll help you."

Her voice also jumped about surprisingly. There was something weird in being in a room with an utter stranger whose existence was only manifested by this apparently erratic voice and by hands which unsnarled my shoe laces, handed me my pajamas, and put me to bed.

"I must run off now and attend to Mrs. Stickney, next door—she is very fussy. The night nurse, Miss Wright, comes on pretty soon, at six. She'll bring you your supper. When you wake up in the morning, ring the bell, here over your head, and I'll bring you breakfast. Good night."

It was when she had gone and I alone there in the strange bed, that I first felt the awful void of the darkness. I do not like to think of it now.

It was probably not many minutes, but it seemed hours on end, before Miss Wright brought me my supper. She sat on the edge of my bed and helped me find the way to my mouth. She was considerate, and tried to be cheering. But I did not like her. Always her very efficiency reminded me of my helplessness. And her voice seemed too large for a woman. It gave me the impression that she was talking to someone several feet behind me.

They had, I think, mercifully drugged my food, for I fell asleep at once. When I woke I had no idea of the hour. For some time I lay there in the darkness wondering about it. I did not want to wake anybody up. But at last I decided that I would not be so hungry before breakfast time. After much futile fumbling I found the bell above my bed. In a few minutes Miss Barton's voice —even after all these years, I think of it as the type of sunny cheerfulness— announced that it was near eleven. When the breakfast was finished, with joking cautions against setting the bed on fire, she filled my pipe and taught my hands the way to the matchbox.

In the weeks which followed, I lost all track of the sun's time. I came to figure my days in relation to her. During the "nights," when she was off duty, the darkness was very black.

It would be impossible for me to give in detail the evolution by which Miss Barton, my nurse, changed into my friend, Ann. It began I think when she discovered how utterly alone I was. The second day in the hospital I was given permission to have visitors, and I sent for my employer's man of law.

"Whom do you want to have come to see you to-morrow?" Miss Barton asked when he had gone.

I could think of no one.

"Do you want me to write some letters to your relatives?"

"No. I haven't any near kin."

"Well. Haven't you some friends to write to?"

In the three years I had lived at Mr. Perry's I had severed all social connections. I had not kept up my college friendships. Benson had been so opposed to my leaving what he called active life that I had lost all touch with him. My only relations with people had been technical, by correspondence. I did not want to trouble even Prof. Meer with my purely personal misfortunes. This seemed utterly impious to Miss Barton. What? I had lived several years in the city and had no friends? It was unbelievable! Unfortunately it was true. I could think of no one to ask in to relieve my loneliness. And there is no loneliness like the darkness.

The next week was the worst, for the nurses changed and Miss Wright, who was on day duty, was not companionable. However, Miss Barton, taking compassion on me, used often to sit with me by the hour at night. How fragmentary was my contact with her! No one who has not been deprived of sight can realize how large a part it plays in the relationships of life. I could only hear. There was always the creak of the rocking chair beside my bed and her voice, sometimes placid, sometimes tense, swinging back and forth in the

61

darkness. It did not seem to have any body to it. Whenever her hands touched me, it startled me.

But from her talk I learned something of the person who owned the voice. She had been born in a Vermont village, where no one had ever heard of a professional woman, but as far back as she could remember, she had set her heart on medicine. Her father she had never known. Her mother, a fine needlewoman and embroidery designer had brought up the children. A brother was an engineer and the older sister a school teacher. But there had not been enough money to send Ann to medical college. Nursing was as near as she had been able to get towards her ambition. But what could not be given her she intended to win for herself. She had taken this position because the night duty was very light and every other week she could give almost the entire day to study. Her interest had turned to the new science of bacteriology. Her vague ambition to be a doctor had changed to the definite ideal of research work.

Somehow the voice, so calmly certain when it dealt of this, gave me an impression of integrity of purpose, of invincible determination, such as sight has never given me of anyone. I did not, any more than she, know how she was to get her research laboratory. But I could not doubt that she would. She had unquestioning faith in her destiny. I find myself emphasizing this phase of her. It impressed me most at the time.

But her conversation was by no means limited to her ambition. She had read a thousand things besides her medicine, and spoke of them more frequently. She was constantly referring to books, to facts of history and science, of which I was ignorant. She talked seriously of ethics and the deeper things of life. It woke again in me all the old questionings and aspirations of prep. school days—the things I had hidden away from in my book-filled library. She was the first person I had met since the doctor at school who showed me what she thought of these things. Benson had talked copiously about the objective side of life, but he had never referred to his inner life. The people I had known wanted to make this world a prayer meeting, a counting house or a playground. Ann was no more interested in such ideals than I was.

She used a phraseology which was new to me: "Individualism," "self-expression," "expansion of personality." She spoke of life as a crusade against the tyrannies of prejudice and conventions. Her viewpoint was biologic. All evolutionary progress was based on variations from the type. Efforts to sustain or conserve the type she called "reactionary" and "invasive." She insisted on the desirability of "absolute freedom to vary from the norm." The authority she quoted with greatest reverence was Spencer. This conversation, much of which I did not understand, showed me clearly one thing—a soul seeking passionately for truth. That she told me was her ideal as it had been the war-cry of Bakounine. "*Je suis un chercheur passionné de la Vérité.*"

When any reference was made to my manner of life, she flared up. It was —and this was her worst denunciation—unnatural.

"I believe in individualism, egoism," she said. "But not in isolation. Man is naturally as gregarious as the ant. An ant that lived alone would be a non-ant. You've been a non-man. It's good your eyes went back on you—if it teaches you sense. Intercourse with one's kind is a necessary food of human life."

And while it was a God-send for me to find someone to talk to, it must have been also a pleasure for her. The stories she told me about the other patients showed that their relations to nurses were barren enough—when not actually insulting. After listening by the hour to Mrs. Stickney's endless little troubles, it was a relief for her, I think, to come to my room and talk of the things which interested her violently. She gave more and more time to me. During the third week, when she was again on day duty, she read me Lecky's "History of European Morals."

## III

It is hard to write about the next week. I can no longer see it as it must have looked in those days. I cannot tell the "why" of it. It was.

There was immense loneliness—and fear. The few hundred dollars I had saved for studying in Oxford would pay the doctor's bill and keep me for some months. But what was there beyond, if my eyes did not come back? At best the chances were only even. In any case the one trade I knew was gone. A bookworm with weak eyes is a sorry thing. Of course I might have gone home. But I have never had much respect for the Prodigal Son. He must have been a poor spirited chap.

Well, in my utmost misery, Ann comforted me—as women have comforted men since the world began. In some inexplicable way, for some inexplicable causes, she loved me.

I try to arrange my memories of those days in orderly sequence. But it is all a blur. Day by day my need grew and day by day she met the need. The patients in that hospital did not require much attention, except in the day. Most of them slept well. They rarely rang for her after midnight. She gave me more and more of her time.

The stress between us grew rapidly, but by gradual steps, almost imperceptibly. Her hand rested in mine a trifle longer. The hand clasp became a caress—then a kiss. The kiss lingered....

So the voice took on a body. Touch came to the aid of hearing as a means of contact with this dear person of the darkness. It is strange in what a fragmentary way she took shape in my consciousness as something more than a paid nurse, more close and intimate than any friend I had known in the light.

In the darkness every other thing seemed strange. What I discovered by touch to be a table, did not fit into the old category of "tables." Even the pipe which I had smoked since college seemed to have undergone some fundamental change in its nature. Ann was the only thing which seemed natural. I had had no intimacy with woman of the light by which I could judge this experience. Coming to me as it did, it did not seem strange—it made subsequent things seem strange. When at last my eyes were opened, I blushed before Ann as before a stranger.

It all seemed so inevitable.

"It's late," she said one night, "I must go. If you want me, ring."

"Of course I want you."

"But you ought to sleep. I mean, ring if anything happens."

"It don't matter whether anything happens or not. I——"

"Don't ring unless you need me."

The door closed behind her. I lay there debating with myself whether or not I needed her. The bell was in reach of my hand. I got out of bed to be further from temptation. With awkward trembling hands, I filled and lit my pipe and sat down by the open window. My head ached with loneliness and desolation. Off somewhere in the night a church bell struck two, some belated footsteps rang sharp and clear on the sidewalk below me. I tried to interest myself in speculating whither or to whom the person was hurrying. But my thoughts swung back to my own loneliness. In all the world there was no one who knew of my blindness and cared except the tin-can merchant who was cursing that he must have the trouble to find someone to finish my work. No. There was Ann.

Quite suddenly a vision of my childhood came back to me, of the time I had been sick at Mary Dutton's, when she had taken me into the warm comfort of her bed. The vision brought quick resolution. I rang the bell. I stood up against the wall and waited—breathless. The door opened and from the darkness came her voice.

"Do you really want me?"

I do not think I spoke, but I remember reaching out my hands to her. My strained ears caught a faint rustle—then came touch—and my arms were about her.

So I was comforted.

# IV

For the night there was rich forgetfulness. But the new day called me back from the Elysian Fields to the cold reality of this ordinary world of ours.

My familiarity with the frank openness of my good friend Chaucer and the early English writers had cleansed my mind of much nastiness. I never had any feeling of Biblical sin in regard to my sudden passion for Ann. It was too entirely sweet and natural to be anything so wrong. But conflicting with this early Renaissance attitude was a modern sense of personal responsibility. The implications of the thing troubled me desperately.

As I sat there in the darkness, thinking it out—with now and then Miss Wright coming in on the routine business of the day—I realized for the first time the difference between love and passion. There was no doubt that Ann loved me. But I did not love her.

She was as far removed from cheap sentimentality as any woman I have known. She was strangely unromantic. There was an impressive definiteness about everything she did. I knew from the first that the love she gave me was for always. It was to be the big human factor of her life, but it was not to be mutual. In my misery I wanted her comfort, in my loneliness I had need of her affection. I had grown greatly fond of her, dependent on her, but I knew from the first that she was not to be the center of my life.

Nevertheless my course seemed very clear. "The Woman Who Did" had not been written in those days. The idea, now so commonly expressed in literature, that sex life outside of marriage might be beautiful and dignified, was not familiar. Although I had no longing for a perpetual mating, no desire to marry her, my conscience told me very clearly that I ought to. I did not think that I could, with anything like decency, do less.

Since Margot had receded, I had not been given to romantic dreams. I was not counting on the grand passion, as a necessary part of life, so there was no especial self-sacrifice in closing the door on that possibility by marrying a woman I did not wholly love. Yet, threatened with blindness without money or a trade, what had I to offer her? The more I thought of these things the more humble I became. However her "fair name" seemed more important to me than any of these considerations. It was regrettable that I could not assure her ease and comfort. It was regrettable that I could not give her the love which should be the kernel of marriage, but all this seemed no reason not to offer her the husk.

When at last Ann came, she laughed at me. What? Get married? Nothing was further from her mind. She had her own work mapped out for her. Set up a home? Why as soon as she had saved a hundred and fifty dollars more she was going to Paris to study with Pasteur. People might laugh at his germs and cultures and serums. Let them laugh! The future was to bacteriology. Marry? Of course she loved me, but where did I get those two ideas mixed up?

She gave me a lecture on free love. It is hard to write about a theory to which I am so strongly opposed. Yet Ann's attitude in this matter is an integral part of my story.

The longer I live the more remarkable it seems to me, how limited is the field in which any of us does original thinking. One of my friends is an exceedingly able physician. Within his specialty he has been startlingly radical. His cures, however, are so amazing that his colleagues are accepting his methods. But in all other departments of thought he is hopelessly conservative. Another acquaintance, a painter, is a daring innovator in his use of colors, but has unquestioningly accepted all those beliefs which Max Nordau has called "The Conventional Lies of our Civilization." To one subject we seem to give all our mental energy, all our powers of original thinking, in other matters we believe what we are taught. It was so with Ann. Her specialty was bacteriology, her ideas on marriage she had inherited.

67

Her mother, whom I afterwards came to know and respect, was a remarkable woman. Mr. Barton, after a fairly upright younger life, had deserted her at thirty-five. Although neither Ann nor Mrs. Barton, ever spoke much of him, I learned that he had died, a hopeless drunkard. At first the mother had supported the children by nursing and sewing among the families of her Vermont neighbors. And everywhere, once she had entered the privacy of a household, she found the same repellent pretense, a carefully preserved outward show of harmony and affection, an inside reality of petty quarrels and discord. Often she found situations of more abhorrent tragedy, jealousy, hatred and strange passions, women heartbroken for lack of love, bodily broken from an excess of child-bearing. From considering her own misfortunes a horrible exception, she came to believe such sorrows were pitifully common. And everywhere women seemed to be the victims. However unhappy a man's married life might be, he found release in his work. To the woman, home was everything, if it went wrong, all life was awry.

By chance apparently, but I suppose inevitably, she had come in contact with some of the leaders of the early "Woman's Rights Movement." She corresponded with them ardently and at length came west to Cincinnati, having decided that she needed education. She supported herself and her children by needle-work and spent half the nights, after they were abed, over schoolbooks. She had to begin at the beginning. By herself, in her garret, she followed the grammar school course, crowding the work which takes a child two or three years, into the half nights of one. Gradually she worked her way up to the position of forewoman in a large embroidery establishment and so was able to send her children through high school, the older ones to college. But her health had given out before Ann's turn came.

Her interest in the Woman's Movement had brought her into touch with all sorts of radicals and shortly after her arrival in Cincinnati she had met Herr Grun, a German Anarchist refugee. The friendship had grown into a beautiful love relationship which had lasted until his death.

Ann had accepted all the libertarian dogmas of her foster father. It seemed very wonderful to me to hear her speak about her "home." It was a barren enough word to me. But to her it meant a wealth of affection, a place of sure sympathy. I listened with sad and bitter envy to her stories of childhood. The loving kindness, the happy harmony which she had known at home, she had been taught to believe resulted from the free relationship between her mother and her lover. Ann had grown up in an atmosphere where free love was the conventional thing.

Persecution is the surest way of convincing a heretic that he is right. I have known a good many Anarchists and the most striking thing about them is their community interest. Whether or not they are seriously offensive towards society, they are all in a close defensive alliance against it. The hostility they meet on every hand forces them to associate with their own kind. Ann had grown up among the children of comrades.

To them love is an entirely personal, individual matter. The interference of the Church or State they regard as impertinent and indecent. They take this whole business of sex more seriously, and in some respects more sanely, than most of us. Their households, as far as I have seen them, are very little different, no better nor worse than the average home. Their advantage lies in the fact that most Anarchists are of kindly nature and that they are seldom cursed with money grubbing materialism. But this is a difference in the people, not in their institutions.

Marriage, for Ann, would have been a repudiation of her up-bringing and the people she loved, comparable to that of a daughter of a Baptist minister who became a Catholic nun or the third wife of a Mormon Elder. But Protestant women sometimes do marry Mormons or take the veil. And Anarchists are no wiser in bending the twig so it will stay bent than Baptists. If Ann had been this type of a woman, she might have kicked over the traces, and have left her people to marry me, as carefully reared daughters have done in similar crises since the world was young.

But she had a very definite theory that love should not be allowed to interfere with life. Each of us, she held, has been given a distinct personality, a special job to do in the world, and the development of this personality, the performance of this individual task, is the great aim of life. Love should not distract one from the race to the appointed goal. Love is an adornment of life. She spoke with biting scorn of a man she knew who "wore too many rings on his fingers." His taste was bad, he tried to over-decorate his life and so missed the reality of life. The goal she had set before her was bacteriology and she had not the faintest doubt that she had chosen it rightly. This was to be her life. If the fates granted her such joys as she called her love for me, it was something to be thankful for. But it must be subservient to—never allowed to interfere with—her career.

Certainly this is not the ordinary attitude of women towards love. But Ann was an exceptional woman, one of those unaccountable exceptions, which we label with the vague word "Genius."

A few months ago I picked up an illustrated French paper and opening it at random came upon a page containing photographs of half a dozen celebrated women. Ann's face was among them. There was an article by an eminent psychologist on "Women of Genius." His conclusions did not especially interest me, but I had never before seen so concise a statement of Ann's accomplishments, the learned societies to which she belongs, the scientific reviews she helps to edit, the brochures she has written, the noted discoveries she had made. It startled me to see on half a page so impressive a record of achievement.

It helps me now to a better understanding of the young woman, who puzzled me sorely twenty odd years ago. In those days I saw no special promise of distinction. I smile with a wry twist to my mouth when I recall my presumption in thinking that it was necessary for her to hide herself under the shadow of my name. I suppose that if she had consented to marry me, we would have somehow found a way to gain a livelihood. In my crippled condition I could not have done much—I have no knack for money making. The burden of supporting the home would have fallen considerably on her.

Perhaps it would have been "better" for both of us, if her strange upbringing had not made marriage distasteful to her. She and I might possibly have been "happier" if she had not been filled by the consuming ambition which drove her to put love in a lesser place. Perhaps. But the race would have been poorer, would have lost her very real contributions to the elimination of disease.

I could not argue with her then about these things. My knowledge was so much less than hers. But although it was a relief to find that she would not marry me, there was still a feeling of deep injustice. There seemed a despicable cheat in taking from her so much more than I could give. It seemed ultimately unfair to accept a love I could not wholly return. But she brushed aside any efforts to explain. She ran to her room, and bringing a copy of the Rubaiyat, preached me quite a sermon on the quatrain about Omar's astronomy, how he had revised the calendar, struck off dead yesterday and the unborn tomorrow. Love, she said, was subjective, its joy came from loving, rather than from being loved. Then suddenly she became timorous. Perhaps she was being "invasive," perhaps I did not want her to love me....

My scruples went by the board with a rush. I surely did want her. And I was able to convince her of it.

# V

Our relations having been for the time determined, Ann set about to reform me. She was really horrified at the isolated life I had been leading. That I took little interest in humanity, none at all in public life and only by chance knew who was mayor of the city, shocked her. Every evening, after her other patients had been settled for the night, she brought me the papers. There was no love-making—only one kiss—until she had read to me for half an hour. It bored me to extinction, but she insisted that it was good for me. I had to listen, because each evening she examined me on what she had read the night before. So I acquired a certain amount of unrelated information about millionaire divorces, murders and municipal politics.

Her next step was to make me associate with the other patients.

"Bored?" she scolded. "It's a sin to be bored. They're people—human beings—just as good as you are. You're not interested in Mrs. Stickney's husband? You're not interested in Mr. Blake's business worries? Those are the two great facts of life. The woman half of the world is thinking about men. The man half is thinking about business. They are the two things which are really most interesting."

She took my reformation so much to heart that I began to be interested in it myself. I familiarized myself with all the symptoms of a husband's dyspepsia. Mrs. Stickney's eye trouble seemed to have been caused by a too close application to cook books—in search for a dish her husband could digest. From Mr. Blake's peevish discourse I got a new insight into business and the big and little dishonesties which go to make it up. I sometimes wonder if he really was robbed during his illness as much as he expected to be. He was convinced that his chief competitor would buy his trade secrets from his head book-keeper. He did not seem angry at his rival nor at his employee for seizing this opportunity to cheat him, but at the fates which, by his sickness, offered them so great a temptation. He complained bitterly because no such lucky chances had ever come to him.

But it was through the newspapers that I gained most.

"Want to hear about a millionaire socialist, who says that all judges and policemen ought to serve a year in jail before being eligible for office?"

"It sounds more hopeful than campaign speeches," I said submissively.

It was Norman Benson. I recognized his quaint way of expressing things, before she came to his name.

"I know him," I laughed.

I had to tell her all about our short acquaintance.

"Why don't you ask him to come up and see you?"

I did not feel that I knew him well enough to bother him. I had not seen him nor heard from him for three years.

The first thing in the morning, without letting me know, she telephoned him of my plight. About eleven o'clock, to my immense surprise, Miss Wright brought him to my room.

Benson was the busiest man I have ever known. In later years when I roomed with him and was his most intimate friend, I could never keep track of half his activities. He was a sort of "consulting engineer" in advertising. Big concerns all over the country would send for him and pay well to have him attract the attention of the public to some new product. He could write the Spotless Town kind of verses while eating breakfast, and although he did not take art seriously, he drew some of the most successful advertisements of his time. One year he earned about thirty thousand dollars, above his inherited income of ten thousand. He did not spend more than five thousand a year on himself, but he was always hard up.

He was director of half a hundred philanthropies—settlements, day-nurseries, immigrant homes, children's societies, and so forth. His pet hobby was the "Arbeiter Studenten Verein." When he did not entirely support these enterprises, he paid the yearly deficit. It was such expenses which pushed him into the advertising work he detested.

It was a wonder to me how, in spite of these manifold activities, he found time for the thousand and one little kindnesses, the varied personal relations he maintained with all sorts and conditions of men. Once a week or so he dined at the University Club, more often at the settlement, and the other nights he took pot-luck on the top floor of some tenement with one of his Arbeiter Studenten. In the same way he found time to remember me and bring cheer into the hospital.

That first morning, in speaking of the newspaper story, I asked him if he was a socialist.

"Hanged if I know," he said. "I never joined any socialist organization. I don't care much for these soap-box people. They talk about reconstructing our industrial institutions, and most of them don't know how to make change for a dollar. They talk about overthrowing Wall Street, and they don't know railroad-stock from live-stock. They don't begin to realize what a big thing it is—nor how unjust and crazy and top-heavy. But sometimes I think I must be a socialist. I can't open my mouth and say anything serious without everybody calling me a socialist. I don't know."

The remaining weeks in the hospital gave me a great fund of things to ponder over. My mind works retrospectively. I have always sympathized with the cud-chewing habit of the cow. The impressions of the hour are never clear-cut with me. For an experience to become real, I must mull over it a long time; gradually it sinks into my consciousness and becomes a vital possession.

Benson's sort of kindness was absolutely new to me. No one had ever done things for me as he did. And as it surprised me to have him take the trouble to send me a can of my favorite tobacco, so the affection, the intimate revelations of love, which Ann gave me, was a thing undreamed of. "Come with me, up on to a high mountain, and I will show you all the wonder of the world"—such was Ann's gift to me. Out of the horror of darkness, from the very bottom of the slough of despond, she led me up into the white light of the summit peaks of life.

As I read back over these pages, I find that I have described Ann as a voice, as a person who thought and talked of serious things, who seemed principally absorbed in an ambition, which up to that time had borne no fruit. I would like to picture the woman who came to me in the darkness with a wealth of cheer and tenderness and love.

Some day I hope our literature and our minds will be purified so that such things can be dealt with sanely and sweetly. But that time has not yet come and I must be content with the tools at hand. Ann brought to me in those desolate days all the wondrous womanly things—the quaint and gentle jests of love, the senseless sweet words and names which are caresses, the sudden gusts of self revelation, the strange and unexpected restraints—of which I may not write.

I was not lonely any more—not even when Miss Wright was on duty— there was so much to ponder over.


# VI


At last the bandages were taken off. I recall the sudden painful glare of the darkened room, the three doctors in hospital costumes, who were consulting on different forms of torture. Especially I remember the mole on the forehead of the chief, a gray haired, spectacled man. It was the first things my eyes, startled out of their long sleep, fixed upon. The ordeal dragged along tragically. It seemed that they were intentionally slow. But the verdict when it came was acquittal. I was lucky. With care I might regain almost normal vision. But for months I must not try to read. Always, all my life, I must stop at the first hint of fatigue.

So, having adjusted some smoked glasses, they sent me back to my room, to pack and go out into a new life. As I entered the corridor, I saw two nurses at the other end. My heart stopped with a jump and I was suddenly dizzy. Somehow I had not thought of Ann in terms of sight. She had come to me out of the darkness, revealed herself as a sound and a touch. I had no idea how she would look. They both came towards me. I could see very little through my dark glasses. I could not guess which was which.

"So. They've taken off the bandages? I'm very glad." It was Miss Wright's strenuous voice.

"I'm glad, too," Ann said.

I tried to see her, but my eyes were full of tears.

"I'll show him his room," Ann said.

When the door was closed on us, she threw her arms about my neck and cried as I had never seen a woman cry.

"Oh! beloved," she sobbed. "I'm so glad. I was afraid—afraid you were going to be blind."

She had always been so cheerful, so professional, about my case—of course it would turn out all right—that I had not seen it from her point of view. It was a revelation to me that her bravery had been a sham.

"Oh. I was afraid—afraid!"

I tried to comfort her but all the pent-up worry and fear of weeks had broken out. And I had not realized that her love had made my risk a personal tragedy for her.

When she had quieted a little, I wanted her to stand away so that I might look at her. But no—she said—she did not want me to see her first when her eyes were swollen with tears. She clung to me tightly and would not show me her face.

There was a knock at the door. I had not lived long enough to realize the seriousness of a woman's wet eyes, and, without thought of this, I said, "Come in." It was Benson.

"Miss Wright tells me—"

He hesitated. He was looking at Ann. I turned too. She was making a brave effort to appear unconcerned, but her eyes were red past all hiding.

"Yes," she said, in her professional tone. "The news is very good. Better than we hoped."

"Fine. I dropped in," Benson said, as though there was nothing to be embarrassed about, "to see how you came out and get you to spend the weekend with me if they let you go. I've got to visit my uncle and aunt—stupid old people—hypochondriacs. But they are going to Europe next week and I really must see them. I'll die of boredom if there isn't someone to talk to. Better come along—the sailing's good. I've got to run over to the club for a few minutes. Can you get your grip packed in half an hour? All right. So long."

Ann was as nearly angry as I have ever seen her.

"At least you might have given me time to dry my eyes."

"I don't believe he noticed anything. Men never see things like that," I said.

But Ann laughed at this and so her good temper was restored.

Her face, now that I saw it, was not at all what I had expected. It was serious, meagre, a bit severe. I had thought of her as blonde, but her hair was a rich, deep brown. Of course I am no judge of her looks. She had brought joy into my darkness. She could not but be beautiful for me.

The expression is what counts most. About her face, emphasized by her nurse's uniform, was a definite air of sensibleness, of New England reliability. Perhaps under other circumstances she would not have attracted me. Her face in repose might not have inspired more than confidence. But when she put her hands on my shoulders and looked up into my face, with the light of love in her eyes, it seemed to me that a mystic halo of beauty shone about her. No other woman has ever looked to me as Ann did. And yet I know that most people would call her "plain."

The hardest thing for me to accept about her was her height. I had thought her considerably shorter than Miss Wright. I had been misled of course by the relative size of their voices. Ann was above average height and Miss Wright hardly five feet.

In the half hour before Benson returned, we had not discussed anything more concrete than opportunities to meet outside the hospital. She was free on alternate Saturdays from supper time till midnight. I was rather afraid that Benson, when we were alone, might ask some questions or make some joke about her, but he talked busily of other things.

His uncle and aunt were a lonely old couple. Their children were established and they had little left to interest them except their illnesses, some of which, Benson said, were real. It was a beautiful house just out of Stamford on the Sound—rather dolefully empty now that the children had gone. I had never seen such luxury, such heavy silver, such ubiquitous servants.

They were planning to live in Paris, near a daughter who had married a Frenchman. Their arrangements had been all made. But at the last moment their trained nurse had thrown them into confusion by deciding suddenly that she did not want to leave America. The aunt told us about it, querulously, at dinner. Ann's desire came to mind.

"How much free time would the nurse have?" I asked. "I know one who is anxious to live in Paris and study with Pasteur. She is very capable. Your nephew has seen her—Miss Barton—she was at the hospital. I liked her immensely."

Benson shot a quick glance at me. It was the only sign he ever gave of having noticed any intimacy between us.

"My aunt expects to live permanently in Paris," he said. "She would not want to take any one who was not willing to stay indefinitely."

"That, I think, would suit Miss Barton exactly."

Benson immediately fell in with my suggestion and recommended Ann enthusiastically. I had to answer a string of questions. The aunt was one of those undecided persons who hate to make up their mind, but the uncle wanted to get started. We talked about it continually during the three Sunday meals, and on Monday morning they went in to see her, with a note of introduction from me.

Ann, as I had foreseen, was delighted with the opportunity. She pleased them, and as soon as she could find a substitute, an easy matter, as her position was desirable, the arrangements were made.

## VII

Ann and I spent together the day before they sailed. We had planned an excursion to the sea-side, but it rained desperately and we found refuge in an hotel. We were too much interested in each other to care much about the weather or our surroundings. Any beauties of nature which might have distracted our attention would have seemed an impertinence.

It was a day of never-to-be-forgotten delight. And yet it was not without a subtle alloy. By an unexpressed agreement, we lived up to Omar's philosophy, we discussed neither the past nor the future. I was afraid to stop and think, for fear it might seem wrong....

Once she brought a cloud by some expressions of gratitude for my having, as she put it, given her this great opportunity to realize her dream of studying with Pasteur. And all the while, I knew it was not solely for her sake that I had picked up this chance, which the fates had thrown me. Despite the joy of her love there was this under-current of incertitude. I wanted to get far enough away from it, to judge it. It is hard to express what I mean, but I was happier, more light-hearted, that day, because I knew she was leaving the next.

But these blurred moments were—only moments. We were young. It was the spring of life as it was of the year. The spirit of poesy, of the great Lyrics, was there in that tawdry hotel room....

In the early morning, through the wet glistening streets we made our way across town towards the river. Of course I knew just where we were going, but somehow the entrance to the dock found me surprised and unprepared. For a moment we stood there, shaking hands as formally as might be. Suddenly tears sparkled in her eyes, she reached up and kissed me. Then she turned abruptly and walked into the bare, shadowy building. She had a firm step, she was sallying out to meet her destiny.

I watched until she was out of sight. And then I surprised myself by a sigh of strange relief.

# VIII

Later in the day I lunched with Benson at the University Club.

"What are your plans now?" he asked as we settled down to coffee and cigarettes.

"Find a job, I suppose."

"You're in no condition to work nor to look for work—just out of the hospital."

"But I've got to eat."

"That's a fool superstition!" he exploded. "You don't have to work in order to eat. None of 'the best people' do. Half the trouble with the world is that so many idiots will sweat—just to eat. If they'd refuse to work for tripe-stews and demand box seats at the opera, it would do wonders. Why people will slave all their lives long for a chance to die in a tenement is beyond me. What kind of work do you want?"

My ideas on that point were vague.

"How much money have you?"

That I had figured out.

"One hundred and eighty-five dollars and ninety-three cents. And then my books—perhaps I could get a hundred more for them."

"Of course if you are sufficiently unscrupulous that's a good start for a fortune. Lots of men have done it on less. But it's a bore to sit back and watch money grow. Did you ever see a hunk of shad-roe—all eggs? Money's a darn sight more prolific than fish. Impregnate a silver dollar with enough cynicism and you can't keep your expenses up with your income. Look how wealth has grown in this country in spite of all our thievery and waste! In the Civil War we burned money—threw millions after millions into the flames—we never noticed it. The nation was richer in '65 than in '60.

"But making money is a fool's ambition. Just think how many dubs succeed in earning a living. Anybody can do that. It isn't original. Look round for interesting work. Something that's worth doing aside from the wages. Take things easy. If you begin worrying, you'll grab the first job that offers and think you're lucky. Come down to the settlement—the board's seven a week. You can live three months on half your money. In that time you'll see a dozen openings. You'll be able to take your choice instead of snatching the first job you see."

This conversation was typical of Benson. He nearly always started off with some generalized talk, but just when you began to think he had forgotten you and the issue, he would end up sharp, with a definite proposition. I accepted his advice and moved to the "Children's House."

So my temporary blindness brought me into contact with two great facts of life I had hitherto ignored, women and want—the beauty of sex and the horror of misery. And these two things occupied my whole mind.

One by one I picked out my memories of Ann and pondered them in all their implications. I tried to arrange them like beads on a thread, in some ordered unified design. Day by day she became a more real and concise personality.

The effect of my encounter with Ann, I could then have found no word to describe. But a very modern term would explain my meaning to some. She opened my spirit to the "over-tones" of life. Last year I heard "Pelleas and Melisande." I sat through the first half hour unstirred. There was much sensuous appeal to the eyes, but the music seemed unsatisfactory. Suddenly appreciation came. Suddenly I understood with a rush what he was meaning to say. All the mystic harmony, the unwritten, unwritable wonder of it swept over me. And now Debussy seems to me the greatest of them all. "The Afternoon of the Faun" moves me more deeply than any other music. In fact, I think, we must invent some newer name than "music," for this more subtle perfume of sound.

In a similar way Ann showed me the "over-tones" of life. Deeper significance, mystic meanings, I found in many things I had hardly noticed before. The sunsets held a richer wealth of colors. I had known Chaucer and his predecessors intimately, somewhat less thoroughly all the world's great poetry. It had interested me not only as a study of comparative philology, not only as a delicate game of prosody—of rhythm and rhyme and refrain. It had held for me a deeper charm than these mechanical elements—fascinating as they are. But somehow it all became new to me. I discovered in the old familiar lines things, which, alone in my study, I had never dreamed of. I began to see in all poetry—in all art—an effort to express these "overtones."

On the other hand, my active life was spent in the appalling misery of the slums—a thing equally new to me. In those days the majority of our neighbors were Irish and German. Decade after decade the nationality of Stanton Street has changed. First the Germans disappeared, then the Russian and Hungarian Jews pushed out the Irish, now one hears as much Italian as Yiddish. The heart-rending poverty, the degradation of filth and drunkenness is not a matter of race. Wave after wave of immigration finds its native customs and morality insufficient to protect it from the contagion of the slum. And so it will be until we have the wisdom to blot out the crime of congestion and give our newcomers a decent chance.

I try to force my mind back to its attitude in those first weeks in the "Children's House" and try to explain to myself how I became part of "The Settlement Movement." I fail. I think very few of the really important things in life are susceptible to a logical explanation.

I have met some people, who from books alone have been impressed with the injustices of our social organization, and have left the seclusion of their studies to throw their lives into the active campaign for justice. Such mental processes are, I think, rare. Certainly it came about differently in my case.

When Benson proposed that I should come to live in the settlement, I felt no "call" to social service. I was lonely, out of work, utterly adrift. The memory of the evening I had spent with him in the Children's House and the interesting people I had met was very pleasant. I had no suspicions that I was going there to stay. It appealed to me as sort of convalescent home, where I could rest up until I was able to go out and cope with the ordinary life of the world.

At first the little circle of workers seemed incoherent. Here were half a dozen highly educated men and women, most of whom had left pleasant homes, living in the most abject neighborhood of the city. Why? What good were they doing? Around us roared the great fire of poverty. Here and there they were plucking out a brand, to be sure. But the fire was beyond their control. They did not even think they could stop it.

I remember one night at dinner we had for guest, a professor of economics from one of the big universities. He prided himself on his cold scientific view-point, he regarded the settlement movement as sentimental, almost hysterical, and he had the ill-breeding to forget that what he scoffed at was a desperately serious thing to his hosts.

"This settlement movement reminds me of a story," he said. "Once upon a time a kind hearted old gentleman was walking down the street and found a man—drunk—in the gutter. He tried vainly to pull the unfortunate one up on the sidewalk and then losing courage, he said, 'My poor man, I can't help you, but I'll get down in the gutter beside you.'"

He laughed heartily, but no one else did. The story fell decidedly flat. It was several minutes before anyone took up the challenge. At last, Rev. Mr. Dawn, the head worker, coughed slightly and replied. He had turned quite red and I saw that the joke had stung him.

"That is a very old story," he said, "it was current in Jerusalem a good many centuries ago. It was told with great *eclat* by a scribe and a pharisee who 'passed by on the other side.'"

"Oh, come, now!" our guest protested. "That's hardly a fair comparison. The Samaritan we are told really did some good to the poor devil. And besides the victim in that case was not a drunkard, but a person who had 'fallen among thieves.'"

"Thieves?" Benson asked, with a ring of anger in his voice. "Do you think there are no thieves but highway robbers?"—and then apparently realizing the uselessness of arguing with such a man, he smiled blandly and in a softer tone went on. "Besides some of us are foolish enough to imagine that we also can do some good. Let's not discuss that, we'd rather keep our illusions. Won't you tell us what you are teaching your classes about Marx's theory of surplus value? Of course I know that phrase is taboo. But what terms do you use to describe the proceeds of industrial robbery?"

I could not make up my mind whether the professor realized that Benson was trying to insult him or whether he was afraid to tackle the question. At all events he turned to Mrs. Dawn and changed the conversation.

This little tilt gave me a great deal to think of. I did not like the professor's attitude towards life. But after all, what good were these settlement workers doing? Again and again this question demanded an answer. Sometimes I went out with Mr. Dawn to help in burying the dead. I could see no adequate connection between his kindly words to the bereaved and the hideous dragon of tuberculosis which stalked through the crowded district. What good did Dawn's ministrations do? Sometimes I went out with Miss Bronson, the kindergartner and listened to her talk to uncomprehending mothers about their duties to their children. What could Miss Bronson accomplish by playing a few hours a day with the youngsters who had to go to filthy homes? They were given a wholesome lunch at the settlement. But the two other meals a day they must eat poorly cooked, adulterated food. Sometimes I went out with Miss Cole, the nurse, to visit her cases. It was hard for me to imagine anything more futile than her single-handed struggle against unsanitary tenements and unsanitary shops.

I remember especially one visit I made with her. It was the crisis for me. The case was a child-birth. There were six other children, all in one unventilated room, its single window looked out on a dark, choked airshaft, and the father was a drunkard. I remember sitting there, after the doctor had gone, holding the next youngest baby on my knee, while Miss Cole was bathing the puny newcomer.

"Can't you make him stop crying for a minute?" Miss Cole asked nervously.

"No," I said with sudden rage. "I can't. I wouldn't if I could. Why shouldn't he cry? Why don't the other little fools cry! Do you want them to laugh?"

She stopped working with the baby and offered me a flask of brandy from her bag. But brandy was not what I wanted. Of course I knew men sank to the very dregs. But I had never realized that some are born there.

When she had done all she could for the mother and child, Miss Cole put her things back in the bag and we started home. It was long after midnight but the streets were still alive.

"What good does it do?" I demanded vehemently. "Oh, I know—you and the doctor saved the mother's life—brought a new one into the world and all that. But what good does it do? The child will die—it was a girl—let's get down on our knees right here and pray the gods that it may die soon—not grow up to want and fear—and shame." Then I laughed. "No, there's no use praying. She'll die all right! They'll begin feeding her beer out of a can before she's weaned. No. Not that. I don't believe the mother will be able to nurse her. She'll die of skimmed milk. And if that don't do the trick there's T.B. and several other things for her to catch. Oh, she'll die all right. And next year there'll be another. For God's sake, what's the use? What good does it do?" Abruptly I began to swear.

"You mustn't talk like that," Miss Cole said in a strained voice.

"Why shouldn't I curse?" I said fiercely, turning on her challengingly, trying to think of some greater blasphemy to hurl at the muddle of life. But the sight of her face, livid with weariness, her lips twisting spasmodically from nervous exhaustion, showed me one reason not to. The realization that I had been so brutal to her shocked me horribly.

"Oh, I beg your pardon," I cried.

She stumbled slightly. I thought she was going to faint and I put my arm about her to steady her. She was almost old enough to be my mother, but she put her head on my shoulder and cried like a little child. We stood there on the sidewalk—in the glare of a noisy, loathsome saloon—like two frightened children. I don't think either of us saw any reason to go anywhere. But we dried our eyes at last and from mere force of habit walked blindly back to the children's house. On the steps she broke the long silence.

"I know how you feel—everyone's like that at first, but you'll get used to it. I can't tell 'why.' I can't see that it does much good. But it's got to be done. You mustn't think about it. There are things to do, today, tomorrow, all the time. Things that must be done. That's how we live. So many things to do, we can't think. It would kill you if you had time to think. You've got to work —work.

"You'll stay too. I know. You won't be able to go away. You've been here too long. You won't ever know 'why.' You'll stop asking if it does any good. And I tell you if you stop to think about it, it will kill you. You must work."

She went to her room and I across the deserted courtyard and up to mine. But there was no sleep. It was that night that I first realized that I also must. I had seen so much I could never forget. It was something from which there was no escape. No matter how glorious the open fields, there would always be the remembered stink of the tenements in my nostrils. The vision of a sunken cheeked, tuberculosis ridden pauper would always rise between me and the beauty of the sunset. A crowd of hurrying ghosts—the ghosts of the slaughtered babies—would follow me everywhere, crying, "Coward," if I ran away. The slums had taken me captive.

As I sat there alone with my pipe, the groans of the district's uneasy sleep in my ears, I realized more strongly than I can write it now the appalling unity of life. I sensed the myriad intricate filaments which bind us into an indivisible whole. I saw the bloody rack-rents of the tenements circulating through all business—tainting it—going even into the collection plates of our churches. I saw the pay drawn by the lyric poet, trailing back through the editorial bank account to the pockets of various subscribers who speculated in the necessities of life, who waxed fat off the hunger of the multitude. My own clothes were sweat-shop made.

I could not put out the great fire of injustice. I could at least bind up the sores of some of my brothers who had fallen in—who were less lucky than I. My old prep. school ethics came back to me. "I want to live so that when I die, the greatest number of people will be glad I did live." In a way it did not seem to matter so much whether I could accomplish any lasting good. I must do what I could. Such effort seemed to me the only escape from the awful shame of complaisancy.

Wandering in and out of the lives of the people of our neighborhood, I looked about for a field of activity. There were so many things to be done. I sought for the place where the need was greatest. It did not take me long to decide—a conclusion I have not changed—that the worst evils of our civilization come to a head in "The Tombs."

The official name for that pile of stone and brick is "The Criminal Courts Building." But the people persist in calling it "The Tombs." The prison dated from the middle of the century and a hodge-podge of official architecture had been added, decade by decade, as the political bosses needed money. It housed the district attorney's office, the "police court," "special sessions" for misdemeanants, and "general sessions" for felons. One could study our whole penal practice in that building.

I was first led into its grim shadow by a woman who came to the settlement. Her son, a boy of sixteen, had been arrested two months before and had been waiting trial in an unventilated cell, originally designed for a single occupant, with two others. His cell-mates had changed a dozen times. I recall that one had been an old forger, who was waiting an appeal, another was the keeper of a disorderly house and a third had been a high church curate, who had embezzled the foreign mission fund to buy flowers for a chorus girl. The lad was patently innocent. And this was the very reason he was held so long. The district attorney was anxious to make a high record of convictions. His term was just expiring and he was not calling to trial the men he thought innocent, these "technically" bad cases he was shoving over on his successor. At last, with the help of a charitable lawyer, named Maynard, of whom I will write more later, we forced the case on the calendar and the boy was promptly acquitted.

In talking over this case with Benson, I found that he was already interested in the problems of Criminology. He was one of the trustees of "The Prisoner's Aid Society." The interview in the newspaper, which Ann had read to me at the hospital, had been an effort of his to draw attention to the subject and to infuse some life into the society.

"They're a bunch of fossils," he said. "Think they're a *société savante.*' They read books by foreign penologists and couldn't tell a crook from a carpet sweeper. We need somebody to study American crime. Not a dilettante —someone who will go into it solid."

I told him I had thought a good deal about it and was ready to tackle the job if the ways and means could be arranged.

"I imagine I could get the society to pay you a living salary. But they are dead ones. If you did anything that wasn't in the books, it would scare them. I'll think it over."

About a week later, I received a letter from the recently elected, not yet installed district attorney asking me to call on him. His name was Brace, his letter the result of Benson's thinking. I found him a typical young reform politician. A man of good family, he was filled with enthusiasm, and confidently expected to set several rivers on fire. There was going to be absolute, abstract justice under his regime. Benson had told him how the actual district attorney was shoving off the "bad cases" on him and he was righteously indignant. He wanted someone whose fidelity he could trust, who would keep an eye on the prison side of the Tombs. He was sure there were many abuses there to stop, and he was the man to do it. The only position he could offer me under the law was that of special county detective. The pay would be eighteen hundred a year.

"It is not exactly a dignified position," he said. "The county detectives are a low class,—but of course you won't have to associate with them."

I was more than ready to take the place. With the rest of the new administration I was sworn in, and so entered on my life work. It was a far cry from my earlier ambition to be a Fellow at Oxford.

# BOOK IV

# I

"Literary unity" can be secured in an autobiography only at the expense of all sense of reality. The simplest of us is a multiple personality, can be described only partially from any one point of view. The text book on physiology which I studied in school contained three illustrations. One of them pictured a human being as a structure of bones, a skeleton; another showed man as a system of veins and arteries; the third as a mass of interwoven muscles. None of them looked like any man I have ever seen. It is the same with most autobiographies, the writers, in order to center attention on one phase of their activities, have cut away everything which would make their stories seem life-like.

"The Memoirs" of Cassanova give us the picture of a lover. But he must have been something more than a *roué*. "The Personal Recollections" of General Grant portray the career of a soldier. But after all he was a man first, it was more or less by chance that he became a victory-machine. How fragmentary is the picture of his life, which Benvenuto Cellini gives us!

I might accept these classic models and tell directly the story of my work in the Tombs. I might limit my narrative to that part of myself which was involved in friendship with Norman Benson. Or again, I might strip off everything else, ignore the flesh and bones and blood vessels, and write of myself as an "emotional system." In one of these ways I might more nearly approach a literary production. But certainly it would be at a sacrifice of verisimilitude. Perhaps some great writer will come who will unite the artistic form with an impression of actuality. But until genius has taught us the method we must choose between the two ideals. My choice is for reality rather than art.

And life, as it has appeared to me, is episodal in form, unified only in the continual climaxes of the present moment. It is a string of incidents threaded on to the uninterrupted breathing of the same person. The facts of any life are related only *de post facto*, in that they influence the future course of the individual to whom they happen. The farther back we strive to trace these influences, which have formed us, the greater complexity we find. It is not only our bodies which have "family trees," that show the number of our ancestors, generation by generation, increasing with dizzy rapidity. It is the same with our thoughts and tastes. From an immensely diffuse luminosity the lens of life has focused the concentrated rays of light which are you and I.

So—in telling of my life, as I see it—my narrative must break up into fragments. Unartistic as such a form may be, it seems to me the only one possible for autobiography. Incidents must be given, which, however unrelated they appear, seem to me to have been caught by the great lens and to have formed an integral part of the focal point, which sits here—trying to describe itself.

## II

For some years I have been continually writing on the subject of criminology. I could not give, here in this narrative, a complete picture of the Tombs and its people, nor show in orderly sequence how one incident after another forced me into a definite attitude towards our penal system, without repeating what I have published elsewhere. But the atmosphere in which I have spent my working life has so definitely influenced me, has been so important a force in my experiment in ethics, that I must give it some space. I must try, at least, to give some illuminating examples of the sort of thing which did influence me and a brief statement of the attitude which has resulted from my work, for without this background the rest of my story would be meaningless.

At first I found myself the object of universal hostility. The Tombs was a feudal domain of Tammany Hall. I was regarded as an enemy.

The "spoils system" had given place to the evils of civil service. Municipal employees could not be displaced unless "charges" had been proven against them. The people of the Tombs did not worry much about the reform administration. They regarded it as an interruption in the even tenor of their ways, which happily would not last long. They were used to such moral spasms on the part of the electorate and knew how little they were worth. Some of the "Reform" officials tried earnestly to clean up their departments. Their efforts were defeated by unruly subordinates, men trained by and loyal to the machine.

The way things went in the Tombs was typical. Brace had a conference with the new commissioner of correction and as a result some "Instructions for the guidance of prison keepers" were pasted up on the walls. But district attorneys change with every election, while the warden—protected by civil service—goes on forever. The sale of "dope" to the prisoners, forbidden by the "instructions" in capital letters, was not interrupted for a day. Within a week the screws had forgotten to make jokes about it.

Having been appointed by the reformer Brace, I was naturally supposed to be his personal spy. I was saved from falling into so fatal a mistake by a queer old prison missionary called "General Jerry." He had lost an arm at Three Oaks, in the hospital at Andersonville he had found "religion." And as the Lord had visited him in prison, he had devoted what was left of his life to similar work. I think he had no income beyond his pension—he was always shabby. He had very little learning, but an immense amount of homely wisdom. If ever a man has won a right to a starry crown it was Jerry. He and the Father—each in his different way—were the most wholesouled Christians I have ever encountered. Such a noble dignity shone from the eyes of this humble old man that I felt it ever a privilege to sit at his feet and learn of him.

First of all, from watching him, I found that a man who was sincere and honest could win the respect of the Tombs, in spite of such handicaps. Before long we became friends, and he gave me much shrewd advice.

"I come here to save souls," he said. "That's all I come for. I don't let nothin' else interest me. I ain't no district attorney. Sure, I see graft. Can't help it. Every year—onct—I talk to each one of the screws about his soul. 'Big Jim,' I says, 'you ain't right wid God. I ain't the only one as seed you take money from the mother of that dago what was hanged. I ain't the only one as heard you lie to that Jew woman, telling her how you'd help her husband out. I ain't the only one as knows the hotel you took her to. God sees! God hears! He knows! You'd better square it wid Him!' That's all I says. They knows I don't go round tellin' it. And they helps me wid my work. Just yesterday Big Jim comes to me. 'General,' he says, 'there's a guy up in 431 what's crying. I guess you'd better hand him a bit of Gospel.'

"What do you come down here to the Tombs for? To help out the poor guys what they've got wrong. Well. Don't do nothin' else. The screws all think you're gum-shoein' for Brace. 'Jerry,' they says to me, 'who's the new guy? What's he nosin' around here for?' 'Don't know,' I says. 'Better keep your eye on him—same as I'm doin',' I says. 'After a while we'll know.'"

I felt their eyes on me all the time. A couple of months later I sat down beside Jerry in the courtyard; he had a Bible on his knees and a cheese sandwich in his hand.

"I ain't no good sayin' Grace," he explained, "so I always reads a Psalm when I eat," .... "Say, young man," he went on, "I got a word to say to you. The screws ain't got you quite sized up yet—but most of 'em agrees you ain't nobody's damn fool. Now I just want to tell you something. You take this here Tombs all together—warden, screws, cops and lawyers, district attorneys and jedges—you can't never be friends wid all of 'em. They's too many what's hatin' each other. So you got to pick. You say you're going to stay by this job. Well, you just better figure out who's goin' to stick wid you. The jedges stay and the screws stay. But the district attorneys don't never stay more'n two years. Figure it out. That's what the good book means by 'Be ye wise as sarpents.'"

Jerry's advice was good. I had already "figured out" that the favor of the judges was more important for me than that of the district attorney. I had to choose whom I would serve, and it was very evident that it was expedient—if I wished to accomplish anything—to make friends with the mammon of political unrighteousness. The reformers were not only pitifully weak, few of them commanded confidence. They had not been in office six weeks before it was evident that their reëlection was impossible. The best of them were rank amateurs in the business of politics and government. Much of their disaster was due no doubt to well intentioned ignorance. But very few of them stuck to the ship when it began to sink. It would furnish some sombre amusement to publish the figure about how many loud-mouthed reformers went into office again two years later—under the machine banner.

Brace, my chief, as soon as he discovered that the walls of Tammany would not fall down at the sound of newspaper trumpets, lost heart. He had no further interest except to keep himself in the lime-light. Just like all his predecessors, he neglected the routine work of his office and gave all his attention to sensational trials which added to his newspaper notoriety.

One of the big scandals of the preceding administration, which as much as anything else had stirred public indignation against ring politics, had centered about a man named Bateson. He called himself a "contractor" and got most of the work in grading the city streets. There was conclusive evidence to show that almost all the work he did was along the routes of the street car lines. The scandal had been discovered and worked up by one of the newspapers in a most exhaustive manner. The facts were clear. The engineer of the street car company would report to his superiors that such and such a street was too steep for the profitable operation of their cars. One of the directors would call in Bateson. Bateson would take up the matter with the mysterious powers on Fourteenth Street, the aldermen would vote an appropriation to grade the street; Bateson would get the contract and after being well paid by the city would get a tangible expression of appreciation from the street car company. The newspapers had already collected the evidence. The fraud was patent. Everyone expected Brace to call Bateson to trial at once. And it seemed inevitable that from the evidence given in this case, indictments could be drawn against both the "Old Man" on Fourteenth Street and the bribe giving directors of the street car company.

Brace began on this case with a great flourish of trumpets. But one adjournment after another was granted by the Tammany judges. It trailed along for months. And when at last it was called, the bottom had, in some mysterious manner, dropped out of the prosecution. Bateson was acquitted. A few months later Brace resigned and became counsel for the notorious traction reorganization. Some recent magazine articles have exposed the kind of reform he stood for.

"Politics" has always seemed to me a very sorry sort of business. I found plenty of non-partisan misery to occupy all my time. Gradually I fitted myself into the life of the Tombs and became a fixture. When the new elections brought Tammany back to power, "civil service" protected me from the grafters, just as it had protected them from their enemies. And so—in that ill-smelling place—I have passed my life.

To one who is unfamiliar with our juggernaut of justice it is surprising to find how much work there is which a person in my position can do, how many victims can be pulled from under the merciless wheels. First of all there are the poor, who have no money to employ an able lawyer, no means to secure the evidence of their innocence. Then there are the "greenhorn" immigrants who do not know the language and laws of this new country, who do not know enough to notify their consuls. Saddest of all—and most easily helped—are the youngsters. We did not have a children's court in those days. But most of my time, I think, has gone in trying to ease the lot of the innocent wives and children of the prisoners. Whether the man is guilty or not it is always the family which suffers most. And if there had been none of these things, I would have had my hands more than full with trying to help the men who were acquitted. Look over the report of the criminal court in your county and see what the average length of imprisonment while *waiting trial* is. It varies from place to place. It is seldom less than three weeks. And three weeks is a serious matter to the ordinary mechanic. About a third of all the people arrested are acquitted. They get no compensation for their footless imprisonment. Besides the loss of wages, it generally means a lost job.

Two stories, which have been told elsewhere, are worth retelling, as examples of the varied work I found to do.

It was in the summer of my first year in the Tombs that I got interested in the case of a redhaired Italian boy named Pietro Sippio. He was only fourteen years old and he had been indicted for premeditated murder.

The prosecution fell to the lot of the most brilliant young lawyer on the district attorney's staff. The Sippio family was too poor to employ counsel and Judge Ryan, before whom the case was tried, had assigned to the defense a famous criminal lawyer. The trial became at once a tourney of wit between these two men. Little Pietro and his fate was a small matter in the duel for newspaper advertising.

The principal witness for the state was Mrs. Casey, the mother of the little boy who had been killed. She was a widow, a simple, uneducated Irishwoman, who earned her living by washing. She told her story with every appearance of truthfulness. During the morning of the tragic day, she had had a quarrel with Pietro in the backyard of the tenement, where both families lived. Pietro had thrown some dirt on her washing and she had slapped him. Instead of crying as she thought an ordinary boy would have done, he had said he would "get even" with her.

When she heard the noon whistles blow in the neighboring factories, she had gone out on the front sidewalk to get her baby for dinner. The youngster was sitting on the curbstone and as she stood in the doorway calling him, a brick, coming from the roof of the tenement, struck the baby on the head, killing him instantly. She rushed out and—she swore very solemnly—looked up and saw "the little divil's red head, jest as plain as I sees yer honor."

The counsel for the defense was unable to shake her testimony in the least.

Other witnesses swore that, on hearing Mrs. Casey's cry for help, they had rushed up to the roof and had met Mrs. Sippio coming down through the skylight with her two younger children, Felicia a girl of eight and Angelo, who was five. When they had asked her where Pietro was she said she had not seen him. But these witnesses were Irish and sided with Mrs. Casey. They testified that it was easy to pass from one roof to another. And it was evidently their theory that Pietro had escaped in this manner.

A few minutes after the tragedy, Pietro had come whistling up the street and had walked into the arms of the police, who were just starting out to search for him.

In his own defense Pietro testified that after quarreling with Mrs. Casey he had played about in the street for some time and then had gone down to the river with a crowd of boys for a swim. They had not left the water until the noon whistles had warned them of dinner time. They had all hurried into their clothes and gone home. He swore positively that he had not been on the roof during the morning. He evidently did not realize the seriousness of his position and was rather swaggeringly proud of being the center of so much attention.

Two or three other boys testified that Pietro had been swimming with them and had not left the water until after the whistles blew. This was an important point as the baby had been killed a very few minutes after noon. But the district attorney, in a brutal, bullying cross-examination, succeeded in rattling one of the boys—a youngster of eleven—until he did not know his right hand from his left. He broke down entirely, and sobbingly admitted that perhaps Pietro had left before the whistles blew.

Mrs. Sippio testified that she had not seen Pietro after breakfast. She had gone upon the roof about half past eleven to beat out some rugs. She had taken the two younger children with her. But Pietro had not been on the roof. She was a very timid woman, so frightened that she forgot most of her scant English. But she seemed to be telling the truth.

After the testimony was in the counsel for the defense made an eloquent, if rather bombastic plea. He turned more often to the desk of the reporters than to the panel of jurymen. No one, he said, had given any testimony which even remotely implicated Pietro, except the grief-stricken and enraged Mrs. Casey. He made a peroration on the vengeful traits of the Irish. He almost wept over the prospect of eternal damnation which awaited Mrs. Casey's soul on account of her perjury. No reasonable man, he concluded, would condemn a fly on such unreliable testimony.

The prosecutor commenced his summing up by referring to his position as attorney for the people of the state of New York. He said that his able opponent was technically called "The counsel for the defense," but that in reality he himself more truly deserved that title. He was engaged not in the defense of an individual offender, but in that of the whole community of law abiding citizens. And in the pursuance of this most serious function he could not allow his personal pity for the youthful murderer to deflect him from his public duty.

He then gave a picturesque and blood curdling account of the Vendetta and Mafia. He called the jury's attention to the well known traditions of vengeance and murder among the Italians.

As for Mrs. Sippio's testimony—despite his high regard for the sanctity of an oath—he could not find it in his heart to blame this mother who by perjury was endangering bar own soul to save her son. He was more stern in regard to the evidence of the boys. Their only excuse for perjury was their youth. They were members of a desperate gang, of which Pietro was the chief. They were corrupted by the false standards of loyalty to their leader, so common among boys of the street.

The only testimony which deserved the serious attention of the jury was that of Mrs. Casey—the estimable woman, who had seen her babe foully murdered before her eyes. Her identification of Pietro had been absolute.

"I am sorry," he ended, "for this boy, who, by so hideous a crime, has ruined his life at the very outset. But you and I, gentlemen of the jury, are bound by oath to consider only the cold facts. The judge may, if he thinks it wise, be merciful in imposing sentence. But your sole function is to discover truth. Here is a boy of fiery disposition and revengeful race. He vowed vengeance. Some one must have thrown the brick. No one else had the motive. Either the defendant is guilty as charged in the indictment or the brick fell from heaven."

The law explicitly states that a person charged with crime, must be given the benefit of any "reasonable doubt." In the face of the manifestly conflicting testimony, I think every one in court was surprised when the jury returned a verdict of "guilty."

I had not then been long enough in the Tombs to get used to it. I had not become hardened. The tragedy of this case amazed me. A little boy of fourteen condemned of deliberate murder! But the thing which impressed me most was the way the lawyers in the court room rushed up to congratulate the prosecutor for having won so doubtful a case. It would be revolting enough to me if any one should congratulate me on having sent an adult to the gallows. But this little boy of fourteen....

I went over the Bridge of Sighs and talked to Pietro in his cell. If ever a boy impressed me as telling a straightforward story he did. I was convinced that he had been at the riverside when the Casey baby was killed.

After lunch I went up to the scene of the tragedy and my faith in Pietro's innocence was considerably shaken although not overthrown by my talk with Mrs. Casey. She was angry, of course, but she did not seem malicious or vindictive. As I talked with her in her squalid basement room, full of steam from the tubs of soiled clothing, I could not doubt her sincerity. She really believed that Pietro had killed her child. Wiping the suds from her powerful arms, she led me out on the sidewalk and showed me the place where the baby had been sitting and pointed out where she had seen the devilish red head above the coping.

The idea flashed into my mind that a boy would have to be surprisingly clever to throw a brick from that height and hit a baby. With Mrs. Casey following me, I went upon the roof. The chimneys were in a dilapidated condition and a number of loose brick lay about. I was a fairly good ball player at college, but when I tried to hit a water plug on the curb stone, six stories below, I over shot at least eight feet. I asked Mrs. Casey to try and her brick lit in the middle of the street. I called up some of the boys, who were watching my operations from the street, and offered them a quarter if they could hit the water plug. Their attempts were no better than mine.

A little further along the low coping some bricks were piled where children had evidently been building houses with them. I asked Mrs. Casey to push one of them over, easily as if by accident. It fell out a little way from the wall and crashed down fair on the curbing.

"Mrs. Casey," I said, "I don't think Pietro threw that brick. He couldn't have hit the baby if he had tried. Somebody pushed it over by accident."

She stood for some seconds looking down over the wall, shaking her head uncertainly.

"Faith, and I'd think ye were right, sir," she said at last, "If I hadn't seen his red head, sir, jest as plain as I sees yours."

And as we went down stairs, she kept repeating "I sure seen his red head." She was evidently convinced of it.

I went to see Mrs. Sippio. She had moved to another tenement, because of the hostility of the Irish neighbors. I found Mr. Sippio at home taking care of his wife, she was half hysterical from the shame and her grief over Pietro's fate. But she told me her story just as simply and convincingly as had Mrs. Casey. Pietro had not been on the roof. There had been only Felicia and Angelo. I was on the point of leaving in discouragement. Apparently one of the women was lying. I could not guess which. I had gained nothing but a conviction that the brick could not have been thrown with an intent to kill. And that would be a very weak plea against the verdict of a jury. Just as I was getting up, there was a patter of feet in the hall-way. Mrs. Sippio's face lit up. "It is the children," she said. As they rushed noisily into the room the whole mystery was cleared up. It had not occurred to me—nor to any one—that there might be two redheaded boys in the same Italian family. But Angelo's hair was even more flaming than Pietro's.

I took him up in my lap and amused him until I had won his confidence. And when he was thinking about other things, I suddenly asked him.

"Angelo, when that brick fell off the roof the other day, why didn't you tell your mother?"

For a moment he was confused and then began to whimper. He had been afraid of being whipped. I gave a whoop and reassuring the family, I rushed down town and caught Judge Ryan, just as he was leaving his chambers. He listened to me eagerly, for he was as tenderhearted a man as I have ever known and he had been deeply horrified at the idea of having to sentence such a youngster for premeditated murder.

The attorneys were summoned to the judge's chambers, and—I guess that the "pathos" writers of the newspapers were notified. For the next morning they attended court in force. The district attorney made a touching speech. He was grandiloquently glad to announce that new evidence had been discovered which cleared the defendant from all suspicion. The judge set aside the verdict of the jury. The district attorney said that Mrs. Casey had so evidently mistaken Angelo for his older brother that there was no use having a new trial and Pietro was discharged. In making a few remarks on the case,

Judge Ryan mentioned my name and thanked me personally for my part in the matter. With increasing frequency he began to call on me for assistance in other cases and in time the other judges took notice of my existence. I found my hands more than full.

Very often I was able in a similar manner to unearth evidence, which the defendants were too poor and ignorant or the lawyers too lazy to obtain.

But it was in another class of cases that I proved of greatest utility to the judges. A large proportion of the prisoners plead guilty, without demanding a trial. If the whole matter is thrashed out before a jury, the trial judge hears all the evidence and so gets some idea of the motives of the crime, of the personality and environment of the accused. But when a prisoner pleads guilty, practically no details come out in court and unless the judge has some special investigation made he must impose sentence at haphazard. Ryan, almost always asked me to look into such cases. The other judges—with the exception of O'Neil—did so frequently. I would visit the prisoner in his cell and get his story, listen to what the police had to say, and then make a personal investigation to settle disputed points.

As time went on Ryan came to rely more and more on my judgment. He felt, I think, that I was honest; that I could not be bribed and that I was more likely to err on the side of mercy than otherwise. His easy going kindliness was satisfied with this and he was only too glad to let his responsibilities slip on to my shoulders. In the last years before he was elevated to the Supreme Court, he practically let me sentence most of his men. Except in the cases where political influences intervened, my written reports determined the prisoner's fate.

Of course I had to manage his susceptibilities. If I had presumed to suggest definitely what sentence he should impose he would have taken offense. He was very sensitive about his dignity. But I worked out a formal phraseology which did not ruffle his pride and accomplished what I intended. After stating the facts of the case I would end up with a sort of code phrase. If I wanted the judge to give the man another chance under a suspended sentence, I would say: "Under the circumstances, I believe that the defendant is deserving the utmost leniency. I am convinced that the arrest and the imprisonment which he has already suffered have taught him a salutary lesson which he will never forget." From that as the circumstances warranted I could go to the other extreme: "During my investigation of this case, which has been seriously limited because of lack of time, I have been able to find very little in this man's favor."

Every time I had to present such a report as this I felt defeated. It meant that the prisoner was an old offender, hardened to a life of professional crime. And that I could see no hope of reformation. But if I had not accepted such defeats, when circumstances compelled them, the judges would very quickly have lost confidence in my pleas for mercy.

I was valuable to the judges because I relieved them from worry. Whenever anyone approached them on behalf of a prisoner, they shrugged their shoulders and referred the suppliant to me. Now-a-days we have a probation law and such work as I have been describing is legalized. But in the early days, when I had no official sanction I found my position very embarrassing. Without having been in any way elected to office I was actually exercising a power which is supposed to be the gift of the voters. However— like so many things in our haphazard government—my position, extra-legal as it was, grew out of the sheer necessity of the case. The theory is that our judges shall be jurists. And a knowledge of the law does not fit one for the responsibility of deciding how we shall treat our criminals. In the old days when the law frankly punished offenders it was a simple matter and perhaps not too much to ask of judges. But today when we are beginning the attempt to reform those individuals who endanger society, the business of imposing sentence requires not so much a knowledge of law as familiarity with psychology, medicine and sociology. Although an expert in none of these lines, I was accepted as a makeshift. The law did not provide for the employment of specially trained men to assist the judges. I was informally permitted to entirely neglect the ordinary work of a county detective and give all my time to the courts.

The danger in such happy-go-lucky arrangements is that of graft. I could have doubled or quadrupled my salary with impunity. The "shyster" lawyers, who infest the Tombs tried for several years to buy my intercession for their clients. I had to be constantly on my guard to keep them from fooling me. And when they found that they could not reach me in this manner, they tried industriously to discredit me, to trick me into some suspicious conditions so they could intimidate me. More than once they set women on my trail.

The politicians also tried to use me. I received a letter one day from the "Old Man" asking me to intercede for a friend of his. I wrote back that I would investigate carefully. A couple of days later I sent another letter containing the prisoner's record, he had been twice in state prison and many times arrested. "Under the circumstances," I wrote "I cannot recommend mercy in this case."

The next day one of the "Old Man's" lieutenants met me in the corridor and leading me into a corner, told me I was a fool. When what he called "reason" failed to shake me, he became abusive and threatened to have me "fired." I took the whole matter to Ryan. He told me not to worry, that he would talk it over with the "Old Man." I do not know what passed between them. But after that I had no more trouble from Fourteenth Street. Whenever I saw the "Old Man," he gave me a cordial nod. Frequently his runners would hand me one of his cards with a penciled note, "See what you can do for this friend of mine and oblige." But with one or two exceptions the "friend" turned out to be deserving. One day he sent word that he would like to see me personally. I called on him in Tammany Hall. He thanked me for "helping out" one of his friends and told me that the city, in some of its departments, or some of his "contracting friends" were always taking on new hands and that he would try to find a place for any man I sent him. This was an immense help to me in my work and a God-send to many a man who had lost his job because of a baseless arrest.

So I gradually found a place of usefulness in the life of the Tombs.

Another typical case happened years later. I would not have known how to handle it at first. The defendant was a Norwegian named Nora Lund. She was about seventeen and the sweetest, most beautiful young girl I have ever seen in the Tombs. She was employed in one of the smartest uptown stores. It had an established reputation as a dry goods house. The founder had died some years before, a stock company had taken it over and was developing it into a modern department store. Besides the old lines of goods they were carrying silverware, stationery, furniture and so forth. Their patrons were most of the very well to do classes.

Just inside the main entrance was an especial show case, where a variety of specialties were exhibited. Nora presided over this display and it was her business to direct customers to the counters they sought and answer all manner of questions. She had been chosen for this post because of her beauty and her sweet, lady-like manners. If you asked her where the ribbons were for sale, you carried away with you a pleasing memory of her great blue eyes and her ready smile.

She was paid six dollars a week. Her father, who had been a printer, was dead. Her mother worked in a candy factory. A sister of fourteen was trying to learn bookkeeping at home while she took care of the two younger children.

Nora's wage, together with the mother's, was enough to keep them in cleanliness, if not in comfort, and to put by a trifle every week for the education of the boy whom the women fondly dreamed of sending to school. But the mother fell sick. Gradually the little pile of savings was swallowed up. Mrs. Lund needed expensive medicine. And six dollars a week is very little for a family of five, especially when one is sick and another must always have fresh clean linen collars and cuffs. At the store they insisted that the girls should always be "neat and presentable." The fourteen year old sister went to work looking after a neighbor's baby, but she only got two dollars a week and two meals.

When the savings had been exhausted Nora took her troubles to the superintendent. She did not want to seem to be asking for charity, she begged to be given some harder work so she could earn more. It was refused. That week Wednesday there was nothing in the house to eat. The druggist and tradesmen refused further credit, and the rent was due. Nora went again to the superintendent and asked to have her wages paid in advance or at least the three dollars she had already earned. The superintendent was angry at her importunity.

When Nora left the store that evening she carried with her a box containing a dozen silver spoons. Unfortunately she did not know any of the regular and reliable "receivers of stolen goods," so she had to take a chance on the first pawnshop she came to. The man suspected her, asked her to wait a moment and telephoned for the police. He kept her at the counter with his dickering until the officer came. Nora did not know the first thing about lying and broke down at the first question.

If she had been a man I would have encountered her sooner, but I very seldom went into the women's prison. It is part of the burden of their sex, I suppose, but the women one generally finds in prison are the most doleful spectacle on earth. Having once lost their self respect they sink to an infinitely lower level than men do. With the first enthusiasm of my early days I used often to dare the horror of that place. But I soon recognized my defeat before its hopelessness and gave it a wide berth. So I did not hear of Nora when she first came to the Tombs. It was two weeks before her case was called. It came up before Ryan. I was not in court when she was arraigned, but the next morning I found a note in my box from the judge.

"Please look into the case of Nora Lund, grand larceny in the second degree. She plead guilty yesterday but she does not look like a thief. I remanded the case till Wednesday to give you plenty of time."

Before Wednesday I had the facts I have already related. It was pitiful to see Mrs. Lund. The shame and disgrace to the family name hurt her much more than the starvation which threatened the household. She was really sick, but she came down every morning to cry with her daughter. They were in a bad way at home, as Nora's wage had stopped since her arrest. I fixed them up with some food, squared the landlord, and did what I could to cheer them. Ryan had already shown his sympathy and I allowed myself to do, what I made it a rule never to do. I practically promised the mother that Nora would be released.

I prepared my report with extra care. It was an unusually good case. All the goods had been restored. The firm had lost no money. I had rarely had an opportunity to report so strongly my belief that the offender could be safely discharged. I recommended the "utmost leniency" with a light heart.

When the case was called, I handed up my report to the judge. He read it rapidly as if he had already made up his mind to let her go.

"You're sure it's the first offense?" he asked perfunctorily.

I assured him it was.

"All right," he said, "I guess suspended sentence...."

The clerk stepped up and gave the judge a card.

"Your honor," he said, "a gentleman would like to speak to you about this case, before you impose sentence."

The man was called up and introduced himself as the regular attorney of the complainants. He was a member of one of the great down-town law firms. He had the assurance of manner of a very successful professional man. His clients, he said, had asked him to lay some information before the court. In the last few years they had lost a great many thousand dollars through such petty theft. The amount of this loss was steadily increasing. Most of the thefts were undiscovered because the employees protected one another. They seemed to have lost all the old fashioned loyalty to the firm. The directors' attention had been unpleasantly called to this very considerable outlet and they had decided to respectfully call it to the attention of the courts. If two or three offenders were severely punished it would have a salutary effect on the morals of their entire force.

My heart sank. I knew how the judge would take it. He was always impressed by people of evident wealth. I am sure that he thought of God as a multi-millionaire. He handed my report to the lawyer. He read it half through and returned it. It could not, he said, affect the attitude of the complainants. They were not interested in the family life of Nora Lund, but in the honesty of employee No. 21,334. Their view-point was entirely impersonal. "Even if my clients wanted to be lenient, they could not, in justice to the stockholders. It is purely a business proposition. The losses have been very heavy."

"Are you asking his honor," I said, "to punish this girl for the thefts of the others you did not catch?"

He ignored my question and went on telling the judge that unless something was done this sort of thing would increase until business was impossible.

"Our whole force," he said, "know of this crime and are watching the result. If no punishment follows there is sure to be a big increase of theft. But if she is sent to state prison it will greatly reduce this item of loss."

"Your honor," I broke in, thoroughly angry, "This is utterly unfair. He whines because the employees are not loyal. How much loyalty do they expect to buy at six dollars a week? They figure out just how little they can pay their people and keep them from the necessity of stealing. This time they figured too low, and are trying to put all the blame on the girl. If they paid honest wages they might have some right to come into court. But when they let their clerks starve they ought not to put silver in their charge. Its...."

"Hold on, officer," Ryan interrupted, "There's a great deal in their point of view. Our whole penal system is built on the deterrent idea. The state does not inflict penalties to repay the wrong done it by an act of crime, but to deter others from committing like crimes. As long as the complainants take this view of the case I cannot let her go without some punishment."

"Punishment?" I broke in again. "I hope we will never be punished so bitterly. The shame of her arrest and imprisonment is already far in excess of her wrong doing. The firm did not lose a cent and they want her sent to state prison."

"I won't send so young a girl to state prison," the judge said, "But I cannot let her go free. I'll send her to one of the religious disciplinary institutions."

I asked for a few days adjournment so I could lay the matter before the members of the firm personally.

"The delay would be useless," the attorney put in. "My clients have no personal feelings in the matter. It is simply a carefully reasoned business policy."

I persisted that I would like to try. The judge rapped with his gavel.

"Remanded till tomorrow morning."

As we walked out of the court room, the attorney condescendingly advised me not to waste much time on this case. "Its useless," he said. But I did not want to give up without a fight.

When I tried to see the members of the firm, I found that my opponent had stolen a march on me by telephoning to warn them of my mission. Their office secretaries told me that they were very busy, that they already knew my business and did not care to go into the matter with me.

I was acquainted with the city editor of one of the large morning papers and I had found that the judges were very susceptible to newspaper criticism. More than once a properly placed story would make them see a case in a new light. I found a vacant desk in the reporters' room and wrote up Nora in the most livid style I could manage—"soulless corporation," "underpaid slaves" and such phrases.

"It's a good story," the city editor said, "Too bad there isn't a Socialist paper to run it. But we can't touch it. They're the biggest advertisers we've got. I'm sorry. It certainly is a sad case. I wish you'd give this to the mother."

He handed me a bank-note. But I told him to go to the father of yellow journalism. It was not money I wanted. I stamped out of his office, angry and discouraged. But my promise to Mrs. Lund, to get Nora out, made it impossible for me to give up. I walked up the street racking my brains for some scheme. Suddenly an inspiration came. They would not listen to me. Perhaps I could make money talk.

My small deposits were in an up-town bank. It did not have a large commercial business, but specialized on private and household accounts. The cashier was a fraternity mate of mine. With a little urging I got from him a list of depositors who had large accounts at the store where Nora had worked. I picked out the names of the women I knew to be interested in various charities and borrowed a telephone.

It is hard to be eloquent over a telephone. The little black rubber mouth-piece is a discouraging thing to plead with, but I stuck to it all the afternoon. As soon as I got connection with some patron of the store, I told her about Nora's plight—most of them remembered her face. I tried to make them realize how desperately little six dollars a week is. I told the story of her hard struggle to keep the home going, how the firm had refused to give her a raise and were now trying to send her to state prison. I spoke as strongly as might be about personal responsibility. The firm paid low wages so that their patrons might buy silk stockings at a few cents less per pair. And low wages had driven Nora to crime. I laid it on as heavily as I dared and asked them to call up the manager and members of the firm—to get them personally—and protest against their severity towards Nora. I urged them to spread the story among their friends and get as many of them as possible to threaten to withdraw their trade.

I started this campaign about three in the afternoon and kept it up till after business hours. It bore fruit. Some of the women, I found out afterwards, went further than I had suggested and called on the wives of the firm. I imagine that the men, who had refused to see me, did not spend a peaceful or pleasant afternoon and evening.

In the morning, when Nora's case was called, the attorney made a touching speech about the quality of mercy and how to err is human, to forgive divine. He said that the firm he represented could not find heart to prosecute this damsel in distress and that if the court would be merciful and give her another chance they would take her back in their employment. Judge Ryan was surprised, but very glad to discharge her. However, I was able to find her a much better place to work.

Her story is a sad commentary on our system of justice. The court did not care to offend a group of wealthy men. The press did not dare to. The only way to get justice for this girl was by appealing to the highest court—the power of money.

It is always hard for me to write about our method of dealing with crime in restrained and temperate language—the whole system is too utterly vicious. I had not been many weeks in the Tombs before I was guilty of contempt of court.

Four of the five judges in general sessions were machine men. It was rare that their judgments were influenced by their political affiliations; in the great majority of the cases they were free to dispense what happened to strike them as justice. It is simpler for the organization to "fix" things in the police courts where there are no juries. But once in a while a man would come up to us who "had a friend." The "Old Man" on Fourteenth Street would send down his orders and one of these four judges would arrange the matter. The impressive thing about it was the cynical frankness. Everybody knew what was happening.

The fifth judge, O'Neil, was a Scotchman. He was said to be—and I believe was—incorruptible. He had been swept into office on a former wave of reform, and had no dealings with the machine. But he was utterly unfit to be on the bench. A few weeks after I was sworn in, I saw a phase of his character which was worse than "graft."

A man was brought before him for "assault"—a simple exchange of fisticuffs. In general such cases are treated as a joke. Two men have a fight—then they race to the police station. The one who gets there first is the complainant, the slower footed one is the defendant. Each brings a cloud of witnesses to court to swear that the other was the aggressor. It is hopeless to try to place the blame. The penal code fixes a maximum sentence of one year and five hundred dollars fine, but unless some especial malice has been shown, the judges generally discharge the prisoner with a perfunctory lecture or, at most, give them ten days.

This man had an especially good record. He had worked satisfactorily for several years in the same place, his wife and her three small children were entirely dependent upon his earnings. O'Neil skimmed over his recommendations listlessly, until his eye caught a sentence which told the nature of the man's employment. He stiffened up with a jerk.

"Are you a janitor?" he thundered.

"Yes, your honor."

"Well, I tell you, sir, janitors must be taught their place! There is no more impudent, offensive class of men in this city. This morning, sir, there was no heat in my apartment, and when my wife complained the janitor was insolent to her! Insulted her! My wife! When I went downstairs he insulted me, sir! The janitor insulted me, I say! He even threatened to strike me as you have wantonly assaulted this reputable citizen here, the complainant. It is time the public was protected from janitors. I regret that the law limits the punishment I can give you. The court sentences you, sir, to the maximum. One year and five hundred dollars!"

The outburst was so sudden, so evidently a matter of petty spite, that there was a hush all over the court.

"What's the matter?" his honor snapped. "Call up the next case."

Of course this sentence would have been overthrown in any higher court, but the man had no money. Such things did not happen very often, but frequently enough to keep us ever reminded of their imminent possibility.

I have sixty fat note-books which record my work in the Tombs. Almost every item might be quoted here to show how little by little contempt of court grew in my mind. It crystallized not so much because of the relatively rare cases where innocent men were sent to prison, as because of the continual commonplace farce of it.

Very early I learned—as the lawyers all knew—that considerations of abstract justice were foreign to the Tombs. Each judge had his foible. It was more important to know these than the law. Judges McIvor and Bell were Grand Army men. Bell was always easy on veterans. He had a stock speech —"I am sorry to see a man who has fought for his country in your distressing condition. I will be as lenient as the law allows." McIvor, if he saw a G.A.R. button on a man before him would shout, "I am pained and grieved to see a man so dishonor the old uniform," and would give him the maximum.

Ryan, the most venal, the most servile machine man of the five, had a beautiful and intense love for his mother. A child of the slum, he had supported his mother since he was fourteen, had climbed up from the gutter to the bench. And filial love, like his own, outweighed any amount of moral turpitude with him. When I found a man in the Tombs who seemed to me innocent, I did not prepare a brief on this aspect of the case. I looked up his mother, and persuaded the clerk to put the case on Ryan's calendar. If I could get the old woman rigged up in a black silk dress and a poke bonnet, if I could arrange for two old-fashioned love-locks to hang down before her ears, the trick was turned. All she had to do was to cry a little and say, "He's been a good son to his old mother, yer honor."

The cases were supposed to be distributed among the judges in strict rotation. It was, in fact, a misdemeanor for the clerk to juggle with the calendar. But the largest part of a lawyer's value depended on his ability to persuade the clerk to put his client before a judge who would be lenient towards his offense.

O'Neil believed that a lady should be above suspicion. So when a woman was accused of crime, she was certainly not a lady, and probably guilty. It was for the good of the community to lock her up. Of course whenever a lawyer had a woman client his first act was to "fix" the clerk so that the case would not be put down before O'Neil.

Yet I would be eminently unfair to the people of the Tombs, if I spoke only of their evil side. Of course this was the side I first saw. But by the end of a year I had established myself. Once they had lost their fear that I was trying to interfere with their means of livelihood—a fear shared by the judges as well as the screws—hostility gave place to tolerance, and in some cases to respect and a certain measure of friendship. I began to think of them, as they did of themselves, as dual personalities. There was sinister symbolism in the putting on of the black robes by the judges. The screws out of uniform, in off hours, were very different beings from the screws on duty.

It is a commonplace that machine politicians are big-hearted. They listened to any story I could tell of touching injustice, often went down in their pockets to help the victim. I have never met more sentimental men. All it needed to start them was a little "heart interest." Frequently Big Jim, the gate man, would raise ten or fifteen dollars from the other screws to help out one of my men.

Judge Ryan met me one day on the street and invited me into a saloon. There began a very real friendship. Off the bench he was a most expansive man; he had wonderful power of personal anecdote. In the story of his up-struggle from the gutter, his mother on his shoulders, he was naïve in telling of incidents which to a man of my training seemed criminal. He owed his first opportunity, the start towards his later advancement, to Tweed. And he was as loyal to him as to his mother. The soul of the slum was in his story. It was an interpretation of the ethics which grow up where the struggle for existence is bitter. An ethics which is foul with the stink of fetid tenements, wizened with hunger, distorted with fear.

The attitude of the people of the Tombs to this dual life of theirs, the insistence with which they kept separate their professional and personal life, was shown clearly when a young assistant district attorney broke the

114

convention. He brought his wife to court! He was a youngster, it was his first big case, he wanted her to hear his eloquence. The indignation was general. I happened to be talking to Big Jim, the gate man, when one of the screws brought the news.

"What?" Jim exploded. "Brought his wife down here? The son of a ——! Say. If my old woman came within ten blocks of the place—or any of the kids—I'd knock their blocks off. Go on. Yer kidding me."

When they insisted that it was true, he scratched his head disgustedly and kept reiterating his belief in the chap's canine ancestry. Two hours later, when I was going out of the Tombs, he stopped me. It was still on his mind.

"Say," he said, "what d'ye think of that son of a ——?"


# III


It did not take me very long to see that the trouble with our criminal courts goes deeper than the graft or ill-temper of the judges. Day after day the realization grew upon me that the system itself is wrong at bottom.

A man can do a vicious thing now and then without complete moral disintegration. It is constant repetition of the act which turns him into a vicious man. Brown may once in a while lose his temper and strike his wife, and still be, on the whole, an estimable fellow. But if he makes a regular habit of blacking her eye every Saturday night, we would hold him suspect in all relations. We would not only question his fitness to bring up children, we would doubt his veracity, distrust him in money matters.

The more I have been in court the stronger grows the conviction that there is something inherently vicious in passing criminal judgment on our fellow men. A Carpenter who lived in Palestine two thousand years ago thought on this matter as I do. His doctrine about throwing stones is explicit. If he was right in saying "Judge not," we cannot expect any high morality from our judges. The constant repetition of evil inevitably degrades.

Unless we can expect our judges to be omniscient—and no one of them is so fatuous as to believe himself infallible—we are asking them to gamble with justice, to play dice with men's souls. We give them the whole power of the state to enforce their guesses. The counters with which they play are human beings—not only individual offenders, but whole families, innocent women and children. Such an occupation—as a steady job—will necessarily degrade them. It would change the Christ Himself.... But he said very definitely that He would not do it.

However, my work in the Tombs has not made me a pessimist. Science has conquered the old custom of flogging lunatics. The increase of knowledge must inevitably do away with our barbaric penal codes, with cellular confinement and electrocution. An enlightened community will realize that the whole mediæval idea of punishing each other is not only a sin—according to Christ—but a blunder, a rank economic extravagance, as useless as it is costly. We will learn to protect ourselves from the losses and moral contagions of crime as we do from infectious diseases. Our prisons we will discard for hospitals, our judges will become physicians, our "screws" we will turn into trained nurses.

The present system is epileptic. It works out with unspeakable cruelty to those who are suspected of crime—and their families—it results in the moral ruin of those we employ to protect us, and it is a failure. The amount of money which society expends in its war against crime is stupendous—and crime increases. All statistics from every civilized country....

But this personal narrative is not the place for me to discuss in detail my convictions in regard to criminology.

# IV

The influence of the Tombs on my way of thinking was slow and cumulative, here a little and there a little. I got a more sudden insight into some of the ways of the world, some of its stupidities and pretenses, from the peculiar circumstances under which Benson and I were thrown out of the settlement. I had been there almost two years when the crash came. In this affair, I was little more than the tail of his kite. That is the fact I wish to emphasize. Benson was I think beyond any doubt, the most valuable "resident" in the Children's House. It was not only that he gave much money into the general treasury and that he gave far more to such subsidiary enterprises as his Arbeiter Studenten Verein, all of which gave added prestige to the settlement, but also his personality was a great asset. Through his professional and social connections he was continually recruiting new supporters. And certainly to the people of the neighborhood, he was the most popular of us all. And yet to preserve certain stupid ideas of respectability, Benson was sacrificed.

The Jewish population—penniless refugees from Russian massacres—had been growing rapidly in our district. They had almost entirely driven out the Germans and Irish. And as a result of their intense poverty, prostitution was becoming frightful. There were red lights all about us. To the thoughtful Jews this had become the only political issue. The machine was cynically frank in its toleration of vice. Two years before a man named Root had been elected congressman on the reform ticket. It was pretty generally known that he had used his time in office to make peace with the machine. And although he still talked of reform, he was so friendly with the enemy that they had nominated a figure-head named O'Brien. But this Democratic candidate was only for appearances, we all knew that Root was to be re-elected and that Tammany votes were promised him.

Benson shared my hatred of hypocrisy. We often talked over this political tangle.

117

"I'd like to get the evidence against him," Norman said one night. "Nothing I'd like better than to shoot some holes into his double-faced schemes."

I gathered a good deal of information, which if it was not legal evidence, was certainly convincing. The Tombs was a great place for political gossip. I was almost the only person there at this time who was not a Tammany man. And as in my two years of work I had taken no interest in politics, I was considered innocuous. From scraps of conversation I learned that there had been a meeting between Root and the Old Man and some treaty made between them. I could guess at the terms. The organization was to throw enough votes to elect Root, and he was to keep too busy in Washington to interfere in local affairs. But I did not dare to ask questions, and had no idea when or where the agreement had been reached. By the barest chance I was able to fill in these details:

Coming up the Bowery late one night, I ran into a crowd who had made a circle around two girls who were fighting. Just as I arrived on the scene one of the girls called out——

"Charley—give me a knife."

Her cadet handed her one with a very ugly looking blade. I seldom used my right as county detective to make arrests. But as this seemed to threaten serious bloodshed, I broke up the fight and collared the cadet. He turned out to be a man of some importance in politics, a runner for "The Old Man." Two or three times he had been arrested, but his pull had always got him off.

He was half drunk and in a great funk over the serious charge I said I would make against him. As I was jerking him along towards the station house, he threatened me with dire consequences if I ran him in—said he was a friend of the Old Man. I pretended not to believe him, and in his effort to convince me that he really was protected, he let the cat out of the bag. He had been the messenger from the "Old Man" to Root, and had arranged for the meeting between them. It had taken place on the evening of September third, in the back room of Billy Bryan's saloon. He did not know what had happened at the meeting, the only person present beside the two principals had been a "heeler" of Root's, named "Piggy" Breen. There was no use in arresting a man with his "pull," so I turned him loose.

I hurried back to the settlement and telephoned for Benson at his club. He brought along Maynard to give us legal advice. Maynard was an erratic millionaire. One-third of the year he played polo, one third he spent in entering his 75-foot sloop in various club regattas, and the rest of the time he lived in the city, leading cotillions at night and maintaining a charity law office in the day-time. He was also a trustee of the settlement. He was wildly indignant over the story of Root's treachery.

"We can defeat Root, dead easy," Benson said. "It's a cinch. Publicity has never been tried in politics" (as far as I know, Benson invented this term "publicity," now so commonly applied to organized advertising)—"it's a cinch. In less than twenty-four hours everybody in the district will know he's a crook."

"What reform man can we get to run in his place?" Maynard asked.

"Hell!" Benson said. "We haven't time to nominate anybody—election is only a week off. I don't care who's elected so we put Root out of business."

"Well, but," Maynard protested, "we don't want to throw the influence of the settlement in favor of Tammany Hall."

"We don't need to. There must be some other candidates—Socialist or Prohibition—just so he isn't a red-light grafter."

"There isn't any Prohibition ticket," I said. "The Socialist candidate is named Lipsky."

"All right," said Benson, "we'll elect Lipsky."

Maynard went up in the air. Help elect a Socialist! He did not believe in political assassinations.

"Oh, devil!" Benson snapped. "Would you rather see one of these cadet politicians in office than an honest working man? I don't know who this man Lipsky is, like as not a fool who sees visions. But the Socialists never nominate crooks. What we want is an honest man."

Maynard, however, did not believe in community of wives, felt it necessary to protect the sanctity of the home—even at the cost of prostitution. And so he left us.

I wish I could remember half the things Benson said about Maynard after he had deserted us. I have seldom seen anything more invigorating than Benson mad. But he did not let his indignation interfere with business. It was far along towards morning, but he set to work at once. He wrote to Lipsky promising to support him, and then began sketching cartoons and posters.

One was a picture of Root selling a girl in "parlor clothes" to "The Old Man." Another read:

"VOTE FOR LIPSKY

if you have a daughter!

If you vote Democratic, you

Vote for the RED LIGHTS!

If you vote Republican, you

Vote for the CADETS!

VOTE THE SOCIALIST TICKET, and you

VOTE FOR DECENCY!"


But the best were a series:

"ASK ROOT

where he was on the evening of September Third?"

"ASK ROOT

what business he had with the Old Man?"

"ASK ROOT

how much he got?"


Having mailed the letter to Lipsky and sent off the copy to the printer, we turned in just at sun-up.

We were awakened a few hours later by the arrival of a socialist committee. There was Dowd, a Scotch carpenter; Kaufmann, a brewery driver, and Lipsky, the candidate. He was a Russian Jew, and had been a professor in the old country. He could speak very little English, but he had served a long term of exile in the Siberian prison mines.

The socialists had no idea of winning the election. The campaign was for them only a demonstration, a couple of months when they had larger audiences at their soap-box meetings. They were suspicious of us.

That consultation is one of the most ludicrous of my memories. Benson, sitting in an arm-chair, in blue silk pajamas, smoking cigarettes, outlined the plan in his fervent, profane, pyrotechnic way—much of which was beyond their comprehension. Kaufmann had to translate it into German for Lipsky. And when we talked German, Dowd could not understand.

"But," said Herr Lipsky, when the posters had been translated to him, "there is nothing there about our principles. There is no word about surplus value. It is not the red lantern we are fighting—but the Kapitalismus."

"The people," Benson raged—"the people with votes don't know surplus value from the binominal theorem. Perhaps they will vote for their daughters —they can see them. But they won't get excited about their great-great-grandchildren."

There was a squabble among the committee-men. The Scotchman was too canny to take sides; he wanted to refer the matter to the local, which was not to meet until two days before the election.

"Aber," said the brewery man, "Ve need etwas gongrete."

Lipsky accused him of being a "reformer."

After an hour's wrangle, it was decided that they could not stop us from attacking Root. But we were to hold up the posters asking votes for Lipsky. He would not permit his name to be used without the consent of the local.

As they were going downstairs, I heard Kaufmann protesting—"Aber, Genossen—ich bin eine echte revoluzionaire!"

So Benson ran the campaign unaided. The effect of his posters was electric. The next day he brought out some more:—

"ASK THE OLD MAN."

Of course they both denied. But as the posters made no specific allegations, they did not know what to deny. Their output was conflicting. During the afternoon, Benson stirred things up again with a series—

"IF ROOT WON'T TELL, ASK 'PIGGY' BREEN."

Breen was rattled, and said it was all a lie, that the red light business had not been discussed at the meeting in Billy Bryan's saloon. Both Root and the Old Man had denied the meeting. So Benson had them on the run. The more they explained the worse they tangled things. The cadet from whom I had forced our information, fearing the wrath of The Old Man, was of course keeping his mouth shut. We did not give away on him. So they could not guess Benson's source of knowledge, and would have given anything to know just how much he knew.

The Socialist local nearly broke up over the affair. A number were absolutely set against accepting aid from a "Bourgeois philanthropist," like

122

Benson. Lipsky was in a violently embarrassing position. Suddenly there was a good chance of his election. The people of the district were manifestly excited over the issue. They were ready to vote for any one who would promise effective war against the cadets. It must have been a frightful temptation to him. But he stood fast for his principles. He did not want to be elected on a chance reform issue. If the people of the neighborhood stood for Marxian economics, he would be glad to represent them. But he would have nothing to do with demagogy.

On the other hand, a young Jewish lawyer named Klein was the Socialist candidate for alderman, and he saw a chance of being elected on the "Down with the red light" cry. He was ready to tear the hesitaters to pieces. He felt that the social revolution and universal brotherhood only awaited his installation in office.

At last it was agreed that a mass meeting should be called in the Palace Lyceum on Grand Street and that Klein and Benson should speak on the red light issue and Lipsky on economics. We brought out the "Vote the Socialist Ticket" poster.

Benson was at the very top of the advertising profession, and he certainly threw himself headlong into this job.

"I've persuaded about fourteen million people to buy Prince of Wales Aristocratic Suspenders," he said. "I don't see why I can't persuade a few thousand to vote right once in their lives."

He certainly did marvels at it.

The night before election, the Palace Lyceum was packed to the roof. And this in spite of the organized efforts of the strong-arm men of the machine. But the meeting was a miserable fizzle. Benson was helpless between those two speakers.

Klein's discourse consisted in telling what he would do if elected—among other things, I recall, he was going to nationalize the railways and abolish war.

Benson was not much of a public speaker. As far as I know, it was his one attempt. But his success at advertising was based on his knowledge of the people and how they thought. They were not interested in Klein or the nationalization of the railroads. The one thing which moved them was the sale of their daughters. Benson went right to the point, reminded them of it in a few words, and then told the story of Root's treachery, piecing together our facts and guesses. "It is not legal evidence," he said, "you can take it for what it is worth. It's up to you—tomorrow at the voting booths."

"To hell with Root!" somebody yelled.

"There's only one candidate better than Root," Benson shouted back, —"Lipsky!"

When they got through cheering, he gave them the words of a song he had written to "Marching through Georgia." He had trained the Männer Chor of the Arbeiter Studenten Verein to sing it. It caught on like wildfire. I am sure that if the meeting had broken up then, and they could have marched out singing that song, Lipsky would have been elected overwhelmingly. But Lipsky spoke.

"Der Socialismus ruht auf einer fasten ekonomischen grundlage...."

For twenty minutes in deadly German sentences he lectured on the economic interpretation of history. Then for twenty minutes he analyzed capitalism. Then he drank a glass of water and took a fresh start. He referred to Klein's speech and pointed out how the election of one or a hundred officials could not bring about Socialism; the only hope lay in a patient, widespread, universal organization of the working class. Then in detail he discussed the difference between reform and revolution, how this red light business was only one by-product of the great injustice of exploitation by surplus value.

When he had been talking a little over an hour, he said "Lastly." He began on a history of the International Socialist Party from its humble beginning in Marx' Communist League to its present gigantic proportions.

On and on he drawled. Many got up and left—he did not notice. Someone in the gallery yelled,

"Cheese it! Cut it out! We want Benson!"

He went right on through the tumult, and at last discouraged the disturbers. The recent International Socialist Congress had discussed the following nine problems: (1) The Agrarian Question, (2) The Relation of the Political Party to Trade Unions…. It was hopeless. The audience melted. And they did not sing as they left.

At last he was through. I remember the sudden transformation. The set, dogged expression left his face, as he looked up from his notes. His back straightened, his eyes flashed—a light came to them which somehow explained how this dry-as-dust professor of economics had suddenly left his class-room and thrown his weak gauntlet at the Tsar of all the Russias. It was the hope which had sustained him all the weary years in Arctic Siberia.

"Working-men of all lands—Unite!" he shouted it out to the almost empty house—his arms wide thrown in his only gesture—"You have nothing to lose but your chains! You have a world to gain!"

There was a brave attempt at a cheer from the few devoted Socialists who remained. The exultation left him as suddenly as it had come, and he sat down, a tired, worn old man. Klein rushed at him, with tears in his eyes. "You've spoiled it all!" he wailed. The old man straightened up once more.

"I did my duty," he said solemnly.

When the returns came in the next night, the Socialist vote had jumped from 250 to 1800. Root had only 1,000. O'Brien, the machine candidate, won with 2,500. At the last moment, the Old Man, seeing that Root was hopelessly beaten, had gone back on his bargain and sent out word to elect O'Brien.

"The funny thing about the Socialists is," Benson said to me, "that they are dead right. Take Lipsky. He's a dub of a politician, but pretty good as a philosopher. Wasn't it old Mark Aurelius who wanted the world ruled by philosophers—not a bad idea—only it's impracticable. They are right to suspect us reformers. Nine out of ten of the settlement bunch are just like Maynard—quitters when it comes to the issue. They'd like to uplift the working class, but they don't want to be mistaken for them. And after all this red light business is only a symptom. You and I and Lipsky can afford to be philosophic about it—we haven't any daughters. But the fathers who live in this dirty district—they ask for bread—not any philosopher's stone. Any way, we fixed Root, and that is what we set out to do."

"It cost me a lot of money," he said later. "And I did not want to go broke just now. There is a bunch of swindlers out in Chicago with a fake shoe polish they want me to market. It will ruin a shoe in two months. They are offering me all kinds of money. I hate to go to it—but I guess I'll have to."

He sat down to his desk and began studying his bills and bank-book.

"How would 'shin-ide' do for a bum shoe-polish?" he said, looking up suddenly. "'Shin-ide. It puts halos on your shoes.'"

Our sudden burst into politics, at least Benson's—my small part in it was never known—attracted a good deal of newspaper notice. Certainly Root realized where his troubles started, and he went heartily about making us uncomfortable.

A couple of mornings after election, the Rev. Mr. Dawn, the head-worker, came to our room, his hands full of newspapers and letters—the "corpus delicti."

I wish I could give more space to Dawn. He was a thoroughly good man. And although we judged him harshly at the time, I think an admirable man. At least, I feel that I ought to think so about him, but some of the old contempt still clings to his memory.

His whole soul was wrapped up in the settlement movement. Socialism was repellent to him because it insisted on the existence of class lines. He had come to America from England because the class distinctions—so closely drawn there—were repugnant to him. He hoped in our young Republic to see a development in the opposite direction. His hope blinded him.

And in spite of his loudly-professed Democracy, he was essentially aristocratic in his ideas of social service. The solution of our manifest ills he expected to find in the good intentions of the "better bred." Their loving kindness was to bring cheer and comfort to the lowly. His faith in the settlement movement was real and great, which of course made him very conservative in the face of any issue which involved its good repute.

"You people seem to have seriously offended Mr. Root," he began.

"You don't say so!" Benson replied. He was shaving.

Dawn could not understand Benson's type of humor.

"I am afraid you have," he said.

Benson cut himself.

"I don't remember having called him anything worse than a cadet," he said sweetly.

"Oh, I see you are joking."

"No. I did call him that."

"I'm sorry to hear you say it. Sorry to have you verify the report that you used intemperate language. I have never met Mr. Root. But he has many friends among…."

"The best people?" Benson interrupted.

"I was about to say among our supporters. It is most regrettable that your ill-advised attack on him may alienate many of them. It seems also that you have dragged the name of the settlement into the mire of Socialism. I must confess that I hardly know—that, in fact, I am at a loss…."

"You needn't worry about it. Whitman and I will leave. All you have to do is to roll your eyes if we are mentioned, and say—'Yes. It was most regrettable—but of course they left the settlement at once!' Invite Root to dinner a couple of times. Walk up and down Stanton Street with him—arm in arm. It will blow over—it will square everything with 'the best people'!"

"I am sorry to hear you speak so bitterly," Dawn said, "But frankly, I think it wisest that you should sever your connection with us. When the welfare of the whole settlement movement is at stake, I cannot allow my personal feelings to blind my...."

"Oh, don't apologize. There is no personal ill-feeling."

And so we left the settlement.

# BOOK V

## I

Benson and I set up housekeeping in the top floor of an old mansion on Eldridge Street. Once upon a time it had boasted of a fine lawn before it, and of orchards and gardens on all sides. But it had been submerged in the slums. You stepped out of the front door onto the busy sidewalk, and dumb-bell tenements springing up close about it had robbed it of all its former glory. Two mansard bedrooms in the front we threw together, making a large study. We put in an open fire-place, built some settees into the walls and before the windows. There were bookcases all about, some great chairs and a round table for writing and for meals. Of the rooms in the back we arranged two for sleeping, turned one into a kitchen and a fourth into a commodious bath. With his usual love for the incongruous, Norman nicknamed the establishment —"The Teepee."

In my work in the Tombs I had one time been able to clearly show the innocence of an old Garibaldian, who was charged with murder. He felt that he owed his life to me, and so became my devoted slave. His name was Guiseppe and he had fought for Liberty on two continents. It was hard to tell which was the more picturesque, his shaggy mane of white hair or his language—a goulash of words picked up in many lands. Within his disappointed, defeated body he still nursed the ardent flame of idealism. The spirit of Mazzini's "Young Italy," the dream of "The Universal Republic" lived on in spite of all the disillusionment which old age in poverty and exile had brought him.

In the Franco-Prussian War, while campaigning in The Vosges, he had cooked for the Great Liberator. We installed him in the kitchen of the Teepee. His especial pride was a pepper and garlic stew which Garibaldi had praised. This dish threatened to be the death of us. It was the trump he always led when in doubt.

## II

During the years I was in the settlement, I received regularly two letters a month from Ann. They were never sentimental. They dealt with matters of fact. Norman's uncle and aunt had interested themselves in her ambition and had allowed her much time to study. At first her work in Pasteur's laboratory had consisted in cooking bouillon for the culture of bacteria. It did not seem very interesting to me, but it fascinated her. She even sent me the receipt and detailed instructions about using it. After awhile she had been promoted to a microscope and original research. She soon attracted Pasteur's attention and he offered her a position as his personal assistant. Her employers were immensely proud of her success and, securing another nurse, released her. She was enthusiastic over this change. She could learn more, she wrote, watching the master than by any amount of original work.

It was part of her character that her letters gave me no picture of Paris. She had no interest in inanimate things, no "geographical sense." I knew the names and idiosyncracies of most of the laboratory assistants, she gave me no idea of Les Invalides, near which she lived. There was much about the inner consciousness of a German girl with whom she roomed, but I did not know whether the laboratory was in a business or residential section of the city. She wrote once of a trip down the river to St. Cloud, and all she thought worth recording was the amusingly idiotic conversation of an American honeymoon couple, who sat in front of her, and did not suspect that she understood

English.

Although she wrote so much about people, the characters she described never seemed human to me. She did not understand the interpretive power of a background. Her outlook was extremely individualistic. Auguste Compte wrote somewhere that there is much more of the dead past in us than of the present generation. I would go further and say that there is much more of the present generation in us than there is of ourselves. If we stripped off the influence of our homes, of our friends, of the contempore books we read, of our thousand and one social obligations, there would be precious little left of us. Ann carried this stripping process so far that even Pasteur, for whom she had the warmest admiration, seemed to me a dead mechanism.

She never referred to our personal relations, never spoke of returning to America. And I avoided these subjects in my answers. I was afraid of them.

I thought about her frequently and almost always with passion. I dreamed about her. Fixed somewhere in my brain was a very definite feeling that such emotions ought not to exist apart from love. I was not in love with Ann. Her letters rarely interested me. It was a task to answer them. Our contacts with life were utterly different.

I kept to the "forms" of chastity. There are those who believe that there is some virtue in preserving forms. I have never felt so. It did not require much effort to keep to this manner of life. I was constantly observing prostitution from the view-point of the Tombs. And to anyone who saw these women, as I did, in their ultimate misery and degradation, they could excite nothing but pity. There is no part of the whole problem of crime so utterly nauseating. Although I held myself back from what is called "vice," the state of my mind in those days was not pleasant,—and I think it was not healthy. It was no particular comfort for me to learn that other men, living, as I was, in outward purity, were also tormented by erotic dreams.

Shortly after we moved into the Teepee a letter came from Ann which was bulkier than usual. The first pages were a statement of new plans. An

American doctor, who had been working with Pasteur, was returning to establish a bacteriological laboratory in this country. He had offered her a good salary to come with him as his chief assistant. The laboratory was to be built in Cromley, a Jersey suburb, thirty minutes from the city. As soon as it was ready she was coming. It would be interesting, responsible work and she could make a home for her mother who was becoming infirm.

The rest, pages and pages, was a love letter. Every night, these years of separation—so she wrote—had been filled with dreams of me. As always she put her work above her love. Bacteriology was the great fact of her life. She held it a treason to reality when, as so often happens, people lose their sense of proportion and allow love to usurp the place of graver things. But now that her work brought her towards her love, she looked forward to a fuller life—a life adorned.

The letter brought a great unrest. Her passionate call to me certainly found an echo. I lost much sleep—tormented, intoxicated with the images her words called up. Years before an immense loneliness had pushed me into the comfort of her arms. This was no longer the case. My life was full, almost over-full of work and friends. But the pull towards her seemed even more irresistible now than before.

Marriage seemed to me the only worthy solution. But even more clearly than in the hospital days I knew I did not want to marry her. It was, I suppose, above all because I did not love her. It was partly because I liked my bachelor freedom, the coming and going without reference to anyone. It was partly my deep attachment to Norman. I felt he would not care for Ann. Anyway it would break up our household in the Teepee.

At last a letter came setting the date of her arrival. It coincided with a long-standing engagement I had made to lecture on criminology in a western college. I had an entirely cowardly sense of relief in the realization that the meeting and adjustment were postponed. But I thought of little else. Returning from my lectures, on the long ride across half the continent, with the knowledge that Ann was awaiting me in the city, that I could postpone things no longer, I won to a decision. I would see her at the earliest convenience—it seemed more straightforward to see her than to write—and tell her that I did not wish to recommence our intimacy. I might not be able to explain why I wanted to break with her, but I could at least make it plain that I did.

On my return, I found a letter waiting me in the Teepee. It contained her telephone number and a query as to when I could come out for dinner. I called her up at once. I would come that very day. The train out to Cromley seemed perversely slow. I was impatient to be through with it, to get back undisturbed to my work. It was only a short walk from the station to her house. The row of gingerbread cottages along her street is one of the fixtures of my memories.

Ann opened the door for me. She held me out at arm's length a minute.

"Woof!" she said, "You've grown old." Then she gave me a sudden kiss. "Come. You must meet Mother."

In the little parlor, Mrs. Barton greeted me cordially. She was a tall, angular New England woman, dried up in body, but her eyes were still young. I have seen many women like her down Cape Cod way. But her presence threw me into as much confusion as if she had been some threatening sort of an ogress. I could not fight out this matter with Ann before her mother. And some instinct warned me that I must plunge into my subject at once, if I wished to do it at all.

"Dinner is ready," Ann said in the midst of my embarrassment.

"This is my little grandson, William," Mrs. Barton said of a tow-headed youngster, of three, who caught hold of her skirt.

Ann picked him up.

"Can't you shake hands like a gentleman, Billy Boy?" she asked. "No? Well, you don't have to."

She swung him into a high chair opposite mine. I have never been more embarrassed in my life. It was all so different from what I had foreseen. I suppose I had expected some heroics. It was entirely common-place. It was hard to keep in mind that a big moral issue was at stake. Mrs. Barton was evidently taking my measure. And "Billy Boy" glared at me across the table out of his big, inane, blue eyes.

Ann did the talking, telling us of the wonders of her new laboratory and something of the personality of her chief. She looked younger than when she went away. She had filled out considerably and her face had lost the oldish, narrow look which I remembered. She had that surety of gesture and tone which comes only to those who have found the work they are fitted to. Above all she seemed happy, and contented and merry. Each glance I stole at her told me it would be harder than I had thought to keep my resolution. It was impossible to look at "Billy Boy," he would have stared the Sphinx out of countenance. So I gave most of my attention to Mrs. Barton.

When the dinner was over, we moved into the parlor for coffee. In a few minutes Mrs. Barton took the youngster to bed. The door had hardly closed behind them when Ann's arms were about me. There was a broken flood of words. I do not remember what she said. But somehow it seemed as if I were saying it myself, so wonderfully her words expressed my own longings. A great happiness had fallen upon me. Perhaps this passion was not right, perhaps it was neither moral nor wise, but it was overwhelmingly a part of me. It would have been utter self-repudiation to deny it.

In the morning I again asked Ann to marry me. It was my last ditch.

"Don't," she said, "dearest, don't talk of marriage. Why? Why do you want to take our love into a courthouse? Once for all—let's fight this out and be finished with it."

It was all very clear to her. Promises of love were futile. She had loved once before, had thought it would last forever. She was glad there had been no promises.

"I'm older now—not so likely to change—but why go to law about it? Why do you want to marry me? Isn't it partly because some people—perhaps your own family—would be shocked at a free love union? Well, haven't I a right to think of my people? My sister, who's dead, Billy's mother—she didn't think it was necessary to have a wedding ring and all that. My people would be grieved if I got married. They'd think I'd conformed—gone back on my principles. It would break mother's heart. It would seem like a repudiation of her way of living. And she's the finest mother anyone ever had. Even if I didn't believe in free love, I'd never get married on her account."

Despite what Ann told me I was decidedly embarrassed to meet her mother at breakfast. But when we appeared, Mrs. Barton kissed me. Her hands on my shoulders, she searched my face with her eyes.

"Ann loves you very much, my boy," she said. "Be good to her."

The breakfast was a far pleasanter meal than the dinner had been. Even Billy Boy's stare was not quite so hostile.

Yet as I rode into town on the early train my scruples came back. To be sure I had very little respect for the "sanctity" of formal marriage. I had seen too much of it in the Tombs. Certainly no amount of legal or religious ceremony is a guarantee of bliss or even of common decency. The minor marriage failures are attended to in the civil divorce courts. The domestic difficulties which are threshed out in the criminal courts show very clearly that there is no magic in church ritual to transform a brute into a good husband. Ten wedding rings will not change an alcoholic woman into a good mother. And then I was always witnessing "forced" marriages. Such was the cheap and easy solution in cases of seduction and rape in the second degree. Our law givers have decreed eighteen as the age of consent. The seduction of a girl under that arbitrary age is rape. Most of our grandmothers were married earlier. But the law is too majestic a thing to consider such details. It deals with general principles. If it has been flouted, Justice must be done though the heavens fall. However, it is an expensive matter to send a man to prison. So he is offered the alternative of marrying the girl. Justice gives no heed to the morality nor happiness of the two young people who have fallen in trouble, cares not at all for the next generation. Send the guilty couple to the altar.

Their sins are forgiven them. The conventions have been vindicated. The juggernaut is appeased. No. I was very little impressed with the virtue of "legal" marriage.

But I had a strong, if rather indefinite, ideal of a "true" marriage, a real mating, a close copartnership, a community of interest and a comradely growth, sanctified by a mutual passion. I saw no chance of this in my relation to Ann.

At the Tombs that day, I tried, and to a large extent succeeded, in forgetting the problem. But back in the Teepee, at dinner with Norman, it seized me again. Even Guiseppe noticed my preoccupation and walked about on tiptoe.

"What's eating you?" Norman asked as we drank our coffee. "Any way I can lend a hand?"

"A woman," I said.

"That lets me out." And after a while he muttered "Hell."

"What do you think," I asked—suddenly resolved to get an outside opinion—"about one's right to be intimate with a woman, outside of marriage?"

"I don't think about it at all," he snapped. "Not nowadays. Time was when I didn't think of much else. It didn't do me any good. The times are rotten—out of joint. Everything we do is out of joint—inevitably. Ninety per cent of us want to do what's right and as it is ninety-nine per cent of us ball things up. I don't think much of marriage. I tried it once—divorced."

This was news to me.

"I don't like to talk about it. No use now. It was a miserable affair. I tried to be decent—did all I knew how to make it right. But I guess the girl suffered more than I did—which is one of the reasons why I hate God. Some people tumble into happiness—but it seems luck to me—pure luck."

I cannot recall that evening's talk in detail. Norman was unusually reticent. It was only by questions that I could draw him out.

"What do you think about free love?" I asked.

"It's a contradiction in terms. There's nothing free about love. It's tying oneself up in the tightest kind of a knot. A man will not only work his fingers off for the woman he loves—he'll have his hair cut the way she likes. A person in love doesn't want to be free. The hell of it is when the slavery continues after the love is dead. Don't try to free love—what's needed is the emancipation of the loveless."

We were silent for a while, very much distressed that we could find no solid anchorage. I was about to ask some other question when he broke out again on his own line of thought.

"Abolishing marriage won't do it. These Anarchists are naïve. They want to make things simple—say free love would simplify the matter. But all progress—all evolution—is towards more complex forms. Our brains are better than monkey brains because they're more complex. This "simple life" talk is rank reaction. I don't want to see laws abolished, but brought up to date. Civilization means ever increasing complexity in the forms of life. And we try to govern it by Roman law, plus a hodge podge of mediæval common law. Not less laws—but modern laws."

For a while his mind played about this idea, then he ended the discussion abruptly.

"Why put your problem up to me? As far as solving the man and woman question goes, my life has been a miserable failure. No matter what you do, whether you quit or go ahead—unless you're lucky as hell—you'll wish you were a eunuch before you're through."

So I got little help from him in this matter. I never really settled it. More or less it settled itself. There were forces at work which were stronger than my scruples. Sometimes it seemed horribly wrong to me and I decided not to go back to Cromley. But as the days passed I began to think more and more of Ann. Sooner or later I telephoned. I did not surrender without many struggles.

But gradually she became an accepted fact in my life and with the years an increasingly valued fact. I am not proud of the moral indecisions, not at all proud of my contentment with what seemed less than perfect. But so it was.

Nothing in my life has seemed to me of so uncertain ethical value. Of course it was a violation of our traditional morality, but there are very few who blindly accept the conventions as always binding. I cannot dismiss it offhand as simply right or wrong; my own judgment in the matter was swung back and forth with almost the regularity of a pendulum.

At first it seemed to me unfair to take so much more than I could give. But after all I think little is gained by trying to treat love like merchandise, by trying to measure and weigh it. Certainly Ann would have been glad if I had loved her more wholly. But she regarded that as a work of fate, which no amount of wishing—by either of us—could change. She would have run away if our intimacy had begun to interfere with her work. She threw herself into her specialty with a wholeheartedness I have never seen equalled. Once I asked her if she had no desire for children.

"Of course I have," she said, "but sometimes I've wanted the moon to wear in my hair. I'd like to live till I could see the triumph of medicine. I'd like to be a pall-bearer at the funeral of the last malignant germ. I'd like a yacht. I never went sailing but once—and it was very wonderful. But I don't want any of these things in the same way I want to work."

She was not entirely satisfied. Who is? She had been taught contempt for the cheap respectability we could have secured for a small fee from a justice of the peace. I think she got as much happiness out of our relationship as most women do from their home lives. I cannot picture her as getting any added pleasure out of sewing buttons onto my clothes or darning my hose. No doubt there were lonely evenings when she wished the fates had given her a more ordinary life and a husband who came home regularly. Although she never complained, I knew that it hurt her if the rush of other—to me more important—affairs kept me in town when she was expecting me. But she would have been more unhappy if she had been in love with a man who interfered in the least in her freedom. It does not seem so unfair to me now as it did at first. We were neither of us getting all we could dream of. But no more was either of us ready to give up the half loaf.

And "half loaf" seems a very inadequate term for my share. I find myself trying to "argue" about this—I am rather vexed by things I cannot call either black or white. But so much of it was utterly unarguable. If we are, as some say, to judge life by the pleasure it brings us, Ann was beyond question the biggest and best thing in my life. I remember one Sunday in the late fall, we were afoot with the first streak of dawn; all day long we tramped through the Jersey mountains. The autumn coloring of the maple groves was unutterably gorgeous. Just at sunset, all the western sky brilliant with red and a hundred shades of hot orange—even more brilliant than the frost nipped leaves had been—we reached a little railroad station and so came back to Cromley and the roaring wood fire and New England supper Mother Barton had prepared for us. I would feel sorry for anyone to whom such a day would not seem glorious. But to me, living six long days a week in the seething slums, in the even gloomier shadow of the Tombs, such outings were a renewal of life, a rebirth.

And besides the evident pleasure of these holidays, Ann brought me a feeling of mental and physical wellbeing and healthfulness I had never before known. My grip on life was surer, my vision clearer, my store of energy was better adjusted, more economically utilized, because of her. I believe that a man, who says he cannot live in celibacy, is lying. But with equal emphasis, I believe that the circumstances which make it wise for a man or woman to live out their lives alone are extremely rare. The hours I spent at Cromley were recreation in the deepest sense of the word.

The rides into town on the early train stick in my mind as a memory apart from all the rest of my life. I seemed at those times to be in a higher mood than usual. Speeding into the city, to my grim task in the Tombs, from the sweet solace of her home, I found inspiration and hope for my daily grind. There was an entirely special sensation, experienced at no other time, when I found myself aboard the ferry, leaning over the fore-rail, watching the sky-scrapers struggle up through the morning mist. Perhaps all of us know some such exhilarating environment, which makes us exult in life and work and purpose. Standing forward on the upper deck, my lungs full of the sweet salt air of the harbor, some foolish association always recalls the lines from the speech of William Tell and makes me want to shout aloud—"Ye rocks and crags, I am with you once again."

None of the obvious objections to such an irregular relationship seem to me to have much weight in the face of the very real good it brought me. And yet—I cannot accept it without qualifications any more than I can condemn it. I have come to feel that its unsatisfactoriness was due to its fragmentary character. I cannot agree with Ann in her theory of keeping work and love apart. A man who divorces his religion from his business finds both of them suffer. I think the same rule holds for our problem. I did not enter in any way into Ann's work, nor she into mine. She gave me new energy for it, rested me from its weariness, but never was a part of it.

I think the fact that I can, in writing of my life, make one section deal with her and another with my work and very seldom mention both in the same paragraph, is the severest criticism which can be brought against our relationship.

## III

Benson persuaded an editorial friend to publish as articles some of the lectures on criminology which I had delivered out west. A supreme court justice attempted to answer my criticisms of the judicial system and carelessly denied some patent facts. The newspapers made a nine days sensation out of our controversy. One effect of the discussion was to awaken the Prisoner's

Aid Society to a realization that something ought to be done. In order to relieve themselves of this responsibility they proposed to employ me as their secretary in the place of an elderly gentleman who had held that position gratuitously—and sleepily—for twenty odd years. The offer did not, at first, attract me. My work in the Tombs held all my interest. Until Baldwin came along, I did not see any chance of real service with the society.

He was assistant superintendent of the state industrial school—a sort of intermediary prison for those offenders who were too young for state prisons and too old for the house of refuge. He had started out as a "screw" in Sing Sing, had been transferred to the state hospital for insane criminals and from there to the industrial school, where he had worked his way up to the position he then held. He really seemed to like the details of institutional management; he knew convicts and he was filled with a great enthusiasm over the possibility of reforming youthful offenders.

He saw my name in the papers, as one interested in criminology and he wrote to me about this enthusiasm of his. After several letters had been exchanged he came to the city so we might talk it over. We put him up at the Teepee. He was getting close to forty-five, but was the youngest man of that age I have ever known. Benson and I went over his project in detail. For three solid days we talked of nothing else. Although my work dealt chiefly with accused persons who were waiting trial, still I was always being brought face to face with the horrors of our convict prisons. The unspeakable stupidity of treating young boys as we mistreat old offenders has always seemed to me the crowning outrage of our civilization.

It is hard to realize today how revolutionary Baldwin's scheme for a reformatory then sounded. Only the most feeble and timid experiments in such matters had been tried. We were still in those dark ages, when orphan and destitute children were sent to jail.

The weak point in his proposal—as is the case with almost every reform —was the expense. The state paid about ten cents a day for the maintenance of its convicts, the per capita for the reformatory would be three or four times as much. Baldwin had foreseen this criticism and had collected endless figures to prove that it was only an apparent extravagance. One of the biggest elements in the cost of crime is the expense of "habitual offenders." Baldwin had the life-story of one man who was serving his twelfth term in state prison and he had figured out just how much this man's various crimes and arrests and trials and imprisonments had cost the community and how much cheaper it would have been to have spent enough to reform him while he was young. It was an impressive document. By a number of such tables he made a conclusive case. The greater expense of the reformatory, would be a real economy if he could save one third of the boys. He believed that two-thirds could be reformed. With the help of a constitutional lawyer he had crystallized his ideas into a bill, which he hoped to have introduced into the legislature.

As I have said, Norman and I gave three days close attention to the project. Baldwin had had much practical experience in such matters and had prepared his case admirably. The scheme looked feasible to us—as indeed it has since proved. We were all unsophisticated enough to believe that a good plan once explained to the people would be immediately accepted.

I went before the executive committee of the Prisoner's Aid Society and offered to accept the secretaryship, if they would pledge their support to Baldwin's bill. They could find no precedent for such a measure in their books on European penology and I doubt if I could have swung them into line single-handed. But Benson was one of their board of directors and they relied on him to meet their annual deficit. He was able to bring more potent arguments to bear than I.

By this time I had become a sort of established institution in the Tombs. With the exception of O'Neil, I had won the confidence of the judges. They were, within certain limits, well-intentioned men and they did not like to condemn young boys to the contagion of state prison any more than you or I would. I got their signatures to a letter endorsing the reformatory idea, and through them arranged with the district attorney for such leaves of absence as

I would need.

I find myself with very little enthusiasm for chronicling this campaign for a reformatory. It was so dolefully disheartening, so endlessly irritating—it dragged on so much longer than we had foreseen. But it is important not only to my own story, it influenced not only my way of thinking; it has also a broader and more compelling significance. There was hardly one of my friends, the people of my generation who were trying to make this world a more livable place, who were not at one time or another involved in a similar fight. One thing we all had experienced in common—the journey up to Albany to try and cajole our legislators into doing something, the value and wisdom of which no sane man could doubt. A new Acts of the Apostles might be written about the endless succession of delegations which gathered in the Grand Central Station, en route for the capital, fired with enthusiasm for some reform—a new tenement house law, some decent regulation of child labor, some protection against the crying evils of the fraudulent immigrant banks or the vicious employment agencies and so forth. It would take a fat book to even list all the good causes which have inspired such pilgrimages. And the ardor with which the delegations set out for Albany was only equalled by the black discouragement which, a few days later, they brought back.

After some trouble we found an assembly man who consented to introduce our bill. It was pigeon-holed at once. Then we went in for publicity. I wrote articles in magazines and newspapers. Benson and Baldwin got out and widely circulated a pamphlet. They were a strong combination, with the former's knowledge of advertising and the latter's familiarity with the subject. I took the stump.

Everyone, I suppose, who has done similar work, has made the same discovery. You cannot win your point with the ordinary audience by an appeal to reason. At first I treated my subject seriously—with dismal effect. But Norman came to one of my New York city meetings and cursed me roundly for a fool when it was over. I took his advice and went up and down and across the state telling "heart-interest" stories; yarns about the white haired mother whose only son was sent to Sing Sing for some trifling offense and was utterly corrupted by evil associates; about the orphan boy who stole a loaf of bread for his starving sister. How I came to hate those two! Once in my dreams I murdered that "white haired mother" with fierce glee. But I could always rely on them to start tears. If I tried to give my audiences our constructive ideal, what we meant by the word "reformatory," I lost my grip on them. They demanded thrills. Well—I gave them thrills. It was the only way, but it made me feel like a mountebank, like a charlatan selling blue pills.

By the end of the year we had worked up enough popular interest to force a discussion of the bill on the floor of the legislature. On the first reading it was referred to the Senate Committee on State Prisons. After several weeks of suspense the committee announced a date for a public hearing. I remember that at the time we thought this meant victory. At last we were to have an opportunity to present our case in a serious manner to serious men. Baldwin and Benson and I put in the preceding week preparing our briefs. On the day set for the hearing we marshalled our forces in the lobby of an Albany hotel. There was Allen, the president of the Prisoner's Aid Society; Van Kirk, a vice-president of the State Bar Association and the three of us. It was arranged that Baldwin and I should speak first, he was to deal with the financial side of the project and I with its broader human phases. Allen and Van Kirk were to add the endorsements of the organizations they represented. I recall how perfect our case looked to us, how utterly impossible it seemed to fail of convincing the committee.

The room in the old state house, where the hearing was held was a dingy place. There was the air of a court about it and the attendants. What seemed vitally important to us was dismal routine to them. When we arrived the committee was listening to a deputation of screws from Sing Sing who were asking for a revision of the rules in regard to vacations. The sight of the three committee men cooled my ardor. The chairman, Burton, was an upstate lawyer, who affected the appearance of a farmer to please his constituents. The other two, Clark and Reedy, were New Yorkers, one a Republican the other a Democrat, both fat and sleepy. At last the screws finished their plea. Burton rapped with his gavel.

"What is the next business?" he asked wearily.

"Hearing in the matter of a bill to establish a reformatory for juvenile offenders," the clerk drawled.

"Does the Commissioner of State Prisons endorse this bill?" Clark asked.

"No"—the Commissioner was on his feet at once. The charter of the Prisoner's Aid Society gave it authority to inspect the penal institutions of the state, to audit their accounts and so forth. It was a thorn in the flesh of all commissioners and they could always be counted on to oppose any suggestion of the society's.

"Well. What's the use of going into the matter, then?" Reedy asked. "It's not our custom to throw down the Commissioner."

"As it's on the calendar we'll have to listen to it," Burton ruled.

"How did it get on the calendar?" Clark growled.

"I was under the impression the Commissioner was in accord," the clerk apologized.

"Well, I want to know where you got that impression," Clark insisted with ill temper.

"Not from me," the Commissioner spoke up.

Burton rapped with his gavel.

"Order, gentlemen," he said. "We are wasting time. We will hear anyone who wishes to speak in favor of the bill."

Baldwin stood up and opened his notes.

"I have an important business matter I would like to attend to," Reedy said. "May I be excused?"

"Hold on," Clark protested, "It's my turn to get off early."

"I can't excuse both of you," Burton snapped. "This is the last business on the calendar. It will not detain us long. Proceed. What's your name? Baldwin? Proceed."

The two other senators scowled sullenly like children who were being kept in after school. Suddenly Reedy began to grin. He leaned back in his chair, so that he could attract Clark's attention behind the shoulders of the chairman who was writing a letter. He held out a coin. "Odd or even?" he whispered. It took Clark a moment to understand, then his scowl relaxed. "Even" he whispered back. Reedy looked at the coin and his face clouded up.

"I have no objection to excusing Senator Clark," he said, interrupting Baldwin in the midst of a sentence.

Burton looked up from his letter in surprise. Clark chuckled audibly as he left the room. Reedy slouched sullenly in his chair. "Proceed," Burton said and turned back to his letter. Baldwin did admirably in the face of his levity, but no one was listening. Just as he was on the point of closing, Burton interrupted him again.

"You have had fifteen minutes. I will give the other side ten and adjourn."

Van Kirk tried to argue with him, but Burton ignored his existence. "Mr. Commissioner," he said, and turned once more to his letter. It was a relief to me that he cut me off. I was too furious to have spoken coherently. The Commissioner, sure of success, took the matter flippantly.

"Mr. Chairman, Senators. The Department of State Prisons is opposed to this bill on the ground that it is a visionary piece of nonsense. The whole talk of a reformatory was started by this Mr. Baldwin, an employee of my department, who is discontented because we have not sufficiently recognized his abilities. I understand that he wishes to be made superintendent of the State Industrial School, in which institution he is now employed in a subordinate position. He has secured the support of the undoubtedly sincere, but visionary theorists of the Prisoner's Aid Society. As far as I know there are no other advocates of this bill. I could not recommend so large an appropriation of the people's money to satisfy the ambition of Mr. Baldwin— nor to please the gentlemen of the Prisoner's Aid Society!"

He had hardly regained his seat when Burton's gavel fell.

"Adjourned."

Baldwin was one of the steadfast kind who do not know the meaning of discouragement. And Benson was so angry that he threw himself into the fight with redoubled ardor. Between them they carried me along.

We started again at the bottom—trying to make an effective demand reach the legislators from the voters. I went again through the state, but stayed longer in each place, until I had formed a permanent committee. That year's work persuaded me that I could have earned my living as a book-agent or by buncoing farmers into buying lightning rods.

I remember especially New Lemberg, a sleepy town on one of the smaller lakes. I was the guest of the Episcopalian clergyman and stayed at the rectory. It took me three days to land him, and he gave in at last from sheer boredom. He had been willing enough to let me come and speak to his congregation after morning prayer, and he had called a conference of the ministers and leading citizens in his parlor on Sunday afternoon. But when I asked him to act as chairman of the county committee he held back. His life was full to overflowing already with his parish work, he was fond of the open country and of books. His hobby was translating Horace. I was asking him to give up some of this recreation for a cause which had never come close to him. I was sorry for him, but I needed him to give "tone," the fashionable stamp, to the committee. On Monday afternoon—I had been harassing him all morning, he proposed to teach me golf. A general discussion of literature carried us as far as the third hole and he had been happy. But as he was teeing for the next drive, I began on him again. He pulled his stroke horribly, and sat down in a pet. I remember those links as the most beautiful spot in all the state. There was softly rolling farm lands, woods and fields in a rich brocade of brown and green, and below us the lake. Here and there a fitful breeze turned its surface a darker blue.

"I'm so busy as it is," the rector pleaded, "I can't take on this. Really— you know all my time is taken up already. I don't get out like this more than once a week. You must—really it's asking too much of me—I'm getting old."

It was his last spurt of resistance. I hung on desperately and in a few minutes he gave in. He was a valuable acquisition, no one worked on any of our committees harder than he. But somehow I was ashamed of my conquest. I am sure he shudders whenever he thinks of me. If he should meet me on the street even now, I would expect him to run away.

After a solid year of this work—I groan still when I think of it—we had committees in almost every assembly district. They called on the various candidates and secured their promises to support the bill. We circulated immense petitions and sent formidable lists of signatures to the successful candidates. We had also stirred the women's clubs to action. The newspapers made considerable comment on the "Petition of the Hundred Thousand Mothers." When the new legislature convened, we had the signatures of over two-thirds of the assemblymen, and a good majority of the senators to pledges to vote for the reformatory.

Instead they gave their attention to the routine jobbery of their trade and just before they adjourned they elected a joint commission, three members from each house, to consider the matter.

I am quite sure, and having travelled so much through the state, I was in a position to know, that if we could have had a referendum, eighty per cent of the votes would have been for our bill. Fifteen of the twenty per cent of hostile votes would have come from the most ignorant and debased districts of the big cities. I doubt if a measure has ever gone before the state legislature with the more certain sanction of the electorate. Democracy is a very fine Fourth of July sentiment. But in those days it had nothing to do with "practical politics."

The new commission did not begin work for six months. As the members received ten dollars a day for each session, they sat for an hour or two a day for several weeks. But at last we had our chance to present our case in a thorough and serious manner. The opposition to the bill was based on the testimony of half a dozen wardens who had been ordered to the stand by the Department of State Prisons. They had nothing to offer but prejudice and ignorance. Van Kirk, his fighting spirit stirred by the snub he had received from the senate committee, acted as our attorney and did it ably. Benson took hold of the press campaign and the newspapers were full of favorable comments. I am sure that when they adjourned after hearing our arguments, every commissioner was convinced of the wisdom of our project.

But our opponents were better politicians than we. We let our case rest on the evidence. Just what wires the Department of State Prisons pulled during the recess, I do not know. But when the commission reconvened, a sub-committee introduced a substitute bill, which was accepted without discussion and unanimously recommended to the legislature. It was a travesty on Baldwin's scheme. The age-limit was raised to admit men of thirty. Instead of being for first offenders, the new bill read for persons "convicted for the first time of a felony"—which opened the door to a large class who have become almost hopelessly hardened by a life of petty crime. Ordinary cellular confinement was substituted for the original plan of cottages. It was not at all what we had been fighting for.

As soon as I read the new bill, I went before the Prisoner's Aid Society and begged them to repudiate it, to stand for the original project or nothing. But in the first place they were not sufficiently informed in the matter to recognize the difference between the two bills and in the second place the four years of unwonted activity had overstrained them. They wanted to rest. Ever since they have boasted of their enterprise in getting this mutilated reformatory established.

I would have given it up in disgust except for personal loyalty for Baldwin. He felt that the reformatory, even in its emasculated condition, was an opening wedge and that as superintendent he might gradually be able to persuade the legislature to amend the charter back to his original design. Certainly he deserved the position, the institution would not have been established at all except for his persistent efforts. Norman and I went into the fight again to bring pressure to bear on the governor to appoint Baldwin. We got no help from the Prisoner's Aid Society; it had fallen hopelessly asleep. A few of our county committees came to life again and circulated petitions. My rector at New Lemberg was the most active. I think he was afraid I would visit him again. But the public was tired of the issue. The governor appointed a political friend.

I resigned from the Prisoner's Aid Society and went back to my work in the Tombs. I felt that I had wasted four years.

# IV

Early in this campaign for the reformatory our peaceful life in the Teepee was shaken up by the advent of Nina.

Norman and I were coming home from the Annual Ball of The Arbeiter Studenten Verein. It was near one o'clock Sunday morning as we turned into the Bowery. At the corner of Stanton Street a girl flagged us.

"Hello, boys. Ain't you lonesome?"

An arc-light sputtered and fumed overhead. I will never forget its harsh glare on her face. It was a north Italian face, wonderfully like a Bellini Madonna. But on it was painted a ghastly leer. Above all she looked too young.

"Aren't you afraid the Gerry Society will get you?" Norman asked good naturedly.

There was elemental tragedy in the foul words with which she answered him. But with a sudden change of mood—as unexpected as her appearance, as bewildering as her blasphemy—she threw her arms about his neck and kissed him.

The look of horror on Norman's face changed slowly to another expression. It was not wholly incomprehensible. There was something exotic —something tantalizing to over-civilized nerves—in her youthful viciousness. Baudelaire would have found her a *"fleur de mal."* He would have written immortal verses to her. Norman was stern with himself in such matters. He had steeled himself against the usual appeals of vice. It was the novelty of the attack that got through his armor. He pulled her hands apart, pushed her away from him and looked at her, his face drawn and rigid. A south-bound elevated roared past us overhead. With a sharp intake of breath he turned to me.

"I've half a mind to take her home."

"It would be a great treat for her," I said, "compared to how she'll spend the night if you don't. I suppose it's you or a drunken sailor."

"Will you come home with me?" he asked with sudden resolution.

"Sure. You don't look like a cheap-skate."

So we started on along the Bowery, arm-in-arm. At first we were all silent. But intent on the business of amusing her clients, she suddenly jerked her feet off the ground, and hanging to our elbows, swung her soiled little red slippers in the air before us.

"Gee!" she said, when we had recovered our balance, "You're solemn guys."

"You're in line with the best traditions of philosophy, kid," Norman admitted. "There's no virtue in sinning sadly. We might as well laugh."

The rest of our progress home was a noisy scramble. A hideous nightmare to me—out of the vague impressions of which, I remember most clearly the complaisant grin of the policeman on the beat; who twirled his stick as we passed.

Guiseppe was dumb-founded at the addition to our number. Norman told him curtly to set a third cover for our supper.

Once seated at the table Nina—that we discovered was her name—did not let anything interfere with the business in hand. Norman ate little. I had no appetite. So she did duty for all of us. Norman made a few remarks about the ball, but always he was watching her. I was unresponsive and conversation died.

When Nina had made way with the last edible thing, the flood gates opened and she began to talk and play. She had an immense animal vivacity, which kept not only her tongue, but her whole body in action. She was full of a spirit of fun entirely foreign to both of us. We were rather serious minded, sombre men. Her love of horseplay was a novelty.

It is hard to characterize her talk. Much of it was utterly unprintable. There were words, words—words! But somehow she seemed innocent of it all, wholly ignorant of any better manner of conversation, any better form of life. She grew immensely in my regard during those few minutes. I have seldom listened to more depraved language and yet a sort of intrinsic virtue— the light of unsulliable youth—shone through.

I left them as soon as might be and went to my room. I passed Guiseppe in the hall, he was muttering to himself strange oaths: *"Dios"*—*"Corpo de Bacco"*—*"Sapristi"*—*"Nom de nom."* I silently echoed his multilingual profanity. My passions had not been stirred and, looking at it in cold blood, I could only disapprove. Norman followed me to my room. Conversation did not start easily. But when at last I took my pipe out of my mouth, he cut me off.

"Oh, don't say it. What's the use? I'm saying it myself. I wish I had long ears to wave, so I could bray. There's only one thing to discuss. These diggings are as much yours as mine. I'll take her to a hotel, if you prefer."

"Here or elsewhere. What difference does the place make?" I growled. "I haven't any geographical interest in the case."

He thrust his hands deep in his pockets, paced up and down a minute, then turned with an abrupt "good-night" and went out. It was a troubled night for me. The brutal strength of the sex-pull had never seemed so malignant before. That I had begun to see something lovable in Nina, only made it worse.

I got up early and although it was Sunday and I had no work at court, I breakfasted in haste, hoping to get out before they appeared. But Norman caught me just as I was leaving.

"Come here," he said, with his fingers on his lips.

He led me on tiptoe down the hall. Through his open door I could see her sleeping. The coil of her black hair and one white arm showed above the sheet. There was an ugly, half-healed bruise near the elbow. The painted leer had been washed from her face. A smile came and went—flickered—on her lips, a wonderful smile of peaceful happiness.

"Am I clean crazy?" Norman whispered fiercely, "or is she beautiful?"

We tiptoed back to the library.

"Can you keep an eye on her for a while?" he said. "I had to have Guiseppe throw away her clothes—they were too dirty. I must get her some new ones. It won't take me long."

But he stopped at the door and came back.

"It's the way she smiles in her sleep, Arnold, that gets me." He hesitated a moment, trying to find words to fit his thought. He, who was usually so glib, had to search now. "You know, they say dreams are just a re-hash of waking experience. But—well—it isn't the kind of smile you'd expect from her. God! I'd like to know what she dreams about! It almost makes me feel religious. Reminds me of 'Intimations of Immortality!'"

Then he gave up trying to say it and rushed out to buy the clothes. I laid out my note-books and tried to work. Half an hour later she appeared in the doorway, sleepy-eyed, arrayed in a suit of Norman's pajamas.

"Where's he gone?" she yawned.

"He had to go out for a few minutes."—I did not tell her why, as I thought he might enjoy surprising her with the new outfit. "He'll be back pretty soon. If you ring the bell, Guiseppe will bring you some breakfast."

"Where's the bell?" she asked, looking on the table.

"It's on the wall. Press the button."

"Oh, it's a door be-e-e-l-l." It ended in a yawn.

"If you wash your face, you may wake up enough to be hungry."

"Aw! Go to hell."

She thumbed her nose at me and departed. She had evidently entirely forgotten the dream which had brought the smile to her lips and troubled Norman. When Guiseppe brought in her breakfast, she came back and sat down. She had no greeting for me and I, thinking of nothing worth saying, went on with my writing. When there was nothing more to eat she began to talk with Guiseppe in rapid Italian. After a while he turned to me.

"It's very sad, Mr. Arnold. She comes from the same district in Lombardy where I was born."

My nerves were on edge. I grunted that I did not see how that made it any sadder. He was surprised at my tone, and was, I think, on the point of reminding me that it was also in the same district that the Great Liberator had been born. But he thought better of it and went off to the kitchen in a huff.

Nina wandered about the room, examining the bric-a-brac with what seemed to me a stupid interest. Her inspection finished, she helped herself to a cigarette and sat down cross-legged on the divan. Out of the corner of my eye, I could see that she was minutely studying her pajamas. She would gently stroke the soft fabric, where it was drawn tight across the knee. The tassels on the belt string held her attention for several minutes.

"Say," she broke out suddenly. "The old man says he burned up my clothes. Is it a lie?"

"No. They are burnt. Your friend thought they were too dirty to wear."

"What sort of a game is this?" she demanded, after blowing out a cloud of smoke. "This here suit of clothes is all right—it's real silk, I guess. But— say—I don't like parlor clothes. See? I won't stand for...."

I interrupted her, seeing at once what was in her mind. "Parlor clothes" are an old device—it was doubtless invented by some pander of ancient Nineveh. The proprietors of "disorderly houses" often keep their girls in bondage by withholding all decent clothes. The "parlor" costume, is one in which no woman would dare to go on the street. They are more effective means of guarding slaves than chains. I tried to reassure Nina, telling her why Norman had gone out.

"Honest?" she asked. "He'll let me go? I'd raise hell—sooner than be in a house. It's the sidewalk for mine—every time. He'd better not try any fancy games on me. I sure would raise hell!"

"You wait and see," I said. "He's on the square."

I began writing again, she lit another cigarette and smoked awhile in silence. But presently she came over and sat on the table.

"Say. He'll give me some money, besides the clothes, won't he?"

"You'll have to arrange that with him."

"I've got to have two dollars, by ten o'clock."

"Wouldn't you rather have some good clothes than two dollars?"

"No. Real money."

I leaned back in my chair and looked her over. At last I ventured what was in my mind.

"I suppose women's clothes wouldn't suit your man. But wouldn't some red neckties please him as well as money?"

"Say"—her eyes narrowed threateningly—"You're a wise guy, ain't you? Think you know it all?"

"Well," I said, "I know some."

I turned back the flap of my coat and showed her the badge of a county detective. She whistled with surprise, but did not seem dismayed. In fact she became suddenly friendly. Everything about her recent experiences, the bath, Norman's attitude towards her, the meals, the rooms, had been strange and confusing. But a policeman! That came within the circle of familiar. She knew dozens of them.

"Gee! I never would have thought you was a cop. Plain clothes man?"

I nodded assent and then asked her.

"Who are you hustling for?"

For a moment she seemed to consider the advisability of answering. But what was the use of trying to hide things from a "cop"? What I did not know, I could easily find out. Her cadet's *nom-de-guerre* was "Blackie." She spoke of him without enthusiasm, without marked revulsion—much as we speak of the unavoidable discomforts of life, such as the bad air in the subway, or the tipping system. With a few questions, I got her story—quite a different one from what she had told Norman.

Ever since they had come to America, her mother had been scraping out a bare living for herself and her daughter by means of a small fruit business, and by letting rooms behind the store to boarders. One of these men had seduced Nina under promise of taking her to the marionette show. This had happened—"Oh, a very long time ago"—at too remote a date to be definitely remembered. She spoke of this man with foul-worded bitterness. It was not on account of the evil he had done her, but because he had not taken her to the show. "Men always cheat us," she said. "It don't matter how foxy you are, they beat you to it." She had not burdened her memory with any precise record of her childish amours. They had been without pleasure—for an ice-cream cone, a few pennies, a chance to go to a show. She was a devotee of Bowery drama. "From Rags to Riches" was her favorite. "That," she said, "was something grand!"

The first person who had come anywhere near making love to her was this cadet "Blackie." She had left her mother, without any regret, to live with him. That also had been "something grand"—at first. As near as she could remember, it was about a month before he drove her out on the street to "hustle" for him. Was he good to her, I asked. She shrugged her shoulders. Was he not a man? Then she showed her first enthusiasm. He had a great "pull," he was a friend of the "Old Man on Fourteenth Street." She gave

"Blackie" this sincere tribute, the cops never troubled her. But he did have a temper. "It sure is hell, when he's mad." She rolled up the sleeve of her pajamas and showed me the bruise on her arm. It had been a kick. What for? She had forgotten.

Then Benson came in, his arms full of bundles. I don't suppose he had spent more than fifteen dollars—things are cheap in that neighborhood. But it was an imposing assortment. I could not have bought so complete a trousseau without minute written instructions.

Nina forgot her troubles in an instant, they never troubled her long. She pulled the bundles to pieces and scattered the garments everywhere. Guiseppe came in on some errand, but one glimpse of those feminine frivolities, strewn about our formerly sedate bachelor chairs finished him. With a wild Garibaldian oath, he rushed back to his kitchen.

It was not in Nina's nature to allow anything to intervene between her and her immediate desire. The things once seen, had to be tried on.

"Come, come," Norman protested. "You'd better do your dressing in the other room."

Nina seemed surprised at his scruples, but, gathering up the garments, followed him docilely down the hall. Shrieks of glee came through the open door, beat against my ears—distressingly. I seemed to hear the bones of some ghastly *danse maccabre*, rattling behind her mirth. But as if to drive away my gloom, she soon dashed into the room, fully booted and spurred. She was very pretty. And how she laughed! She seemed a sort of care-free and very young bacchante—the daughter of some goddess of gayety. She jumped on the table and, imitating a music hall artiste, danced a mild mixture of fandango and cancan. And as she danced, she sang—a ribald, barroom song. But the words meant nothing to her, she was just seeking an outlet for her high feelings, expressing her childish joy in her new possessions.

Our neighboring church bell began to strike the hour. Nina brought down the foot which was in the air and, in a strained attitude, listened.

"Gee!" she said, jumping down to the floor. "It's ten o'clock."

For a moment she stood irresolute, and then her face hardening, she walked up to Norman.

"Gim'me two dollars."

The sudden demand hit him like a blow.

"Won't you stay to lunch with us?" he asked lamely.

"No. I've got to go—now! I want two dollars."

Such bargaining is unbearable to me, I fled to my room. In a few minutes, Norman came to my door.

"What can I do about this, Arnold?"

"Oh pay her her wages, and let her go," I said, "what else is there to do?"

"My God," he swore and stamped into my room. His face was white, his lip was bleeding a little where he had bitten it. "Somehow I can't! What rotten creatures we all are! Of course I've known all about this—but we have to touch it—to realize it…. Why did I ever let her come into my life? I can't send her back to it. She's such a kid. And—Good God!—those damned, drunken Bowery sailors!"

"Look here, Norman, you're only making matters worse for her. She'll get a beating if she don't have the money to give her cadet. He's…."

"Cadet?" Norman interrupted me, as though he had never heard the word before. He threw himself down on my bed. I had never seen him so moved.

"Isn't there any way out of it?" he groaned.

I hate to plead absolute despair, but I could see no way out. So I tried to talk reasonably.

"Don't take it so hard. She's bred to it. It isn't half as bad to her as you think. It's all she knows. She doesn't despise this cur of a cadet, she hustles for—the way we do. He's her man—the pivot of her existence." And I told him what she had said about Blackie. "He doesn't beat her as often as he might. She feels rather fortunate, because he's not worse. There isn't any way out. They call it the most ancient profession. Her hard times haven't begun yet,—she's young. She's living on the fat of the only land she ever knew. It isn't exactly a bed of roses—but she's never known a softer one."

"You're a sophist!" he cried, jumping up. "Lies. Damn lies! She has known something better. My God—you should see her smile when she's asleep! I can't stop prostitution, but I can keep her out of the worst of it. She's too young for these Bowery dens. I won't let her go back to that damn pimp."

"Go slow," I said. "What have you got to offer in exchange—for this cadet? I tell you, he's the big factor of her life. Are you willing to take the time and trouble to fill his place? Money won't do it. She can't count above fifty. How are you going to amuse her? She's used to excitement, to street life, the buzz of the Bowery. You're going to offer her a gilded cage, an upholstered cell. It won't work. And suppose you do succeed in giving her a taste for a finer life—what then? After you get through, she'll only find the old life harder. What's to become of her when you're tired?"

"You're the devil's advocate," he said vehemently.

"Perhaps. But are you a God? It would take all of a pretty lively God's time to help—to really help—the lady."

"We'll see what a man can do," he said and stamped out, back to the library. In a few minutes he called me.

"It's beyond me," he said. "It looks like fright. She seems to like me and the place. I think she'd stay, if she wasn't afraid of her old gang. See if you can reassure her."

"Nina," I asked, "are you in love with Blackie?"

She did not seem to be sure what the term meant.

"He ain't so bad."

"Well, if he were dead," I tried again, "would you stay here with Mr.

Benson?"

"Sure," she said. "Sure!"

"You're afraid of Blackie?"

She nodded.

"Well. Cheer up. He can't hurt you here."

"He'd have me pinched," she insisted, doggedly. "He's got a pull with the cops. He'd sure have me sent to the Island, if I tried to shake him."

"Look here,"—again I flashed my badge—"It's gold. That means I'm the same as a captain. I've got ten times more pull than Blackie. If he gets gay, I'll lock him up. I'll plant a gun in his pocket and send him up the river for concealed weapons. You don't need to be afraid of him."

"Gee," she said, "I'd like to stay. But he'd sure get me. He's a bad one."

"He'll be a dead one," I said. "If he starts anything with a friend of mine."

I talked a few minutes more, but not till I showed her a pair of handcuffs, which I kept in my room by way of a curiosity, did she really believe she was safe and begin to smile again.

Having established the family, I made an excuse to go out. I came back late at night and found Benson sitting alone in front of the fire.

"She's asleep," he said.

"Must have had a lot of excitement," I replied, "to be sleepy at this hour."

Having spent all the day outdoors, tramping in the open air, my brain had cleared a little. The thing had lost its distorted proportions, had fallen into focus. I could not understand how the affair had seemed so momentous to me. Such things, I knew very well, were happening on all sides, all the time. I was sorry for Norman. He would take it seriously and that, I felt, meant days of stress and sadness. My work in the Tombs had made me realize more certainly than he could the immense chances against his helping the girl. How many futile efforts I had made at first to lend a hand to some of these unfortunate women! I had given it up in defeat. For her, even if the powers of darkness pulled her back at last, it would mean at least a little oasis of comfort and consideration in the barren desert life the gods had mapped out for her.

"There's one thing, I must say for my soul's good," Norman said. "It's a hard business, this analyzing of our motives. I'm sure I do want to save her, if I can, from being a public prostitute. But it's equally true I want her for myself. I certainly despise this cadet, Blackie—but it's also true that I'm suddenly become just ordinarily, humanly jealous of him. I don't want to pretend that I'm wholly occupied in trying to be God-like."

"Well—I suppose I'm a cynic," I said. "But I don't expect any wonderful reformation—in either of you. Only don't be unfair to her—don't expect too much of her."

And so Nina became an accepted member of our household.

# V

Norman certainly set earnestly about the work of filling the place in Nina's life previously held by Blackie.

A few nights later I joined them in the middle of the performance at Koster and Bials. Nina looked away from the stage only long enough to say "Hello." She was vibrant with excitement. Norman and I sat back in the box much more interested in her than in the commonplaces of the stage. We were both rather ill at ease in so senseless and light-minded a place.

"This experience," he said and I thought I caught a tone of apology in his voice, "is bringing me a closer understanding of the life of the poor. Of course they'd resent my saying that Nina helped me to understand them. The poor are the worst of all snobs. We 'reformers' believe in the working-class a lot more than they do in themselves. It's hard to get at them—we only meet the kind who know how to talk and most of them are mute. The chaps in my Studenten Verein long for education. They envy us who had it forced on us—and, of course, pose before us. You can't really get to people who envy you.

"But Nina never studied—barely reads—don't want to. This sort of thing is her *summum bonum*. I haven't found anything that makes her happier than for me to put on evening clothes and take her to a flashy up-town restaurant. And she can't help talking. She has no self-consciousness—no pose. What she says is reality. It's the wisdom of the tenements she babbles out—the venerable philosophy of the poor. I'm learning a lot from her."

"You needn't apologize to me," I said.

"I wasn't apologizing," he retorted. "Why should I?"

"I said you needn't."

"But you meant that I ought to—not to you, but to somebody. To whom? To God? To Mrs. Grundy? No—why should I apologize?"—He threw his arm back so that his hand lay on my shoulder, it was the nearest our great love for each other ever came to the expression of a caress—"I know you don't approve, Arnold. But after all whom am I harming? You and I have been leading a pretty glum sort of a life…."

"You have," I interrupted. "I'm in no position to chuck any self-righteous stones."

"Oh," he said. "That's what you meant when you said I need not apologize to you."

"I suppose so."

"Well, to whom then? Tell me," he went on when I did not reply at once. "I'm really glad to have the opinion of a disinterested onlooker. It always helps. Tell me."

"Good God," I replied to his challenge, "I'm no oracle—no omniscient voice of conscience. But it looks to me as though apologies were coming to Nina."

"Nina?" he said in surprise.

"Yes. Don't you see what's happening? She's falling in love with you. The real thing. She never saw anybody like you before. You're like the shining white hero of the Bowery melodrama, who rescues the distressed heroine at the last minute—and *marries her*. Of course you and I know that the young millionaires with tenor voices don't marry the distressed damsels. But remember the kind of dope her mind is filled with. The wedding march always starts up, just before the curtain goes down."

The slap-stick comedians had finished their turn, the lights flared up and for the first time I noticed Nina's resplendent gown. It was really a beautiful dress. If her hair had been done up with a little more skill and if Norman had not set all his authority against an excess of powder and paint she would have looked quite like an uptown lady, of the Holland Houses or Rector's, like those who go up Fifth Avenue to a ball or like those who turn over to Broadway and strut about in the theater lobbies to attract the attention of some gentleman from out of town.

I complimented her on her appearance and, she, pleased as a child, told me how they had bought the dress that afternoon at a second-hand place on Sixth Avenue. The most glorious experience of her life, before she had met Norman, was a short acquaintance with the woman who played the "lady villain" at "Miner's." They had had rooms in the same house for a while. And this tragedienne had confided to Nina where she bought her second-hand clothes. Norman in a dinner jacket and Nina in a shirtwaist had attracted a good deal of attention, so he had decided that she must have a more suitable outfit for evening wear. She had led the way. And she told me with great animation—and frequent profanity—of the long and complicated dickering which had preceded the final purchase. The shop woman had asked $27.50 and Nina had stuck out for $17.50. At one stage of the wrangle the woman

164

had led Nina aside and called her a little fool.

"'He's rich,' she says to me. 'He'll pay. Don't you know enough to stick him. I'll knock off fifty cents, you say all right. He'll pay it. And tomorrow you come round and I'll give you three dollars.' Now wot do you think of that? Say. Do you know wot I did?"

I could not guess.

"I spit at her. I said 'You ....'" (Among the other epithets were "cross-eyed" and "hook-nosed.")

"Well—how much did you pay at last?" I asked.

"I think," said Norman, "she could have got it for the seventeen...."

"Sure, I could," Nina interrupted. "But he was in a hurry and gave the ... thief twenty. It...."

The lights went down, the curtain up and a woman, whom I would not have trusted to be kind to her own children, brought on a troupe of pitiable dogs. Nina turned back to watch the stage.

"So you think," Norman reverted to the former subject, "that I ought to marry her?"

"Of course not."

"If you have any reasons why I shouldn't that are not pure snobbishness, I'd like to hear them."

"Good God," I said. "You're not seriously thinking of that, are you?"

"Hardly. But the idea has occurred to me. Why are you so frightened by it?"

It is strange what illogical creatures we are! Up to that moment I had been sorry for Nina. Every day I liked her more. And I saw with a sore heart the wondering, dazed admiration grow within her for her new master. Love is one of the most primeval passions of the race. It is likely to be stronger—grander or more devastating—with primitive people than with those of us who have been civilized away from the parent type. I knew that Nina was falling in love with Norman in a way no woman of our class ever could. He had taken her into a fairy land and she could not, I felt, help expecting the fairy denouement.

But the hint of the possibility of his really acting the part of the fairy prince, switched me about entirely. Nina became a negligible quantity. I worried only for him. It is needless to repeat the arguments against such a marriage which flooded me. They will occur to anyone. But to oppose it—I knew Norman too well—to try that.

"Perhaps that would be the best solution of the matter—for her."

"And for me?" he insisted.

"Well. You're in a better position than I to decide that."

He laughed and leaned forward and pinched her ear. Suddenly she forgot the stage and getting up—reckless of all observers,—came back and kissed him.

"Nina," I asked, "if I pinched your ear, would you kiss me?"

"No," she said, convincingly. "I'd slap your face."

"There's only one thing I know about this, Arnold," he said when she had returned to her seat. "It's bringing me to life again. I don't think I had really laughed for months. I'd forgotten there was such a thing as amusement in the world. I never was very strong on play. Of one thing I'm sure. It's giving me a new insight—a new point of view—into lots of things. Only God knows how it will turn out."

# VI

I can only guess how it would have turned out, if Nina had not fallen among thieves. The most insoluble mystery of life is the way in which the very highest human values sometimes spring out of the coarsest, most brutal wrongs.

Although to Nina, I had spoken of Blackie in a flippant tone, I knew that he might cause trouble. I had spoken seriously about it to Norman, advising him to avoid as much as possible, and especially after dark, those parts of town, where Blackie's gang was likely to be encountered. And together we had impressed on Nina and Guiseppe that she was never to go out alone. But as nothing was heard from him for some time, we all began to worry less.

Nina had been with us about three weeks when the storm broke. I came home from my work about five one afternoon—and found bedlam. Guiseppe's head was wrapped in a bloody bandage, Nina was sobbing wildly on the divan.

It took some minutes before I could get a connected explanation from them. After lunch they had gone out to pay the butcher's bill. Nina, having come from "his district" had won Giuseppe's heart and he allowed her the pleasure of playing at housewife. It pleased her especially to pay the bills, so she was carrying the money—about thirty dollars. At the corner of Second Avenue and First Street, they had been surrounded by Blackie's gang. Guiseppe had fought like a true Garibaldian until his head had been laid open with a knife and he had been thrown to the ground by the young toughs. As quickly as they had come, they ran away. When he picked himself up, Nina was nowhere to be seen. He had asked the aid of a policeman, but had been laughed at. Then he had come to the Teepee, not finding either Benson or me, he had bound up his head, and rallying some Garibaldian comrades, had set out on a search. This about three o'clock. A little after four they had found her sobbing desperately behind an ash can in an alley-way. He had had some trouble in persuading her to come back. She was afraid of Blackie's wrath— but more afraid that Norman would be angry on account of the money.

Her story came out brokenly between spells of crying. At the first attack,

Blackie and another cadet had hustled her around the corner and up some stairs to a rented room. There they took away the money and beat her at leisure. The three who had manhandled Guiseppe came in shortly and kicked her about some more. There was nothing unusual in this—it is the well-established custom, by which the cadets keep their girls in slavery. I doubt if a day ever passes in this great metropolis of ours when the same scene is not enacted. They would probably have beaten her worse, if the windfall of money had not tempted them out to other pleasures. One after another the five men swore, emphasizing their words with blows, that if she ever threw down Blackie again, they would kill her. Their parting advice to her was that if she had not earned five dollars by ten o'clock next morning, she could expect a fresh beating.

Such stories had come to my knowledge before, they are the commonplaces of the police courts. But as Norman had said the first morning, such things must happen to someone near us, before we realize them. I took the handcuffs out of my desk, put fresh cartridges in my revolver. I had never set out after a man before in a like frame of mind....

When I think back to that evening's work, the Tombs and our convict prisons and all the bitter horror of our penal system, is no longer inexplicable. It is only crystallized anger. The electric chair is only a formal symbol of collective hate. I am not at all proud of that man-hunt. A friend of mine had been hurt. "A friend of mine"—how many of man's and nature's laws have been broken with that preface! The political bosses look after their "friends." More corrupt legislation has been passed because of "friendship" than for bribes. Well. A friend of mine had been touched. Everything by which I like to recognize myself as a civilized man dropped away. Suddenly I became an ally of the thing I was fighting against. As I rushed downstairs, with handcuffs in one pocket and a revolver in the other and murder in my heart, I was just adding my contribution to the maintenance of the system which seems to me—when not angry—the most despicable element in our civilization.

I left word for Benson to stay in when he came home, so that I could reach him by telephone. I had no definite plan when I left the Teepee—only somehow I was going to "get" Blackie. It was about an hour before I was able to locate him. The first fury of my anger had passed, it had had time to become cold and to harden.

Pinning my badge on the outside of my coat, I kicked open the door of the "Tim O'Healy Social and Civic Club," and covered the crowd of twenty young toughs who were in the room.

"Hands up," I ordered. They obeyed sullenly.

"I want Blackie," I said, "and no funny work from the rest of you."

For a moment they were irresolute.

"Say. You're making a damn fool of yourself," one of them protested, "Blackie's president of this club—he's right next to the Old Man. You'll get broke sure."

"Shut up. The Old Man sent me," I lied. "Blackie's been getting too fly."

"Hell!" another piped up. "I seen the Old Man shake hands wid him an hour ago."

"Cut it out, kid," I replied. "You talk too much. How long's the Old Man been in the habit of warning guys he's going to light on?"

My lie worked—and saved bloodshed. It was the old tragedy of Cardinal Wolsey acted over again. None of the gang was really afraid of my revolver. One rush would have finished me. But they were all afraid of the Old Man's ire. They drew away from Blackie.

"It's a lie," he growled. "Me and the Old Man's friends."

"You can talk that over with him in the morning. Come on."

He grew suddenly pale, half believing my story. He was such an ill-visaged, rat-eyed scoundrel, I regretted that they had not made a rush—at least I could have stopped his career. Single handed now, he submitted sullenly.

"Wot's the charge?" he asked, holding out his hands for the irons.

"Murder in the first."

From the way he wilted, I think he must have had a murder on his conscience.

"Now," I said to the gang, "I don't need any help from you. You'd better go right on with your game. You can call on him later on in the station house and bail him out—if you want to get in wrong with the Old Man."

But instead of taking him to the nearby station house, I rushed him down town to the Tombs. The sergeant at the desk did not know him, so I entered him under a false name. A search revealed quite an arsenal on his person, a short barreled revolver, a knife and some brass-knuckles. I plastered him with all the charges I could think of—disorderly conduct, concealed weapons, robbery in the first degree, felonious assault. Nina might be too frightened to testify to the robbery, but Guiseppe would swear to the assault.

As soon as I had him in a cell, I telephoned to Norman that all was going well and rushed uptown to the home of the district attorney. The fates were playing into my hands, for at that time—as is usual between elections—there was civil war within the organization. The district attorney was a machine man, but was one of the leaders of the rebellious faction. He heard my story with great glee, a serious criminal charge against one of the Old Man's lieutenants was fine gist for his mill. He promised to push the case and put it on before O'Neil, whom the Old Man could not reach.

Then I went to the "Old Man." I have already written of my encounters with him. In general I had established friendly relations with the machine politicians. Some of them, especially the judges, liked me personally. Ryan's friendship for me was, I think, real. But of what was back of the Old Man's easy going familiarity, I was less certain. I could not count on his friendship. But he was sure to find out what I had done. And there was nothing to be gained by letting some one else tell him.

That night I found him in the back room of his brother-in-law's saloon. He looked up at me, his eyes, usually cordial, decidedly hostile.

"Say, young man, haven't you been getting pretty gay?"

"I sure have," I admitted. "And I've come round to tell you what I did and why I did it." I gave him the story from beginning to end, even my talk with the district attorney.

"Well," he said, when I was through, "you've played it pretty slick—so far. But how are you going to keep that gang from shooting you up, when they find out what you put over on them?"

"It'll be a poor friend of Blackie," I said, "who takes a shot at me. I've got too many friends on the bench. And the district attorney would sure hand him a dirty deal."

He nodded assent. According to his lights the Old Man fought fairly. He had no mean personal animosity. He handed me a cigar. I smoked it silently while he was thinking things out.

I had put a knife into a vulnerable spot—had thrown the apple of discord where it was most likely to cause trouble. Tammany Hall is a latter-day feudalism. Ability to protect one's vassals is the keynote of the organization. The "ward heeler" is a petty count, the "district leaders" are the great dukes. And the kingship of this realm is not hereditary—it is not even a life-tenure. I do not think it has ever happened, certainly not in my time, that a boss has held his position till death. And there have been very few voluntary abdications.

The Old Man was facing a determined rebellion. Not to be able to save Blackie would be a great blow to his prestige. Many a district leadership has been lost on a lesser issue. He knew he could get no help from the district attorney's office, without patching up a humiliating peace. I could see only one outlet for him—to repudiate Blackie. He could easily have found some excuse for backing up my lie. I am sure this thought was in his mind, written all over with the word "discretion." But in expecting him to take this easy way out, I misjudged him. He loved a fight. These factional struggles were what made life interesting within the organization and attractive to men of his type. He had never been defeated. He did not like to lie down before me, who in his eyes was not even a regular warrior—just a sort of banditti.

"I've sent a man down to bail him out," he said abruptly. "I guess there is going to be a fight. You'll get my answer in the morning. Goodnight."

I found Norman in a Berserker fury. He was inclined to quarrel with me for not having shot Blackie on sight. A doctor had sewed up the gash in Guiseppe's head. Beyond some angry black and blue blotches, Nina had sustained no injuries. As soon as she had been reassured about the lost money, she had recovered her spirits.

The Old Man's answer would have caught us unawares—as he intended it should—if it had not been for a fortunate enmity of mine. I suppose there were many people in the Tombs who disliked me, but no one hated me so cordially as Steger, the agent of the society for the Protection of Childhood. Our feud was of long standing. He was an insignificant little man, to whom no one ever paid any attention. He was employed by the society to push the charges against everyone accused of violating the laws for the protection of childhood and to urge the heaviest penalties against all who were found guilty. My business was to persuade the court to temper justice with mercy. Inevitably we came into conflict. He would urge the judge to impose the maximum sentence, and I would plead for leniency. My personal standing was better than his and I invariably won out in these frequent tilts. His rancor against me had always made me smile. I met him as I entered the court house.

"Seems to be a nice sort of fellow—that room-mate of yours," he sneered.

"What's up?"

"You'll know quick enough. Take my advice and disappear. It will be hard for you to disprove complicity."

It was enough to give me the tip. Within five minutes I had the whole story from one of my fellow "county detectives," who had seen the warrant. Blackie and the Old Man had got Nina's mother to make an affidavit that her daughter was only seventeen years old. Steger had joyfully sworn out a warrant against Benson, charging him with rape in the second degree—states prison, ten years.

In the language of the Tombs, they "had the goods on him." There is no getting away from this charge if the girl is under eighteen. The question of whether or not she has "led a previously chaste life," has no bearing in rape cases.

It did not take me long to reach a telephone. Benson had left the Teepee. As the detective was on the way with the warrant, I told Guiseppe to take Nina at once to the Café Boulevard—not to wait a minute! I luckily caught Norman at the club, just as he was calling for his mail. The fact that I was "compounding a felony," did not occur to me till hours afterwards.

I reached the café and transferred Guiseppe and Nina to a private room, before Norman arrived. He was certainly in a belligerent frame of mind when he did come. He had brought his family lawyer with him, a pompous old man, with gray mutton-chop whiskers and a tendency towards apoplexy. His dignity was sadly ruffled by having been drawn into a vulgar criminal case.

Norman and I went with him into another room for a council of war. He was of course ready, he told us, to act as his client directed, but he felt it his duty to point out that he was an older man than we, with some knowledge of worldly affairs. He hoped that I with my familiarity with the criminal courts might point out some more satisfactory solution than the marriage which his client in a nobly Quixotic spirit was contemplating. We must allow an older and more experienced man to say that marriage was a serious—if not actually a sacerdotal affair. It was a gamble under the best circumstances. And in this case, socially so inexpedient, financially so disproportionate, and personally —well—so unprecedented it would be…. He hemmed and hawed, ruffled his scanty hair and patted his paunch—in short could not I offer a suggestion.

"Go ahead and talk," Norman growled. "Get it out of your system."

"They could skip to Canada, temporarily," I said. "If we drop the case against Blackie, they'll squash this warrant."

The lawyer nodded approval.

"Are you all through?" Norman asked. "Well, then, listen to me. I'm not going to skip. I'm not going to let up on that scoundrel. I'm not going to 'quit'! Not for a minute! I'd be on my way to the City Hall marriage bureau already, if old law-books here didn't say I needed the consent of Nina's mother. If you want to be helpful—produce a mother-in-law. Buy the old lady, kidnap her, club her—anything—but produce her in a consenting frame of mind. If you don't want to help—run along. I'll turn the trick myself. It's a cinch. We'll give ourselves up and be married in the Tombs."

The lawyer tried to say something, but Norman was looking at me.

"All right," I said. "I'll fix that. Don't take any chances by going out of this private room. As soon as I snare the old lady, I'll telephone. It may be a long hunt, but sit tight."

It was not a long hunt. The Old Man, never dreaming that a rich young man like Benson would cut the Gordian knot by marrying a prostitute, had not taken the precaution of hiding the mother. I found her dozing in front of her fruit store. She had not heard of Nina for several months, until the night before when they had made her sign the affidavit about her age. She would have consented to Nina's murder for fifty dollars, the marriage was arranged for ten.

When she had made her mark on a legal paper drawn up by the lawyer, we sent Guiseppe home to prepare lunch and entertain the police. He was not to tell them anything, except that we would be back soon. Norman and Nina, the lawyer and I, rode down to the City Hall in a closed carriage. It rather startled me, the speed with which they tied the knot. Back at the Teepee we found a detective and a policeman. There was a tableau.

174

"Good day, gentlemen," Norman said. "Allow me to present you to Mrs. Benson."

He handed the certificate to the detective.

"Now," he said, when the man had read it, "get out. And look here—you policeman. Tell your captain that my wife has been brutally attacked in his precinct. It's up to him to protect her. Tell him that if I have to commit murder, it will be his fault."

Half an hour later, while we were eating, the telephone rang. It was the Old Man.

"Hello," he said. "Give them my congratulations. Say. You beat me to it in great shape. Too bad you ain't in politics. I'd like to have you on my staff. And say—Blackie has gone on a railroad journey for his health. Now you fellows ain't going to be nasty are you and make me pay that five thousand dollars bail? The club's got a new president. He's just been round to see me, says the boys are sorer than hell over the job you put up on them. I told him to keep the lid on. I says to him, 'Those two young gentlemen are my friends.' You are, ain't you?"

"Well," I said, "when I've got what I want, I quit fighting. Forgotten all about that case. The only thing which might remind me of it, would be the sight of Blackie's face."

"Fine," he replied. "That's cleaned up. And say—they're taking on some more men in the dock department to-morrow—room for any of your friends. And—don't forget to give my best wishes to the bride—and groom. I like a fellow that's a real sport."

An hour later a messenger boy arrived with a great bunch of white roses for the bride. On the card, the Old Man had scrawled: "Good luck." So peace was reëstablished.

# VII

The morning after the wedding, Norman found me in the library reading what the newspapers had to say about it. "Eccentric Millionaire Weds Street Walker." "Prominent Socialist Leader, to avoid state prison, married a little girl he had seduced." When my friend, the protector of children, found that we had beaten the warrant, he had taken this way of venting his spleen.

"I'm glad," Norman said, as he glanced at the headlines, "that Nina doesn't read newspapers. These might bother her."

But he made me read them aloud as he drank his coffee. And all the while his look of amused contentment deepened.

"God! That sounds good," he commented. "I never knew just how to do it. I've spent many a sleepless night trying to think out some effective way of telling the 'best people' to go to hell—some way of spitting in the eyes of the smug citizens—so they wouldn't think it was a joke. Every time I get mad—really open up—and tell the gang what I think of them how the stench of their hypocrisies offends my nostrils, it adds to my reputation as a wit. I guess this will fix them! You know that thing of Heine's...."

He jumped up and pulled the "Memoirs" from the shelf and read me the passage where Heine tells of his boyish encounter with "Red Safchen," the hangman's little daughter. Although the good people of the village where he went to school tolerated the office of public executioner, they would have no dealing with the officer. His family was mercilessly ostracised. Heinrich took pity on the daughter and once in a sudden exaltation he kissed her. In these words he ends his account: "I kissed her not only because of my tender feeling for her, but in scorn of society and all its dark prejudices."

"That's it," Norman said gleefully. "I've always wished I could find a hangman's daughter and kiss her somewhere in public—show the empty-headed, full-bellied gang how I despise them. Nina's done it for me."

Nina had taken a very passive part in all these proceedings. She had done what she was told to do, said what she was told to say, without question. How passive a part it had been none of us realized at the time. But that afternoon when I came back from the Tombs, I found her in earnest conversation with Guiseppe.

"Say," she said, after he had gone, "I want to talk to you."

But she found it hard to begin.

"What is it?" I encouraged her.

"The old man, Guiseppe, is a fool," she blurted out. "Says your friend married me."

"Well. That isn't foolish. He did marry you."

"Aw hell! Don't lie to me. Fine men like him don't marry girls they pick up in the street."

"Not very often," I admitted. "But Benson certainly married you."

She sighed profoundly, as though there was no hope of getting the truth in a world of men.

"You must think I'm easy," she persisted. "He won't never marry me. Of course it don't matter how poor you are. Sometimes rich men from uptown marry factory girls, like in 'From Rags to Riches'—but not girls like me. Not girls that have been bad."

I tried to translate into the lingo of the Bowery the old proposition that it is never too late to mend. And then I asked her, "Didn't you go to the City Hall with him?"

"Don't I know? Haven't I seen people get married?" she retorted half in discouragement, half in anger. "Don't I know you have to have a white dress

177

and a priest? Wot's the game?"

I did my best to explain that in America, we have civil marriages which are just as binding as the ones in a church. But all I could get from her was a reluctant admission that there might be two varieties of marriage—a half way kind at the City Hall and a truly kind with a priest. She insisted that it was a sin to have children without a white dress and a ring.

When Norman came in, I took him to my room and, closing the door, told him about it. He rolled around on the bed and kicked his heels in the air.

"Think of it!" he howled. "Me—done up in orange blossoms! Me—going to a priest! Arnold, get out your white gloves—polish your silk hat—you'll have to see me through with this."

He dashed out to order Nina's dress. But he said nothing to her about it, pledged me to secrecy. It was a complete surprise to her when it came.

I have never seen anything in all my life so wonderful as her face, when she opened the package—the gradual melting away of doubt, the gradual awakening of certainty—and then the way she walked over to Norman, her eyes so wide with joy, and threw herself sobbing into his arms. I had to go to my room to hide my tears.

In a few minutes, Norman came in—his voice was also stiff and husky.

"What in hell do you think is the latest?" he asked. "She's gone off with Guiseppe—to confessional! Says it would be a sin to get married without it. My God! My God!"

I was the "best man" and Guiseppe gave her away in the crypt of the Jesuit Church. We came home and dressed—all four of us—and went up to Delmonico's to dinner.

We made something of a sensation as we threaded our way between the tables to our place. Guiseppe, in evening clothes, with all his campaign medals, looked like the veriest nobleman. Nina was wonderful. Usually she was gay beyond words when taken to a restaurant, but this evening she was very solemn and a little pale. Of course a number of people recognized Norman and gossip started in vigorously. But of this Nina was unconscious. Her solemnity went deeper than that. When the cocktails were brought, she refused hers.

"Why not?" Norman asked.

A little blush started in her cheeks, fought its way to her temples and down her throat.

"What's the matter?" he asked.

"I'm married now," she stammered. "Good women don't drink cocktails."

We both glanced about and saw that if Nina's statement had been audible, it would have caused a protest:

"Why—there's Mrs. Blythe over there," Norman said. "She built a church. She's drinking a cocktail—she's awfully good."

"No, she ain't," Nina insisted doggedly. "She's painted herself. She's a sporting girl."

Norman looked very solemn. It was several seconds before he spoke.

"All right, little wife. I'll never ask you to drink any more cocktails."

The problem of what to do with Nina's mother troubled us somewhat for a time, but it solved itself with rather dizzying simplicity. She told Norman that with five hundred dollars for capital she could buy a larger fruit store and live in comfort. He investigated the matter carefully and, as it seemed to him a sound business proposition, he gave her the money. That was the last we saw of her. The gossips of the neighborhood said that one of her boarders, attracted by this magnificent dowry, had married her and that they had returned to Italy. I could not discover the man's name. And we never heard of her again.

It was a joyous thing to watch Nina in the weeks and months that followed her marriage. Always I had a sort of impatience with Norman. It did not seem to me that he realized what was going on within her, how her soul under the strains and stresses of her new surroundings, was being shaped to beauty.

There was much discussion in the scientific circles of those days over the relative force of heredity and environment in the formation of character. Most of the pundits were inclined to the belief that the congenital element, the abilities and tendencies with which we are born, is the greatest part of us. Watching Nina, kept me from this error. It may be that she was unusually plastic, peculiarly adaptable. But the change was amazing. It was not only that she left off swearing, learned to handle a fork as we did, came to wash her face without being urged. It went much deeper than this.

I thought that Norman was giving small account of the change. I did not realize I was unjust to him for a good many months. But one day I went to the station to see him off on a western trip. Just before the train started, he laid hold of my arm.

"We—Nina is expecting a baby."

He swung aboard the train and waved his hand to me. The news meant that he was not afraid of Nina's heredity. That he had not told me until there was no chance of discussing it, gave me a sudden pang of jealousy. Without my noticing it, a new element had come into my friend's life, which was too holy for him to talk over with me. It made me feel very lonely for awhile.

In the months which were left to her time, Nina went about the Teepee— singing. The wonder grew in her eyes, as did also the certainty of her high calling. To me—an outsider—there was something uncomfortable in the sight of their happiness those last weeks before the baby came. I felt like a trespasser, a profaner of some high mystery. But Norman begged me not to leave.

# BOOK VI

## I

Of course Ann was immensely interested in Nina's adventure. From the first she was sure it would turn out well. Ignoring the shell, as she always did, the kernel of the matter did not seem at all strange to her. She went much further than the Professor in "Sartor Resartus," who thought of people without clothes. She stripped them of their vocations as well. For her there existed no such categories as "street car conductors," "actresses," "bank presidents," "seamstresses." She saw only men and women. The way they earned their living was as unimportant to her as the *mode* of their garments. It was not what people did, but the way they did it, which mattered. A man, who had chosen cooking as a career and cooked passionately, threw all his energy into soups and *soufflés* ranked higher with her than a listless, perfunctory poet. The doing heartily of any job whatsoever would sanctify it in her eyes. Of course she knew that working at the match trade or with white lead poisons a person, that some of the "dusty trades" ruin the lungs. But it would have been hard to get her to admit that pleasant, stimulating work might make a person more moral or that a vile job can damn a man. Nina's success in her new rôle, seemed to Ann, to depend entirely upon the intensity with which she entered it. It mattered not at all whether she had been previously a street walker or a queen. This point of view—utterly different from mine—I found very common among the people I met at Cromley.

Sooner or later I made the acquaintance of most of the leading anarchists of this country and many from abroad. They were sure of a welcome from the Bartons, sure of a meal and of any bed or sofa in the house which chanced to be vacant. They were an interesting and in many ways an attractive group. Like Ann, they were little interested in the outward accidents of a person's life, but very intense in regard to a rather indefinite inner life. They were, of course, vehemently opposed to the police. But I was accepted without question. I remember old Herr Most said, one time, his long gaunt forefinger tapping my badge.

"It's not that which makes a policeman. It's not the symbol we're fighting but the habit of mind."

The anarchists are beginning to take the place in our fiction which was formerly held by the gypsy. Half a dozen novels of the last few years have had such types as their heroes. It is hard to resist the romantic charm of a person who is utterly unattached. The vagabond who, in a land of conventional dwelling houses, sleeps out under the stars, casts a spell over us. These anarchists are intellectual nomads. In order that they may be free to wander according to their fancy in the realm of thought, to stroll at will in the pleasant valleys of poesy, to climb at times up onto the great white peaks of dreams, that in the winter days they may trek south to meet their friend, the sun, they have foresworn the clumsier impedimenta of our traditional ideas. As the Beduoin and the tramp despise the "Cit" who is kept at home by his business engagements, by the cares of his family and of his lands and goods, so these anarchists look down on us who are held stationary in the world of thought.

I remember a young Russian exile, who spoke English so faultlessly, after the manner of Macaulay's Essays, that it seemed queer, saying that he was "a cynic of the material." It struck me as a wonderfully apt phrase to distinguish their way of thinking from the more usual. Of all the "kitchenside of life,"—the meals we eat, the clothes we wear, the beds we sleep in, bankbooks, and property deeds, of vested rights and established institutions, of the applause and approbation of the mob—which most of us consider important, they were cynical. I, for instance, must admit to a certain unreasoning respect for clean linen. It is hard for me, even in the face of ocular demonstration, to separate it from clean straight thinking. But this group which gathered at Mrs. Barton's was certainly indifferent in the matter.

Ann's bacteriological training had made her a fervent apostle of cleanliness. "Germs," she would say, "are only filth." But as often as not, some of the guests were evidently unafraid of microbes. Some of the dirtiest of them were the cleanest, straightest thinkers.

I have never met any other group of people who so sympathetically understood how I felt about life. In one way or another they had come to see life as I did—as I believe anyone, having the energy to avoid hardening, would see it, if they worked long in the Tombs. Try it yourself. Go into the Tombs—there is one in every town—if you have any love of justice and rectitude in your being you will come out in violent revolt against the smug complacency of our social machine. You will find anarchists pleasant people to talk with.

But when they tried to convert me, I was cold. I could go with them all the way in their criticism of and contempt for things as they are. Much of what they said and wrote seemed to me platitudes—I had seen it also keenly myself. I knew the things of which our civilization can boast, its universities, and culture, its music and painting, the triumphs of its sciences, its marvelous subjugation of nature, its telegraphs and transcontinental trains, and all this seemed very small return for the frightful price we pay. For years I had been living in the slums. I knew the debit side of the ledger also—the tuberculosis laden tenements, the sweat-shops, the children who never grow up, the poverty, the crime. The time they spent in trying to convince me that society was bankrupt, was wasted. And the dream of communism they offered in its place was enticing. I do not see how anyone can object to the ideals of anarchism, unless they are of the turn of mind which enjoys the kind of arrangements we now have—where one can steal and murder and still be respectable. Of course a scamp would have a pretty bad time in a communist society. But the means by which they hoped to realize their dream—well—that was a different affair.

It is possible to believe in all the miracles of Jesus—from his birth to his resurrection—but it takes "faith." It is possible to believe that, if by some miracle we were all made free we would be very much better than we are. The anarchists hold that our vices come from our manifold slavery. That is their creed. But it also takes "faith." I have not been able to believe anything in that way, since I was sixteen.

But I was quite ready to agree with them that much work such as mine was pitifully futile.

# II

There were two incidents in my work which grew to great proportions in my mind. They happened close together, when I had been about seven years in the Tombs.

Walking one day along a corridor of the prison, past the cells, my attention was caught by an old man. He sat on a low stool, close to the grated door, his face pressed against the bars. On it was written appalling, abject despair.

"What's wrong?" I asked.

He glared at me sullenly. It was some time before he replied.

"They've got me wrong," he said.

The date on the door of his cell gave the history of the case. His name was Jerry Barnes. Arrested three weeks ago, without bail, he had pled guilty the day before to burglary in the third degree, and was awaiting sentence before Justice Ryan.

"What did you plead guilty for?" I asked, "if they had you wrong?"

"Wot's the use? You won't believe me."

With a little urging his story came in a rush. He was an old-timer, had done three bits in state prison, but coming out four years before he had decided to "square it." He wanted to die "on the outside." He had no trade, but had wrung out a meagre living, stuffing straw into mattresses. In the rush season he earned much as a dollar a day. Sometimes only twenty cents. And sometimes there was no work at all. He slept in a ten-cent lodging house, ate ten cent meals—forty cents a day, plus twenty cents a week for tobacco. What was left went into the Bowery Savings Bank. He wanted to have enough so he would not be buried in the Potters' Field. It had been a barren life. But the fear of prison—the fear which only an old-timer, who wants to die outside, knows —had held him to it.

Coming home from work one night he had stopped to watch a fire. As the crowd broke up he saw on the sidewalk several bags of tobacco and some boxes of cigarettes. He picked them up and almost immediately was grabbed by two detectives.

While the crowd had been watching the fire, someone had broken into a tobacco store and looted it. The detectives led Jerry to Central Office, identified him by the Bertillon records, and charged him with burglary in the second degree, for which the maximum sentence is ten years.

Jerry said that he knew nothing of the burglary. When he had been brought into court the district attorney had told him that if he would consent to plead guilty of burglary in the third degree, for which the maximum is only five years, he would intercede with the judge and ask for a light sentence.

Jerry had been hopeless of proving his innocence in the face of his previous record and the fact that some of the proceeds of the burglary had been found on his person. He had no friends. He did not believe that a poor man had any chance in court. So he had pled guilty in the hopes of a short sentence.

His story rang true, but I took great pains to verify it.

The police believed that Jerry was one of three or four who committed the burglary. One hundred dollars in money and twice as much stock had been taken. They had no evidence against Jerry except the packages of tobacco found in his pockets, and his record.

Mr. Kaufman, his employer, spoke highly of him. Jerry had been a regular applicant for work, and a preferred employee. If there was any work at all it was given to him. And sometimes in slack seasons, he had been employed out of charity. Kaufman said he would be glad to come to court and testify to Jerry's regular habits during the last three years. The lodging house keeper was also willing to appear on his behalf. Jerry had earned a definite reputation for quietness and sobriety. He had kept very much to himself and certainly had not been associating with professional criminals.

I took the whole story to Judge Ryan. He always placed great reliance on my judgment in such matters, and I was convinced of Jerry's innocence. Ryan said he would allow him to withdraw his plea of guilty and stand trial. I had a harder time persuading Jerry to do so. He was inclined to take his medicine— let well enough alone. He might live through a couple of years in prison and die outside, but he was afraid to take a chance on a long term. But finally I argued him into doing it.

When at last the case came up for trial, Ryan was off on his vacation, and it was set down before O'Neil, with whom I had less than no influence. Mr. Kaufman had been called out of town by the death of his father. No one appeared to speak for Jerry except the lodging house keeper, who made a poor showing, being mightily frightened under the cross-examination. The district attorney produced a handful of Rogues' Gallery photographs of Jerry. The police expanded their memory to the point of swearing that they had seen Jerry in the rifled premises. The jury convicted him without leaving the room, of burglary in the second degree. And the judge gave him eight years....

I sneaked out of the court room and locked myself in my office. It is not a pleasant thing to think about or write down even now.... I am sure he was innocent. If I had not meddled—he had not asked me to—he would have gotten off light. And eight years was the same as "life" for him.

The next two days when duty took me into the prison, I kept as far as might be from Jerry's cell. What could I say to him?

But on the afternoon of the second day, I met him by accident face to face. He was one of a line of ten men, old and young, chained together—just starting up the river. He jumped at me so hard, it threw the entire line off their feet. His slow, desperate curses as they led them out to the prison-van still haunt me, sometimes, at night.

Now that Jerry is dead—he died during the fourth year—I, more than ever before, wish I could believe in a life beyond death. I cannot imagine another life in which we would not understand and forgive the wrongs done us in this. And I cannot think of anything I would rather have than Jerry's forgiveness.

About the same time, I had taken up the work of supervising the men "on parole" from the reformatory. It was very hard to find satisfactory employment for these boys. I wrote an article which was translated and printed in one of the Yiddish dailies. I described the reformatory, told of the conditions on which the inmates were paroled and the civic duty of encouraging them to make good. And I appealed to the Jews to help me find work for the sons of their race. Many offers of employment came as a result of this article.

One day a fine old Russian Jew, named Lipinsky, came to my office on this business. He was a fur merchant on Second Avenue. He and his son, about nineteen, worked together, and he could use an assistant who would accept apprentice wages and live in the family. I liked the old man; he was a sturdy type, had worked up through endless hardships and reverses to the point where he was beginning to make a surplus and win respect in his trade. He was ambitious for his son, on whom all his hopes centered.

It seemed to me an unusually fine opening, the home conditions I felt sure would be good, and the first Jewish boy who came down—his name was Levine—I sent to Lipinsky. I called two or three times and everything seemed to be going well. But after about three months the crash came. Levine and young Lipinsky were arrested in the act of burglary in a large fur warehouse. They had several hundred dollars' worth of choice ermine skins in their bags. Young Lipinsky went to pieces under the "third degree" and confessed everything. They had been at it for more than a month. It had been a strong combination—his knowledge of furs and Levine's skill with the "jimmy." In an apartment on Fifteenth Street, where they had been keeping two girls, the police recovered large quantities of expensive furs.

Levine got seven years in state prison, and young Lipinsky, because he had turned state's evidence and because of my influence, got off with a sentence to the reformatory.

Old Lipinsky was utterly ruined. His rivals accused him of complicity. The detectives raided his store. They found nothing, but it was enough to ruin his credit. He peddles shoe-strings now on Hester Street.

But greater than this material loss was the blow to his heart—his hope in his only son shattered. He knocks at the door to my office now and then to ask news of his boy. It is sad news I have to tell him. His son is now doing his second term in state prison, a confirmed crook.

Old Lipinsky does not curse me as Jerry did—he relies on me to pay his rent and coal bills. He weeps.

I tried to look at these discouraging incidents, with reason. I tried to tell myself that my intentions had been good, and that intentions counted more than results. I tried to recall the very many families to whom I had brought a blessing. It is not a matter to boast of—nor to be modest about. The work I had chosen gave me daily opportunity to bring help to those in awful need. But try as I would to preserve what seemed to my reason proper proportions, the curses of Jerry, the wailing of old Lipinsky, drowned out all else. It obsessed me.

Looking back over those years it is hard for me to decide whether Norman was the determining element in my thinking, or whether from different angles, by different processes of mind, we reached the same conclusions. Certain it is that many times a conversation with him would precipitate fluid-vague feelings of mine into the definite crystals of intellectual convictions. A talk on this subject—of intentions and results—stands out as clear in my mind as any memory I have of him.

It started, I believe, by some jovial effort of his to lift me out of my profound discouragement. We had lit our pipes, Guiseppe was clearing the supper litter from the table. Nina was dividing her attention between a pile of to-be-darned stockings in her lap and Marie, who was safe in her cradle and needed no attention at all. Nina was a constant factor in all our arguments in those days. She was always silent. Much of our talk must have been far above her comprehension, but she would sit on the divan, her feet tucked up under her, and listen for hours on end. Her presence in some subtle way contributed to our discussions. The ancient Egyptians brought a skeleton to their feasts to remind them of death. Nina was to us a symbol of life—a silent chorus of actuality. Some word or look of mine that night showed Norman how desperately serious was my discouragement, and he dropped his flippant tone.

"After all intentions don't justify anything. We must demand results. But what results? When I see a chap, whose efforts I know to be good, get discouraged, I'm sure he's looking for the wrong kind of results. Of course, our unseen, unintentional influence is much greater than the influence we consciously exert. Some little of it we know about, the greater part we ignore. You're worried because some of your well-intentioned efforts have gone wrong, because our fight for a reformatory ended in a fizzle. These two cases, you speak of—Jerry and Lipinsky—are on your mind. There are probably dozens of others, just as bad, which you don't know about. Are they the kind of results on which you have a right to judge your work? I think not.

"The one real result of human activity is knowledge. Zola makes a character in 'Travail' say that science is the only true revolutionist. And if science is something more than dead laboratory data, if it's live workable human knowledge, a real aid to straight thinking, he is right.

"That must be the test of your activity—the judging result. What does it matter to the race that Jerry is beating his head against the walls of Sing Sing? In all the black history of the race, in all the long up-struggle, which rubbed off most of our hair, what does a little added injustice signify? Nothing. Unless—and this is the great chance—unless you can make the race realize the stupidity of such injustice. If you could make Jerry's tragedy bite into us like Uncle Tom's—well—then you and he would have earned the right to wrap the draperies of your couch about you and all that.

"It's the same with good results. They are insignificant! In terms of the race, they matter as little as the half hundred slaves Mrs. Stowe helped to escape via the underground railroad. Take Tony—this wreck you've dragged into dry-dock and repaired. It's important to him that you came along at the right time. But what does it matter to all the other immigrant craft that are trying to find safe anchorage on this side of the world? There's a new Tony launched every minute.

"Seven years you've been in the Tombs—had your nose in the cesspool. What have you learned—not just subjective acquisition of information, but what has it taught you for the race? Sooner or later, you'll begin to teach. You can't help it. It's too big for you—it will force an outlet.

"Prisons are a stupidity. Why do we cling to them? Natural viciousness? Innate cruelty? You don't believe that. It's ignorance! Dense black ignorance! Sodden ways of thinking. You've seen, you know. Well—that's footless— unless you can make the rest of us see and know. One man can't add much to this great racial mind. But if you can do the little, the very little, that Beccaria did, that John Howard and Charles Reade did—one lightning gleam—these little results you are worrying about now will sink into insignificance.

"You won't solve the problem of crime. That's too much to expect. What you teach about reform—reforms of judicial procedure, reforms of police and prisons—won't interest me much. I know these things seem big to you, but it will be mostly out of date before it's off the press. What I will look for is some help in understanding the problem. That will be your contribution—the judging result of your living. Perhaps some youngster, one of the generation to come, will read your book and go into the Tombs, see it for himself and in two years understand all it has taken you ten years to learn. That's human progress!

"We must saturate ourselves with the idea of evolution. Think of ourselves, our little lives, as tiny steps in that profound procession. Knowledge is the progressive element in life, just as nerve cells are the only progressive tissue in our bodies. We won't develop any more legs as we evolve through the ages ahead of us—the change will be in our brains."

The conversation rambled off into some by-paths which I forget. But it was this same night, I think, that he struck the main road of his philosophy, mapped out before me his idea of the country the race has yet to explore.

"The impediment to progress," he said, "is our fool idea of finality. It's funny how humanity has always been looking for an absolute, final court of appeal. The king can do no wrong. The pope is infallible. God is omniscient! Now we have the age of reason. The old gods have been driven from Olympus. And in place of Jehovah and Zeus our college professors have made a god of truth, the absolute, the final! Sooner or later we've got to learn that progress—growth of any kind—is in exact antithesis to this idea of finality.

"A large part of the scientific world and, I suppose, ninety-nine per cent of what is called "the enlightened public," believe that Darwinism is the last work in natural science. There are a thousand question marks strewn about the theory of natural selection. Only those biologists, who have sense enough not to accept the finality of anything, are trying to answer these questions.

"Socialism is a spectacular example. What did Karl Marx do? He stumbled along through the life which was given him, doing kind things and mean things by the way, all of which is, or ought to be, forgotten. The real thing he did—his contribution—was to keep his eyes open, to look at life without blinders. In the long process of thinking, this is the most important, the fundamental thing. And what he saw he pondered over, sweated over, prayed atheistical prayers over—and then he spoke out fearlessly. The people about him were hypnotized by the wonderfully growing industrialism of the day. It was going to solve all the ills of the race. No one had any responsibility any more. *Laissez faire!* Virtue and happiness and the next generation were automatic. The praise of the machine became an enthusiasm, a gospel. Marx had looked at it harder than the rest, had seen through its surface a glitter. And like Cassandra he shouted out his forebodings, careless of whether the world listened or not. 'It's a sham,' he said, 'this industrialism of yours is fundamentally immoral. It bears within itself death germs. They are already at work. This thing in which you put your trust is already putrid.' I don't know anything more amazing in the history of the human mind than Marx prophecies. Wrong in some details of course. He didn't claim any divine inspiration. But those three volumes in German are stupendous. And the secret of it is that he turned his penetrating eyes on the life about him. He looked!

"But the socialists of today—are they following his example? No. Marx did not believe in finalities; they make a finality of him. He sought new knowledge. They are defending what is already old, and like everything old, some of it is wrong now. Marx was a revolutionist—one of the greatest. The Marxists are conservatives. Think of it. Not an American socialist has tried to analyze Wall Street! Instead of scrutinizing the life about them, they spend their time arguing over his agrarian theory. No country in the world offers such glaring examples of industrial injustice as these United States and the books they circulate are translations from German. Some day they'll wake up —then I'll join them.

"The trouble comes from thinking there are finalities in life—ultimate truths. We've got to get it into our heads that truth itself evolves.

"It's coming to me stronger and stronger that the point of attack ought to be on our ideals of education. My God! You quit college at the end of your freshman year and wasted exactly three years less than I did. I feel so sure that this is the real issue that I'm losing interest in everything else.

"A system of education which wakes up the human mind instead of putting it to sleep! Education which begins where it ought to! At the beginning! the process of seeing, of looking at life with our own eyes— instead of through some professor's spectacles. If we could only teach the trick of original observation!

"The trouble isn't so much that we think incorrectly. We don't see straight. I remember our professor used to tell us that logic is a coffee-mill. If we put coffee in at the top it will come out at the bottom in a more usable form. But if we put in dirt—it stays dirt, no matter how fine we grind it. And then he switched off to train our coffee-mills—a lot of rigamarole about syllogisms, the thirteen fallacious ones—perhaps it was fourteen. But not a single word about how to distinguish dirt from coffee. It's the original assumptions that need questioning. I don't believe Darwin was a better logician than Saint Augustine. But he went out into the world and looked. He used observed facts for his coffee-mill. Saint Augustine ground up a lot of incoherent beliefs and dirty assumptions. Anyone can learn the laws of logic in a three months college course, or in as many weeks from a text-book. But I don't know of any place where they even try to teach original observation.

"Education, everybody says, is the bulwark of democracy. And we Americans really want democracy in a way the most radical European never dreamed of. Yet we are content with our schools! Nobody really worries about improving them. We assume that our system is the best in the world, perfect. Final! Damn finality! I'm not sure that our system isn't the worst. We consistently kill all originality. The minute the kids strike school the process begins. 'This, my child, is what you must believe,' you say. 'This block,' the kindergarten teacher says 'is red.' Of course what she should say is, 'What color is this block?' The college professor says to his senior seminar, 'Goethe is the greatest German poet; if you prefer Heine, you are a barbarian. Milton's epics are the pride of English letters; if you prefer L'Allegro, you show your lack of culture. Shelley was undoubtedly a great poet, but, I regret to say, an incendiary. Of course you must read The Ode to the West Wind and the Clouds, but I warn you against the Revolt of Islam.' From grammar school to university it is all this business of predigested tablets.

"Just look at the effect this sort of business has had on our politics! We Americans are dead. New ideas, discussion of fundamental political principles are fomenting everywhere but here. A Paris cab-driver thinks more about the theory of government than our congressman. We Americans sit back—our feet on the table—puff out our chests and say 'complete and absolute liberty for all time was decreed by the fathers in 1789.' How many men do you know who ever seriously questioned that proposition? How many Americans really believe that it takes 'eternal vigilance' to be free? No. Our Constitution is the most glorious document penned by man. It's final—it's stagnant and stinking!

"If we don't revolutionize our education, we'll rot or give up democracy. It's a clear choice. A national Tammany Hall and dizzy Roman decadence or Neo-aristocracy with restricted suffrage and hare-brained experiments in human stock breeding. If we don't learn to educate in a truer way, if we don't manage to kill this folly of finality, it's a choice between physiological decay and eugenics.

"I'm getting out of everything else—can't see anything but education. No more personal charity, no more checks to shoddy philanthropies. All the money I can lay my hands on goes into a trust fund to finance an educational insurrection. It's the only revolution I'm interested in.

"I tried to write about it. But—hell—people won't take me seriously. I knew somebody would giggle if I talked, so I ground out an article. I found a man in the club laughing over it—said it was 'clever.' Well—I've put what I think about it in my will. Perhaps they won't laugh when they read that."

As I said I am not sure whether Norman gave me my ideas, or whether he voiced conclusions which were forming already in my mind. At least I owe him their concrete shape.

My work in the Tombs took on a new visage. I began to think of it as something to communicate. I went about it with the feeling of a showman or a guide. There was always someone at my shoulder, to whom I tried to explain the essentials back of the details. The routine which had begun to be mechanical was revivified. I began thinking out my book. What I wanted to do was to draw a picture of the complex phenomena of crime and to contrast with it the dead and formal simplicity of our Penal Code, to show its hopeless inadequacy. I began work on a section devoted to "Theft." From my notes and my daily experience, I tried to show the kind of people who steal, the motives which drive them to it, the means they develop towards their end, petty sneak thieves, swindle promoters, bank robbers, pickpockets, fraudulent beggars, defaulting cashiers. The reality of theft is an infinitely more tangled thing than one would suppose from reading the meagre paragraphs in our statutes which deal with "Larceny." The book grew slowly. I felt no hurry. Now and then I published sections in the magazines—"Stories of Real Criminals."

# III

It was when I was getting close to thirty-five that I first saw the name: Suzanne Trevier Martin—attorney and counsellor at law. We had heard rumors of women lawyers from the civil courts. But I think she was the first to invade the Tombs. It was Tim Leery, the doorman, of Part I, who called my attention to her.

"Say," he greeted me one morning about noon, "There's a fee-male lawyer here today—looking for you. And say—she's a peach!"

I do not know why I thought he was joking. I suppose I shared the comic paper idea that most professional women were pop-eyed and short-haired. Anyhow it was a definite surprise when I caught sight of her. Leery was pointing me out to her.

Yes. I am sure surprise was the chiefest element in the impression she made on me. Everything about her was different from what I expected of women. She was the most matter-of-fact looking person I have ever seen— and the most beautiful. I cannot describe her way of dressing, all that sticks in my mind is the crisp, white collar she wore. Somehow one's attention centered on that clean, orderly bit of linen. There was no suggestion of aping man-fashion about her, nor were there any frivolous tweedledees nor tweedledums. It was all as straightforward as that collar.

She had a mass of Titian red hair. A complexion so delicate that the sun had freckled it already in early spring. The lines of her face were altogether beautiful. Her mouth was firm and immobile. Her shifts of mood showed only in her eyes. They were always changing color, from deep tones of brown to a glowing chestnut almost as red as her hair. The way her head balanced on her neck, made me want to cheer. It seemed a victory for the race, that she—one of us—could carry her head so fearlessly.

"Here is an introduction," she said.

It was a letter from a young lawyer. The junior member of his firm, he was sometimes sent into the Tombs to defend the servants of their rich clients. I had often given him pointers on the practice of our courts, which differs materially from that of the civil courts. He asked the same courtesies for his friend, Miss Martin.

I felt with some embarrassment the amused stares of the crowded corridors.

"This isn't a very convenient place to talk," I said. "Let's go round to Philippe's and lunch."

As we walked downstairs, I sized her up as about twenty-five. I noted that the grace of her neck extended down her spine. I have never seen a straighter back. There was something definitely boyish in the way she walked, in her stride and the swing of her shoulders. This impression of boyishness was always coming and interfering with realization that she was a beautiful woman.

We found a quiet table at Philippe's and she explained her case. She was counsel for the Button-Hole Makers' Union. They were on strike and one of the girls had been arrested on the charge of assaulting a private policeman. The question at issue invoked the legality of picketing. If the girl had been within her rights in standing where she did, the watchman, who tried to drive her away, was guilty of assault. It was a case to fight out in the higher courts. The unions demanded a definite decision. Miss Martin wanted to have her client convicted, and still have grounds to take it up on appeal. It was simple and I had given her the necessary points before we had finished our coffee.

The very first sight of her in the Tombs had stirred me, as the first sight of no other woman had ever done. It was not so much a desire for personal possession as a vague feeling that the man to whom she gave her love would be happy above other men. In the back of my brain, as I sat talking to her, was a continual questioning. She had said she was a socialist. I saw that she had the fearless, open attitude to life, which is the hallmark of the revolutionists. I wondered if she had a lover. Was the friend, who had given her the introduction, the lucky man? What were her theories in such matters?

But if she made a more direct sensuous appeal to me than other women, to an even greater degree she seemed to ignore the possibility of such ideas being in my mind. I have never known even an ugly woman who was less coquettish. She was strangely aloof. She made the purely business side of our meeting dominate, did not seem to realize there might be a personal aspect. The way in which she made it quite impossible for me to suggest paying for her lunch was typical. She shook hands with me firmly, frankly, as a boy would with a man who had given him some slight help, and strode up the street to her office. I was surprised.

In and out of the Tombs, she walked for the next few weeks. Judge Ryan, before whom she tried her case, and who believed that all women should marry and keep indoors as soon after eighteen as a man would have them, was mightily exercised over her invasion.

"Damn her soul, Whitman," he said, "she isn't a woman—she's just brain and voice. She sits there before the court opens and looks like a woman —good-looking woman at that—then she gets up on her hind legs and talks. Hell! I forget she is a woman—forget she wears skirts. And, so help me God, there aren't a dozen men in the building who know as much law as she does. She's got the goods. That's the devil of it. You can't snub her. You can't treat her the way she deserves. You want to call her unwomanly and she won't let you remember she's a woman."

She had made Ryan, facing her from the bench, feel the same aloofness, she had impressed on me across the table at Philippe's. But if the judge found it impossible to snub her, it was just as impossible, I found, to be friendly with her. We had frequent encounters in the corridors. I frankly sought them, and she did so as frankly—when she wanted some information. Away from her, I thought of her as a desirable woman. Face to face, she forced me to consider her as a serious minded socialist.

Aside from the details of her case, we had only one talk. The second day she was at court she cross-questioned me on my politics. I had none. "Why not?" she demanded. She had all the narrow-minded prejudice which most socialists have towards the mere reformer, the believer in palliatives, the spreaders on of salve. Did I not realize the futility of such work as mine? I was more keenly aware of it than she. Well, why did not I go to the root of the matter? Why not attack the basic causes? I was not sure what they were. She was. Although she had not been in the Tombs as many days as I had years, she knew all about it. The whole problem of crime sprang from economic maladjustment. Socialism would cure it. It was all so beautifully simple! I have unspeakable admiration for such faith. It is the most wonderful thing in the world. But all I can do is to envy it. I cannot believe.

Her aloofness increased noticeably after she had sounded the depth of my unbelief. When the case was finished, she sought me out to thank me for the very real service I had rendered. Despite my intentions in the matter, her hand slipped out of mine quicker than I wished. I hoped to see her again. She was uncertain how soon, if ever, her work would bring her back to the Tombs. I suggested that I might call on her. She seemed really surprised.

"Why," she exclaimed; "thank you. But you know I'm very busy. I have five or six regular engagements a week—committees and all that. And this strike takes what time is left. I am too busy for the social game. I'm sorry. But we'll run into each other again some time. Goodbye. No end obliged."

It was the snub direct. Her friendship was only for those who saw the light. She had no time for outsiders, for "mere reformers."

She filled more of my mind after she was gone than in the few days of our intercourse. For the first time in my life romance laid hold on my imaginings. I am not sure whether it was real love or simply wounded *amour propre*. But I dreamed of all sorts of extravagant ways of winning her esteem and love—generally at the cost of my life. I was not nearly unhappy enough to want to die, but I got a keen, if somewhat lugubrious delight in picturing her kneeling at my bedside, realizing at last the mistake she had made in snubbing me—repenting it always through a barren, loveless life.

The memory I held of her was altogether admirable—the straight line of her back, the glorious poise of her head, the rich brown of eyes, her frank and boyish manner. But pride held me back from seeking her out. I knew a snub would be the result.

Once, a month or so later, I passed a street corner crowd, under a socialist banner. She was just getting up to speak. I walked a block out of my way for fear she would see me and think I was trying to renew our acquaintance. But I also was busy. Too busy to waste time over a phantom, gradually she sank back into a vaguer and vaguer might-have-been. A year later I ran across her name in the paper in connection with some strike. For a day or two her memory flared up again. That sentimental spasm I thought was the last of her. I was deep in proof-reading.

# IV

That my book brought recognition from professional penologists was a surprise to me. I had written it with the intent of interesting laymen. But a German psychological journal gave it a long review. It was quickly translated into French and Italian. I was made contributing editor of "La revue penologique." Last of all the American Prison Society took notice of me and chose me as a delegate to the International Congress at Rome.

Europe never attracted me, and I doubt if I would have gone, except for the urgings of Norman and Ann. I was sea-sick for five days, and bored beyond words the rest of the way over. It rained so hard the day I spent in Naples that I got no good view of Vesuvius.

Arrived in Rome, I found that they had put down my name for the first day's program, and I spent the time, till the congress opened, in my room writing up my paper. I had chosen for my subject: "The Need of a New Terminology in the Study of Crime." More and more this reform seems imperative to me. The effort to express the modern attitude towards crime in the old phraseology is like putting new wine in old skins. Just as we no longer say that a man is "possessed of the devil," but use such newer words as "paranoia," "paresis" and so forth, we must give up such terms as "burglary in the second degree." It is a remnant of mediæval scholasticism and means nothing today. It is a dead concept of an act and gives no account of the live human being who is supposed to have committed it. "Murder," the code implies, "is always murder, just as oxygen is always oxygen." But while one atom of oxygen is exactly like every other, no two murderers are at all alike. Crime is infinitely complex. "Larceny"—a fixed and formal term—cannot describe the intricate reactions from the varied stimuli of environment, which lead a particular bunch of nerve cells to steal. We must turn our back on the abstract words of the ancient law books and develop a vocabulary which expresses actualities.

That first day of the congress, seemed to me the very apotheosis of absurd futility. Half a hundred delegates from all corners of the world assembled in one of the court rooms of the palace of justice. We were supposed to be serious, practical men, come together to devise means of improving the methods of combating crime. We sat for an hour and a half through tiresome, bombastic exchanges of international greetings. The election of a chairman, of honorary presidents and vice-presidents, of a real secretary and a host of honorary secretaries took up the rest of the morning. A nation's parliament could have organized in less time and we had only come together to exchange ideas, we had no power.

When we convened after lunch, I was called on. There were three delegates from England, one from Canada and another from the United States. The rest had only a long-distance knowledge of English. I have rarely felt more uncomfortably foolish than I did, reading my paper to that uncomprehending audience.

The first two to discuss my thesis were Germans. Neither had completely understood my argument, they attacked me with acrimony. The third speaker was an Italian, who shook his fist at me. I have not the faintest idea what he was talking about. Then one of the English delegation, a bishop, got up and said that it was well to have a note of humanism in our discussion, after all criminals were—or at least had been—men like us. As Archbishop Somebody had said on seeing a prisoner led out to execution—"There, but for the grace of God, go I."

Then a Frenchman, with carefully groomed beard and equally carefully groomed cynicism, said I was a sentimentalist. He told us that he was a "positivist." He referred frequently to Auguste Compte—a philosopher whom I had up till that moment always regarded very highly. My mawkishness he felt was a most regrettable incident in a scientific assembly. Criminology unless it could be reduced to an exact science like mineralogy or mathematics was no science at all. He ended up by telling us that he was glad to report that the sentimental objections to corporal punishment were rapidly dying out in France and that there was every prospect of the cat-o'-nine-tails being reintroduced into their prisons in the near future. What that had to do with my subject I could not see.

How to reply to such critics? It was not only the difficulty of language. Somehow I was oppressed with loneliness. I was a barbarian, an outlandish person among them. In their thoughts they were "officials," they were "pillars of society"—what Norman scornfully called "the best people." It was a stupid mistake which had brought me before them. They knew nothing about crime, except a jumble of words. They never would.

And so—being weary of soul—I said, that as far as I had understood, they were all against me except the gentleman from England. I wanted as far as possible to repudiate his attitude. I protested against the blasphemy of his archbishop. I was no churchman, but I could not find heart to blame the Deity for our outrageous human injustice. I was sorry that he believed in a God so immoral as to exercise special acts of grace to keep him and me out of prison. I felt that a better motto for prison reform would be—"There but for pure luck, go we."

This was taken as a witty sally by everyone but the English delegates who understood what I said and we adjourned to a state reception at the Quirinal; there was a dinner afterwards given by the Italian prison society. The congress reconvened the next day at two in the afternoon. The subject was "Prison Ventilation." I sneaked out and found my way to The Forum. There I encountered a congenial soul—a youthful guide who had learned to speak English in New York. We sat down on a piece of ancient Rome and he told me about his adventures in the new world.

"Ever arrested?" I asked.

"Twict."

"In the Tombs?"

"Sure," he said with a broad grin. "Fer a fight."

I engaged him for the rest of my stay in Rome. He led me to a little restaurant near-by and after supper we sat in the very top gallery of the Coliseum and talked about Mulberry Square. So I missed the dinner tendered us by the municipality.

The next day the great Lombroso was to discuss head measurements. Antonio and I visited the Vatican. He was an anti-clericalist and the indecent stories he told me about the dead popes, as he showed me their tombs in Saint Peter's were much more vivid than the sing-song guide book phrases he used in commenting on the wonder and the beauty of the place. He took me to supper with his family in a tenement district of Rome. So the "sights" I saw were not so much the pictures and the ruins as the souls of the down-trodden peasant folk bitter against church and state. I lost a chance—undoubtedly—to increase my meagre store of "culture," but I do not regret it.

My fellow delegate from America was shocked at my desertion of the congress. He thought I was in a pet over the reception given my paper and said it was not decent to stay away. So I went the next day and listened to a discussion on the advisability of introducing drugs into prison diet to reduce unpleasant nervous disorders among the inmates. Everyone seemed in favor of the proposition, the only opposition came from a realization of the expense involved. The chairman expressed the hope that some drug might yet be discovered which would be effective, and at the same time cheap.

When the congress was finished the delegates were taken as guests of the government to visit a model prison, recently opened in North Italy. Our inspection consisted of a hurried stroll through the cell-blocks and a banquet in the warden's palatial apartments. We drank several toasts to members of the royal family and then, someone proposed a bumper to the International Prison Congress. I noticed by chance that the bottle, from which a convict waiter filled my glass, was labelled, "*Lacrimae Christi.*"

"Tears of Christ!" I said to my next neighbor. "It would be more fitting to drink this toast of the water in which Pilate washed his hands."

My neighbor was a Frenchman with a loud laugh—so the thoughtless jibe had to be repeated. The English delegate seized the opportunity to return my accusation of blasphemy. There was considerable angry comment. It was a regrettable incident, as it did no good.

The Hungarian government had also invited us to visit some of their blue-ribbon prisons. But in the railroad station at Milan, where we were waiting to take train for Trieste and Budapest, I heard the *Chef de Gare* call the Paris express. It came over me with a rush. I could get home a week earlier. Why waste more time with these barren old gentlemen? I bolted, had just time to rescue my baggage.

Arrived in Paris in the early morning, I drove at once to Cook's and reserved passage on the first boat home. As I was turning away from the steamship desk, I had to walk past the window where mail is distributed. I do not think I was consciously looking at the crowd of men and women who were waiting for letters, in fact I remember quite well that I was losing my temper over an effort to put a too large envelope into my pocket, but suddenly I saw Suzanne Martin's back. It was impossible to mistake it, or the glorious pile of hair above her slender neck.

I walked on, intending to hurry away. But I stopped at the door. I picked up one of those highly colored tourist pamphlets—I think it was an advertisement of a "Tour to Versailles in motor cars"—and over the top of it I watched Suzanne gradually approach the window, get her handful of letters, and sit down in one of the easy chairs to read them.

At last she finished with them and started towards the door. I wished that I had not waited, but was ashamed to let her see me run away. I became deeply interested in the little book. She would have to walk right past me but if she did not care to recognize well—-she should not know that I had seen her.

# V

"Why—hello—Mr. Whitman."

It was not till I heard her voice that I realized how much it mattered to me, whether she spoke or not. Somehow or other we got out of the door onto the Avenue de l'Opera.

"Which way are you going?" she asked.

"Nowhere in particular. May I walk along with you?"

So here I was in Paris walking beside Suzanne. I suppose it had been a beautiful day before—it was early June, but it had suddenly become resplendent. The day had begun to laugh. I found out that she was intending to spend several weeks in Paris, so I lied and said I also was there for a month. With selfish glee I learned that Suzanne was lonely. She was evidently glad to have some one to talk to. Afraid that if I did not keep busy some other way, I might shout, I launched into a whimsical account of the prison congress. This carried us as far as a bench in the garden of the Tuileries. And there some chance word showed her that this was my first visit to Paris, that I had arrived hardly an hour before we met.

"Oh!" she said, jumping up, "Then, the very first thing you must do, is to climb the tower of Notre Dame. That's the place to get your first look at Paris."

"*Allons donc,*" I cried. I would have said the same if she had suggested the morgue.

I remember that, as we rode along, Suzanne pointed out various places of interest, but I doubt if my eyes went further afield than the gracious hand with which she pointed. Then suddenly we turned a corner and came out into the place before the cathedral. The charm of youth beside me was broken for a moment by the wonder of antiquity. How alive the old building seems with the spirits of the long dead men who built it! They say that Milan Cathedral is also Gothic. But my fellow delegate must have stood in my way. I had not seen it as for the first time I saw Notre Dame.

"You can look at the façade afterwards," Suzanne said—her voice breaking the spell. "The important thing is to get the view from the top first."

The twisting, worn stairs of the North Tower was one of the treasures of my memory. A strange impression—the thick masonry, our twinkling little tapers in the darkness, stray wisps of Hugo's romance and of even older stories, the beads of moisture on the stones, the chill dank breath of very-long-ago and dominating it all, Suzanne's two tiny and very modern tan shoes and little glimpses of her stockings. I remember the sudden glare of the first balcony. I caught a quick view down the river and wanted to stop. But Suzanne, who was "personally conducting" this tour, said we could climb higher. So we entered the darkness again and came at last to the top.

I could not tell you how Paris looks from the tower of Notre Dame. I only remember how Suzanne looked. The stiff climb had shortened her breath and heightened her color. The breeze caught a stray wisp of her hair and played delightful tricks with it. And how her eyes glowed with enthusiasm.

"This is my favorite spot on earth," she said. "It's the very center of civilization. From here you can see the birthplace of almost every idea which has benefited the race, the battle-fields where every human victory was won. See! Over there on the Mont Ste. Genevieve is where Abelard shattered mediævalism and commenced the reformation. And over there in the Latin Quarter is the oldest faculty of medicine in the world. It was in one of those houses on the hillside that men dared for the first time to study anatomy with a knife. And there—further to the west—is where Voltaire lived. Nearby is the house of Diderot, where the encyclopedists met to free the human mind. And here—on the other side of the river—is the Palais Royal. See the green clump of trees. Under one of them Camille Desmoulins jumped upon a chair and made the speech which overthrew the Bastille. And there—see the gold statue of victory above the housetops—that's all there is left of the grim old fortress. And so it goes. All the history of man's emancipation spread out before you in brick and mortar."

How lifeless it sounds now, as I write down the ghosts of her words which haunt my memory! But how wonderfully alive they sounded that dazzling summer morning—Paris spread out at our feet—we two alone on the top of the world! Even then her words might have seemed dead things, if they had not been illuminated by her vibrant beauty, by the glorious faith and enthusiasm within her. All this history was vitally alive to her. So had passed the first acts in the great drama of progress. And she saw the last act—the final consummation of universal brotherhood—as something near indeed, compared to the long centuries since Abelard had rung up the curtain. We are always attracted by what we lack and her faith threw new chains about me.

A swarm of German tourists broke in upon us, and to escape them we went down to lunch. At this second meal with her she told me something of her life. She had been bred to the faith. Her mother, a Frenchwoman, had married an American. Suzanne had been born in New York. But her three uncles had been involved in the Communard revolt of 1871. One had died on the barricade. The other two had been sent to New Caledonia. The younger, living through the horrors of that Penal Colony, had escaped to America and had brought the shattered remnant of his life to his sister's home. He had been the mentor of Suzanne's childhood.

Six months before I encountered her in Paris, she had fallen sick from overwork, and had come to relatives in Southern Prance to regain her strength. Recovered now, she was spending the last month of her vacation sight-seeing in Paris. She asked me where I was stopping, which reminded me that I had not yet secured a place to sleep. I blamed it on her for having taken me off to the cathedral when I should have been looking up a hotel.

"Why waste money on a hotel?" she asked. "If you're going to be here several weeks a *pension* is lots cheaper."

She told me of the place where she was staying over on the Left Bank. There were vacant rooms. I dashed away to cancel my sailing, to collect my baggage and, before I had time to realize my good fortune, I was installed under the same roof with her. My memory of the next few days is a jumble of Suzanne in the Musée Carnavelet, Suzanne in the Luxembourg, Suzanne in the Place de la Concorde, pointing out where they had guillotined the king, Suzanne under the dome of Les Invalides, denouncing Napoleon and all his ways.

Coming back from Versailles one evening, I asked her if she ever thought of living permanently in France.

"No," she said emphatically. "I love France, but I don't like the French. The men don't know how to treat a woman seriously. They always talk love."

"I envy them the *sang froid* with which they express their feelings."

Suzanne's eyes shot fire. Displaying all her storm signals, she flared out into a denunciation of such flippancy. This business of telling a woman at first sight that she made your head swim, disgusted her. This continual harping on sex, seemed nasty. "Why can't men and women have decent, straightforward friendships?" she demanded. She liked men, liked their point of view, liked their talk and comradeship. But Frenchmen could not think seriously if a woman was in sight. Friendship was impossible with them.

"It's pretty uncertain with any men, isn't it?" I asked.

"Well. Anyhow American men are better. I've had some delightful men friends at home."

"And did the friendships last?" I insisted.

"Well, no." She was wonderfully honest with herself. "Why is it? It wasn't my fault."

"Probably nobody's fault," I said. "Just the grim old law of nature. You don't blame the sun for rising. You can't blame a man for....."

"Oh, don't you begin it," she interrupted. "I give you fair warning."

We sat glum on opposite seats until the train reached Paris.

"Oh, bother!" she said, as we got out. "What's the use of moping? Let's be friends. Just good friends."

She held out her hand so enticingly I could not help grasping it.

"Honest Injun," she said. "No cheating? Cross your heart to die."

So I was committed to a platonic relation which even at the first I knew to be unstable.

The next morning, as though to prove the firmer basis of our friendship, she told me that she was expecting two comrades, a Mr. and Mrs. Long, who were then in Germany, to arrive in Paris in a few days. They were planning a tramp through Normandy—to take in the cathedrals. Would I join them? We spent the afternoon over a road map of North-western France, plotting an itinerary.

And then, two days before we expected to start, came a telegram from the Longs. They were called home suddenly, were sailing direct from Hamburg.

"Let's go, anyhow," I said. "We can put up the brother and sister game. These French don't know whether American brothers and sisters ought to look alike or not. Anyhow, what does it matter what anybody thinks?"

Well. We had bought our rucksacs. The trip was planned. All its promises of pleasures and adventures had taken hold on both of us. She hesitated. I became eloquent. After a few minutes she broke out—evidently not having listened to me.

"Would you keep your word?—Yes—I believe you would. I'll go if you promise me to—well—not to get sentimental—really treat me like a sister."

"Isn't there any time limit on the promise? Am I to bind myself to a fraternal regard till death us do part? I don't approve of such vows."

"You're either stupid or trying to be funny," she snapped. "You propose that we go alone on a tramping trip. You could make it miserably uncomfortable—spoil it all. I won't start unless you promise not to. That's simple."

"Well," I said. "Give and take. I'll promise not to get sentimental, if you'll promise not to talk socialism. Agreed? We'll draw up a contract—a treaty of peace."

And in spite of her laughing protests that I was a fool, I drew it up in form. Suzanne, Party of the First Part, Arnold, Party of the Second Part, do hereby agree, covenant, and pledge themselves not to talk sentiment nor sociology during the hereinafter to be described trip....

So it was ordained. We started the next morning—by train to St. Germain-en-Laye.

## VI

One of my treasures is a worn road map of Northwestern France. Starting from Paris, a line traces our intended course, down the Seine to Rouen, across country to Calais. It is a clear line. I had a ruler to work with, and the map was laid out on the marble top of a table in the little Café de la Rotonde. Also starting from Paris is another line, which shows the path we did follow. It is less dearly drawn, traced for the most part on a book balanced on my knee. Stars mark the places where we stopped, at night. From St. Germain-en-Laye, we doubled back to St. Denis, then a tangent off to Amiens, a new angle to Rheims. It stops abruptly at Moret-sur-Loing.

I can command no literary form to do justice to that Odyssey—it led me unto those high mountains from which one can see the wondrous land of love.

What did we do? I remember hours on end when we trudged along with scarcely a word. I remember running a race with her through the forest of Saint Germain. I remember a noontime under the great elm in the Jardin of a village café. There was delectable omelette and *Madame la patronne* chattered amiably about her children and chickens and the iniquitous new tax on cider. I remember the wonder of those century old windows at Rheims and Suzanne's talk of the Pucelle. I remember trying to teach her to throw stones and her vexation when I laughingly told her she could never learn to do it like a man. And here and there along our route, I remember little corners of the Elysian Fields where we rested awhile and talked. Suzanne had found me unappreciative of Browning. Often by the wayside she would take a little volume of his verse out of her rucksac and make me listen. The first poem to charm me was "Cleon." It led us far afield into a discussion of the meaning of life and Suzanne—to make more clear Browning's preference for the man who lives over the man who writes about life—read "The Last Ride Together." Her voice faltered once—she realized I think how near it came to the forbidden subject—but she thought better to read on. After that I belonged to Browning.

Those verses seemed written to express our outing. Whether she looked beyond our walk or not I do not know. I did not. What would happen when our pilgrimage was over I did not ask. The present was too dizzyingly joyful to question the future.

At last we came to Moret on the border of the great forest of Fontainebleau. It had been our intention to push on and sleep at Barbizon, but we had loitered by the way, and at the little Hotel de la Palette, they told us the road was too long for an afternoon's comfort. So there we stopped, to stroll away some hours in the forest and get an early start in the morning.

They gave us two garret rooms, for the hotel was crowded with art students and the better part was filled. I recall how the bare walls were covered with sketches and caricatures. There was a particularly bizarre sunset painted on the door between our rooms.

Lunch finished, we started for the forest. We came presently to a hill-top, with an outlook over the ocean of tree-tops, the gray donjon keep of Moret to the north. Suzanne as was her custom, threw herself face down in the long grass. I seem to hold no sharper memory of her than in this pose. I sat beside her, admiring. Suddenly she looked up.

"Tomorrow night Barbizon," she said, "the next day Paris and our jaunt is over."

She looked off down a long vista between the trees. I do not know what she saw there. But no matter which way I looked, I saw a cloud of tiny bits of paper, fluttering into a waste-paper basket.

"And then," I said, "a certain iniquitous treaty of peace will be torn into shreds."

My pipe had burned out before she spoke again. Her words when they did come were utterly foreign to my dreaming.

"Why did you write that kind of a book?"

There was earnest condemnation in her voice. To gain time, I asked.

"You don't like it?"

"Of course not. It's insincere."

I filled my pipe before I took up the challenge.

"You'll have to make your bill of indictment more detailed. What's insincere about it?"

"You know as well as I do."

Never in any of our talks did she give me so vivid an impression of earnestness. With a sudden twist she sat up and faced me.

"It's cynical. There are two parts to the book—exposition and conclusions. The conclusions are pitiable. You suggest a program of reforms in the judicial and penal system. And they are petty—if they were all accepted, it wouldn't solve the problem of crime. You imply one of two things, either that these reforms would solve the problem, which they wouldn't, or that the problem is insoluble, which it isn't."

"Count one," I said. "Pleading deferred."

"And then—this is worse—you know there is no more chance of these reforms being granted under our present system, than of arithmetic being reformed to make two and two five."

"Count two. Not guilty."

"No jury would acquit you on it. But there's a third count—perhaps the worst of all. The book is horribly superficial. Hidden away in your preface you mention the fact that the worst crimes against society are not mentioned in the code. You gently hint that some Wall Street transactions are larcenous, even if they are not illegal. All hidden in your preface!"

"That's entirely unfair," I protested. "You are quarreling with me over a definition. My book deals with the phenomena of the criminal courts. I have no business with what you or the newspapers call crime. If I wanted my work to be scientific I had to get a sharp definition. And I said that crime consists of acts forbidden by the legislature. I pointed out that it is an arbitrary conception, which is always changing. Some things—like kissing your wife on the Sabbath day—are no longer criminal and some things—like these Wall Street transactions—probably will be crimes tomorrow. Your third count is not against me but against the 'Scientific Method.'"

"Tommyrot!" she retorted. "You try to evade a big human truth by a scientific pretext. You know that ninety per cent of the criminal law, just as ninety-nine per cent of the civil law, is an effort to make people recognize property relations which are basically unjust. If our economic relations were right it would eliminate ninety per cent of crime. And justice—socialism—would do more, it would result in healthier, nobler personalities and wipe out the other ten per cent. There's the crux of the problem of crime and you dodge it.

"You have a chapter on prostitution. It's splendid, the best I've seen—where you describe present conditions. But the conclusions are—well—

sickening. Do you really think that taking the poor women's finger prints will help? Of course you don't! It's all wrapped up in the great injustice which underlies all life. You come right up to the point—you say that most prostitution comes because the daughters of the poor have no other alternative but the sweatshop—and then you shut your mouth like a fool or a coward.

"Your book might have been wonderful—a big contribution. Oh, why didn't you? It's only half-hearted—insincere!"

I cannot recall my defense. I tried to make her see how we came at the problem from the opposite poles, how her point of departure was an ideal social organization, while I started from the world as it is, how she spoke in terms of the absolute, and I thought only of relative values, how she saw an abiding truth back of life and I believed in an all-pervading change. We fought it out bitterly—with ungloved words—all the afternoon. Neither convinced the other, but I think I persuaded her of my sincerity, almost persuaded her that "narrow" was not the best word to express my outlook— that "different" was juster. The sun was down in the tree-tops when at last she brought the argument to a close.

"We'll never agree. Our points of view are miles apart."

"But that," I said, "need make no difference, so long as we are honest to each other—and to ourselves."

"I'm not sure about that," she said. "I must think it out."

She stretched out on the grass again and began to poke a straw into an ant-hole. I sat back and smoked and blessed the gods who had moulded so perfect a back. Then she looked at her watch and jumped up.

"Do you realize, Suzanne, that you have violated the treaty? You've talked sociology and socialism. Now—I'm free..."

"Oh! Please don't!" she interrupted. "Not now. We must hurry to dinner."

I got up laughing and we walked in silence, between the great trees, in the falling dusk, back to the Hotel de la Palette. The joviality of that troupe of young artists forced us to talk of trivial things. After supper we stood for a moment in the doorway. Behind us was noisy gayety, before us the full moon illumined the gray walls of the citadel, shone enticingly on a quiet reach of the river.

"Come," I said. "Let's go down to the bridge—the water will be gorgeous in this light."

For a moment she hung back reluctantly; then suddenly consented. But in the village, she wasted much time looking for the house where Napoleon had slept in hiding on his return from Elba. When we came at last to the bridge she clambered up on the parapet. I leaned against it beside her. The light on the river was gorgeous. Although there was no wind for us to feel, the great clouds overhead were driven about like rudderless ships in a tempest. For a moment the moon would be hidden, leaving us in utter darkness, the next it would break out, its glory bringing to life all the details of the picturesque old houses by the riverside. Suzanne made one or two barren attempts at conversation. At last I plunged into the real business of the moment.

"Of course," I began, "if you really wish it, I will postpone this till we get to Paris."

There was a perceptible tightening of her muscles—a bracing. But she did not speak.

If I was eloquent that night, persuasive, it was because I did not plead for myself, but for love. It is sometimes said that love is egoistic, subjective, to me it seems the most objective thing in the world. It is—at its grandest—I think, a complete surrender to the ultimate bigness of life. Without love we have nothing to fight for except our little personalities, no better occupation than to magnify our individuality. Love shows us bigger things. At least it was this I tried to tell Suzanne. She had looked on love as a disturbing element in life. I tried to show it to her as the goal, the apotheosis of life.

It seems to me, as I look back on it now, that I was hardly thinking of Suzanne—not at all of my desire for her. I was talking to something further away than she, perhaps to the moon. I was trying desperately to formulate a faith—to give voice to a belief.

And then she laid her hand on mine—and I forgot the moon. I saw only the glory of her face, different from what I had ever seen it. It was paler than usual and dreamy. It seemed surprisingly near to me. When I kissed her, she did not turn away.

Suddenly it rained.

Much of my life has hinged on just such stupid, ludicrous chances. It poured—soaking and cold. It was a serious matter for us. We were traveling light, with nothing but our rucksacs nearer than Paris, no outer clothes except those we wore. Although we ran all the way we were drenched to the skin before we reached the hotel. The rain stopped as abruptly as it had commenced. We were too breathless to talk as we clambered up the stairs to our garret rooms.

After a hard rub, dry underclothes and pajamas, I wrapped myself in a blanket and lit my pipe. Through the thin partition I could hear Suzanne giving directions to the bonne to dry her clothes by the kitchen fire. Then her bed creaked. From the café downstairs came sounds of riotous mirth. Our talk had been so inconclusive.

"Suzanne," I said, knocking on the door between our rooms. "May I come in? Please. It's awfully important."

There was no answer and I opened the door. The moon, having escaped from the clouds, shone in through the mansard window, full on her bed, painting her hair a richer red than usual. I must have been a weird sight, with that blanket wrapped about my shoulders. But she did not smile. I can find no word to name her expression, unless wonder will do. There was a suggestion of the amazed face of a sleepwalker. Instinctively I knew that she would not repulse me. That moment she was mine for the taking. But I did not desire what a man can "take" from a woman. I wanted her to give.

I sat on the foot of the bed and tried to talk her into the mood I hungered for. It was not self-restraint on my part. I was not conscious of passion. What I wanted seemed finer and grander. If she had reached out her hand to me, all my pent up desires would have exploded. If she had tried to send me away, it might have inflamed me. If she had spoken—I do not remember a word. She lay there as one in a dream. There was a strange, dazed look in her eyes, perhaps it was awed expectancy. I did not read it so.

Hoping to wake her, I kissed her hands and her forehead. The great coil of her hair moved in my hands like a thing alive. Its fragrance dizzied me. Fearful of intoxication, I went apart for a moment by the window, looked out at the sinking moon, until my head was clear again. I came back and knelt by her bed.

"Suzanne. What I want is not a thing for the night, not a thing of moonlight and shadows. What I want must be done by day in the great open air—at high noon—for all time and whatever comes after. To-morrow in the blaze of the sun...."

I could not say what was in my heart. The last rays of the moon touched the profile of her face so glowingly that suddenly I wanted to pray.

"Oh, Suzanne, I wish that we believed in a God—we two. So I could pray his blessing on you—on us."

Then I kissed her on the lips and went away.

The hours I spent in my window that night were I suppose the nearest I ever got to Heaven. It seemed that at last my torturing doubts were over, that I had read in the Divine Revelation, that the way, the truth and the light had been made plain to me. For the second time in my life I had the assurance of salvation.

Just as the rim of the sun came up over the eastern hills, I heard her get out of bed, heard the sound of her bare feet coming towards the door. I jumped down from my seat in the window. My dream was fulfilled—she was coming to me in the dawn.

The door opened barely an inch. Her voice seemed like that of a stranger.

"Arnold. Please go down in the kitchen and get my clothes."

I was ready to open my veins for her and she asked me to walk downstairs and bring her a skirt and blouse and shoes.

"Don't stand there like an idiot," the strange voice said. "I want my clothes."

Well—somehow I found the clothes and brought them back. She took them in hastily through the door, closed it in my face—locked it. I think the grating of the bolt in the lock was the thing I first realized clearly. She was afraid I would force myself on her. We were utter strangers, she did not know me at all.

Once in a strike riot I saw a man hit between the eyes with a brick. It must have knocked him senseless at once, but he finished the sentence he was shouting, stooped down to pick up a stone, stopped as though he had thought of something, sat down on the curb in a daze—it must have been a full half minute before he groaned and slumped over inert.

After Suzanne drove the bolt of her door through the dream, I got dressed and sat down dumbly to wait. I heard her moving about her room, heard her putting on her shoes—I remember thinking that as they had been wet, they must be stiff this morning—then she unlocked and opened the door.

"Arnold," she said in that constrained voice I did not know. "I've got to go away—I want to be alone. There's a train for Paris in a few minutes."

I suppose I made some movement as if to follow her.

"No. Don't you come. I've got to think things out by myself. I've got to"—the strained tone in her voice was desperate, almost hysterical—"Let me go alone. I'll write to you—Cook's. I'm...."

She turned without a word of good-bye and I heard her footsteps on the stairs of the still quiet house. And presently, perhaps fifteen minutes, perhaps half an hour, I heard the whistle of a train.

# VII

After a while I "came to." I went into her room and looked about it. In her haste to be gone she had forgotten her rucksac, it lay there in plain sight on the tumbled bed. I went downstairs and drank some coffee and paid the bill. I remember a foolish desire to cry when I realized that I must pay for both of us. In all the trip she had scrupulously insisted in attending to her share. With only our two bags for company I went up to Paris. She had taken her baggage from the pension an hour before I arrived, she had left no address. I spent most of my time in the garden of the Tuileries, going every hour or so to Cook's in quest of the letter she had promised. There were times when I hoped she would come back, when it seemed impossible that I should not find her again, sometimes I despaired. But mostly it was just a dull, stunned pain, which was neither hope nor despair. After three days the letter came. It was postmarked Le Havre.

"Dear friend Arnold,

"It has taken me longer than I had thought to be sure of myself. I cannot marry you. It has never been hard for me to say this before. It is hard now. I know how much it will hurt you. And I care more than I ever did before. More, I think, than I ever will care again. For I can imagine no finer way of being loved than your way.

"If it were not for the pain it has cost you—I would be glad of the chance which threw us together in Paris. The days which followed were the most joyous I have ever known—almost the only ones. I have not found life a

219

happy business. Surely you won't, I doubt if anyone does, realize how sad the world seems to me. But somehow, out of the overwhelming misery about us, you helped me to escape awhile, helped me to snatch some of 'the rarely coming spirit of delight.' They were perfect—those never-to-be-forgotten days on the open road.

"I can't—even after all this thinking, and I have thought of nothing else —understand clearly, what happened at Moret. When you began to talk love to me—well—it was the first time in my life, I did not want to run away. We all have our woman's dream hidden somewhere within us. I don't remember what you said to me there on the bridge but suddenly my dream came big. Love seemed something I had always been waiting for. I kept asking myself 'can this at last be love'—and because I did not want to run away I thought it was.

"When you came to my room I was drunk with the dream. That you did not take advantage of my bewilderment—well—that's what I meant when I said I could think of no finer love than what you have given me. I could not have reproached you if you had. God knows what it would have meant. It might have turned the balance, I might have loved you—in a way. But it would not have been *you*, and it would not have been what you wanted.

"When you went away, I began to recall your words—I had scarcely heard them—and then I realized what you wanted. It seemed very beautiful to me and—will you believe it—I wanted to give it to you, be it for you. But as the hours slipped by the fear grew that I could not, grew to certainty. And I was afraid that if I stayed, I would cheat you. And so, in fear, I ran away.

"I know I must have seemed very cruel to you that morning. And I am writing all this in the hope that you will understand that I was harsh because I was afraid, it was the cruelty of weakness. I wanted to put my arms about you and cry. You will see that it was better that I did not. For now—with a cool head—it is very clear to me, not only that I could not be to you what you wish, but that at bottom I do not want to. I do not love you.

"I would like to make this sound less brutal, but it is true. It's not only in regard to socialism that our view-points are miles apart, but also in this matter of love.

"The porter is calling the 'bus for my steamer. I must stop or miss the tender. It is just as well. If I have not shown you in these few pages what I feel, I could not in twice as many."

I was not man enough to take my medicine quietly. The letter jerked me out of my lethargy, threw me into a rage, the worst mood of my life. I cursed Suzanne, cursed love, cursed Europe. I engaged passage on the first boat home. I took along Suzanne's rucksac with the intention of having its contents laundered and returning it to her with a flippant, insulting note. I occupied most of the time till the boat sailed, on its composition. On board I drank hoggishly, gambled recklessly—and as such things often go—won heavily.

But the last night out, anchored off quarantine, the fury and the folly left me. After all I had been making an amazing tempest in a teapot. What did it matter whether my love affair went straight or crooked? I felt so much the spoiled child, that I was ashamed to look up at the eternal, patient stars. After the vague open spaces of the sea, the crowded harbor, the distant glow and hum of the great city, seemed real indeed. A flare of rockets shot up from Coney Island, dazzled a moment and went out. I laughed. The lower lights along the shore were not so brilliant—but abiding.

I leaned over the rail and strained my eyes towards the city. And it seemed as if life came to me through the night as a thing which one might hold in the hand and study.

The Tombs and all its people, corrupt judges and upright criminals. In a few days I would drop back into the rut among them. What had become of Sammy Swartz? A pick-pocket of parts, he had, when I left, been virtuously scrubbing floors in an office building—a deadly grind, compared to the dash and adventure of his old life. What held him to it? Was it only fear of prison or some vague reaching out for rectitude? Was he still "on the square" or had he gone back to the "graft?"

The Teepee, Norman, Nina and little Marie. What were they doing? Probably wondering when I would return—planning some fête. My questionings shot back to the old home in Tennessee. The Father and Margot —what were they doing, what had been done to them? And Ann? I would have to hurt her in the morning, with my news. Life had driven a wedge in between us.

And Suzanne? She was somewhere in the city. I pictured her in council with her comrades in some grimy committee room, some tenement parlor— the light of the glorious vision in their eyes—planning the great reconstruction, plotting the coronation of justice. She had turned her back on the love I offered that some greater love might be made manifest. It seemed to me wrong. But right or wrong, I loved her better that night than ever before. It was as though a comet had become a fixed star.

And I was sorry for her—while admiring. Like all the rest of us, she was caught in the vast spider web of life, beating her wings to pieces in the divine effort to reach the light. All the people I could think of seemed in the same plight—admirable and pitiable. Is not this immense, spawning, struggling family of ours as much alike in the uncertainty of life as in the certainty of death?

Once ashore, I called up Ann on the telephone. Her laboratory had been moved into the city, and so we could arrange to lunch together. I was glad of the public restaurant, I would have found it harder to tell her about Suzanne, if we had been alone. When once Ann understood, she made it as easy for me as possible.

"And so," she said at last as we reached the entrance to her laboratory, "you won't be coming out to Cromley?"

"I would be a decidedly glum guest, I'm afraid,"

She stood for a moment on the step, her brows puckered.

"Well," she said, "If you really want her—go after her. Hit her on the head and drag her to your cave. Oh, I know. I'm too matter of fact and all that. But it's the way to get her—beat her a little."

"I had my chance to do that," I said, "and couldn't. Perhaps you're right —but I love her a bit too much. I shan't go after her."

Ann sniffed.

"If I was a man, I'd go after what I wanted." Then her eyes softened. "But I'm only a woman. All I can do is to tell you—you're always welcome at Cromley."

She turned and ran up the steps to her laboratory.

In this conversation I realized the basic difference between Ann's point of view and mine, more clearly than before. Her philosophy taught her to be, if not satisfied, at least content, with half things. If she could not get just what she wanted, nor all of it, she tried to be happy with what was available. Doubtless she found life better worth living than I did. But such an attitude towards Suzanne would have seemed to me a desecration. Perhaps if I had sought her out, argued with her, tried to dominate her will—tried figuratively to "beat her a little"—I might have persuaded her to marry me. Perhaps. But what I might have won in this way, would not only have been less than what I wanted, but something quite different.

It had taken no "persuading" to make me love Suzanne. I had seen numberless women, had met, I suppose, several thousands. Many I had known longer than Suzanne. But she stood out from the rest, not as "another" woman, not as a more beautiful, or cleverer or more earnest woman— although she was all these—but as something quite different—my woman. If she did not recognize me, in the same sudden, unarguable way as her man, there was nothing I could do about it. She did not.

The wise man of Israel said that the way of a man with a maid is past all finding out. It would be truer to say that the ways of men with maidens are too varied and numerous for any classifying. My way was perhaps insane.

Very likely I was asking of life more than is granted to mortals. But that is small comfort.

Perhaps Suzanne did love me and had, in running away, obeyed some age-old, ineradicable instinct of her sex. It is possible that she mourned because I did not play the venerable game of pursuit. Perhaps if I had taken advantage of the hour when she was wholly mine, it might have "turned the balance." I might have entered into the glory. I do not understand the forces of life which rule our mating. But one thing I know—I was not in love with any Suzanne who could have been "persuaded."

I sat for some time on a bench in Union Square, thinking this out, after I left Ann. I had a strange reluctance to plunge back into the old life. I remember watching with envy two tramps who sat in contemplative silence on a bench opposite me. I was tempted to wander away, out of the world of responsibilities, out into that strange land where nothing matters. There are two sorts of wanderlust; the one which pushes the feet and the one which pushes the spirit. But at last I shook this cowardly lassitude from me and walked downtown to the Teepee.

Nina threw her arms about my neck. Norman pounded me on the back, the little lassie Marie kissed me shyly, and Guiseppe hobbled in from the kitchen to complete the welcome. While they were still storming me with questions, Norman went back to his work. He had a large sheet of drawing paper thumbtacked to the table and was sketching an advertisement for a new brand of pickles. When the rest of them disappeared to kill the fatted calf, he put a hand on my shoulder and looked me over carefully.

"Been on the rocks?" he said.

I had not realized that it showed. I nodded assent.

He laid on a dash of crimson alongside some glaring green.

"Isn't it fierce?" he said. "They wouldn't hang this sort of thing in the Louvre but it's what makes the public buy." He squinted at it ruefully—"This love business is beyond me. Who would think that I could stumble on Nina where I did? You know that song of Euripides.

'This Cyprian

Is a thousand, thousand things

She brings more joy than any God,

She brings

More woe. Oh may it be

An hour of mercy when

She looks at me.'

I'd given the whole matter up in disgust—and it was solved for me.—Say. I need to work in a little raw blue here. Green pickles, red pepper, blue—oh yes —a blue label on the bottle. Sweet! isn't it?

"You know sometimes I think we are all wrong trying to join brains. You wouldn't call Nina exactly my intellectual equal, but I don't know any chap married to a college graduate who's got anything on me. I'll put up Marie against any highbrow offspring."

He pulled out the tacks and set his sketch up on the mantel-piece and walked across the room to get the effect. He jerked his head, gestured with his hand and his lips moved as though he were arguing with it. He pinned it down again and began putting in the lettering.

"Of course," he took up the thread of his thoughts, "there are people who say that it isn't marriage at all, that I've just legalized my mistress. But I've seen a lot of people striving, breaking their necks, for something they'd call finer, more spiritual—and getting nothing at all. I know I'm happier than most. I'm satisfied with *my* luck. That's the point. I can't call it anything but luck—By the way. There's a pile of letters for you."

And so I dipped back in the rut. In the Tombs I sought out new duties, tried to lose myself—forget the mess I had made of things—in work. Nina and Norman stood beside me in those days with fine sweet loyalty. They asked no questions, but seemed to know what was wrong. Always I felt myself in the midst of a conspiracy of cheer. It was during these dreary months that I first began to like children. Marie's prattle, after the gloom and weariness of the Tombs, was bright indeed.

I know nothing more beautiful than the sight of a little child's soul gradually taking shape. The memory of my own lonely, loveless childhood has given me, I suppose, a special insight into the problems of the youngsters. The fact that I succeeded in gaining this little girl's love and confidence has compensated me for many things which I have missed.

# VIII

Shortly after my return from Europe, I came into communication again with my family. First it was a letter from the Father. He regretted that so many years had passed without hearing from me. Knowing him as I did, I recognized in this a real apology for having tried to starve me into obedience. He had read my book with great pleasure and had been especially proud to learn that I had been chosen to represent our nation abroad. Then there was a little news of the village—a list of those who had died and been born and married. Oliver, he wrote, had recently been called to a pastorate in New York City. He gave me his address so that I might call. And he ended with the hope that I had conquered the doubts which had troubled my youth and won to the joy of religious peace.

It was a hard letter to answer. I had no more of the bitterness I once felt towards him. I wanted very much to give him news which would cheer him. And yet I knew that the one question which seemed really important to him—in regard to my religious beliefs—I could not answer frankly without giving him pain. I did the best I could to evade it.

About Oliver I was less certain. I had never liked him. I did not want to revive the connection. But I knew that it would please the Father to have me. I resolved to call, but having no enthusiasm for it, other engagements seemed more important, I kept postponing it.

But coming home to the Teepee one winter afternoon about five, I found that he had forestalled me by calling first. As I opened the door, I heard Nina's voice and then one that was strange—but I knew at once it was a clergyman's voice. They had not lit a lamp yet and the library was illumined only by the open fire. Norman was sitting on the divan playing with Marie's pig-tail—it was a habit with him, just as some men play with their watch charm. Nina had on her company manners and was doing the entertaining. The clergyman rose as I entered. He was tall and broad, on the verge of rotundity. He wore a clerical vest and collar and the fire light sparkled on a large gold cross which hung from his watch chain.

"Here he is," Nina said as I came in. "I—am—very—

glad—to—see—you—again—Arnold." I did not

realize who it was, until Norman spoke up. "It's your

cousin, Dr. Drake."

"Oh. Hello, Oliver," I said, shaking hands.

I realized at once that this had not been an entirely fitting way to respond to his dignified, almost pompous greeting. I find it hard not to portray Oliver in caricature. He was so utterly foreign to the life I was leading, so different from the people I knew that inevitably he looked outlandish—at times comical. I have always regretted that Browning did not write another poem, the reverse of "Bishop Blougram's Apology," giving us the free thinker's account of that interview.

At first Oliver seemed to me appallingly affected. But as I got to see more of him I changed the adjective to "adapted." Just as a practicing physician must develop certain mannerisms so had Oliver adapted himself to his *metier*. His voice was most impressive. It was his working capital and he guarded it with infinite care. He was as much afraid of a sore throat as an opera singer. He belonged to that sub-variety of his species which is called "liberal." He had accepted the theory of evolution end higher criticism. He prided himself on being abreast of his time. He strove—successfully—to give the impression of a broad-minded, cultured gentleman.

I think he enjoyed the flattery of success and he had the brains to win it. His wife, whom I met later was, I think, dominated by "social" ambitions. She also had brains. They were a strong team. Their progress had been a steady upward curve. From a small town to a small city, then from a mission chapel in Indianapolis to its biggest church, from there to Chicago and at last to a fashionable charge in New York. And when you saw Oliver this progress seemed inevitable.

Spirituality? I do not think he had need of any. It would have been an impediment to his progress. It was very hard to remember that he was the son of Josiah Drake.

"How long is it," he said in his suave, modulated voice, "since we saw each other. Not since I left you at your prep. school—at least fifteen years."

"More," I said, "twenty." I could think of nothing to say. His presence was rather oppressive. But it was part of his profession never to be awkward.

"Well. Now that we are in the same city, I trust we will see each other more frequently. You were in Europe when we arrived. I wasn't quite sure whether you were back yet or not. But I came in on the chance—I got your address from your publishers"—he made a congratulatory bow—"to see if we could have you for dinner next Friday. It's been a great pleasure to meet Mr. and Mrs. Benson, I envy you such friendship...."

"Nina," Norman interrupted, "has been chanting your praises for the last half hour."

"Ah. You cannot dodge your responsibilities that way, Mr. Benson," Oliver remarked, with rather heavy playfulness. "You have been a most effective chorus. Of course, Arnold,"—he turned to me—"your friends will always be welcomed at our house. I would be very glad, and I am sure Mrs. Drake would be also, if you could bring them with you on Friday night."

Norman bounced off the divan, as if someone had exploded a bomb under him.

"Oh, no," he said. "We're very much obliged to you. But Nina and I never go out in society,"—as Oliver looked a bit taken aback, Norman went on to explain. "You see our marriage was—well—picturesque. I've forgotten the date, but you can find the details in the files of any of our newspapers. Fortunately, my wife has no social ambitions, so we don't have to risk embarrassing people who are kind enough to invite us."

Oliver had regained his poise.

"Being a stranger to the city," he said, "I am of course ignorant of the matter to which you refer but"—he gracefully took Nina's hand—"I am quite sure that Mrs. Benson would honor any society. However if it would expose you to any embarrassment, I cannot, of course, insist."

Nina's attitude to Oliver after he was gone was amusing. She had evidently been impressed with his grandeur. But when Norman jokingly accused her of having fallen in love with him, she shuddered.

"No," she said with real but ludicrous solemnity—"I wouldn't like to be his wife."

Marie, who had had to undergo the ordeal of sitting on his knee, remarked that he did not know how to play.

But in spite of the dislike she had taken to him Nina made me tell in detail everything about the dinner party. It had, I am sure, been a great success from Mrs. Drake's point of view. There had been two Wall Street millionaires at the table, a great lawyer, a congressman and an ambassador. Because French came to me easily I had to entertain the latter's wife. The food and the wine had been exquisite. Socially a success, but humanly a barren affair.

I made my duty call on Mrs. Drake and would never have gone near them again, if it had not been for a letter I received from Oliver about a month later. He asked me to come for lunch to talk over a scheme he was working out for penal reform. It interested me immensely to see him and his wife working together. He began with a sonorous peroration. The reason the church was losing influence was that it did not take sufficient interest in social problems. He was developing this idea at some length when Mrs. Drake coughed.

"The idea is familiar," she said.

"Yes, my dear."

Coming, as he did, to the direction of one of New York's most influential churches, a congregation which included many people of great wealth, many people of great influence in the world of business and politics.... Mrs. Blake coughed.

"I'm sure Cousin Arnold knows about the church."

"Yes, my dear. I was about to say...."

He was about to say that he felt it his duty to try to utilize this great force in the cause of human betterment. In a few minutes Mrs. Drake coughed again and said, "Naturally." He had given a good deal of consideration, prayerful consideration, to the subject: personally he was opposed to the church going into politics. He spoke of several well-known clergymen who had gone into the fight against Tammany Hall, he doubted their wisdom. Of course if one could be sure that all their congregation were republicans.... The lunch was finished at this point and we went into the sumptuous library. Mrs. Drake took the subject out of his hand.

"You see, Cousin Arnold," she said, "we think that the role of the church should be conciliating. It is our object to attract people—all people to the church—not to alienate anyone. And the church cannot mix in any of the issues which are vexed—which have partisans on each side—without offending and driving people away. It is evident that the church must interest itself in social questions, must show that it is a power to overcome this horrible unrest. But it is very hard to find a social problem which is consistent with the conciliatory rôle which the church must preserve.

"When Oliver and I read your book, we both had the same inspiration. Here is just the very problem. What you wrote about the prisons is awful. And no one can object to the church taking a definite attitude on this question. The Master, himself has instructed us to visit those who are in prison."

"Exactly," Oliver put in.

But she did not give him time to go on. She rapidly laid before me their plan. Oliver was to call together a group of a dozen fellow clergymen, the most influential—I presume she meant the most fashionable—in each denomination. I was to speak to them and help him to get them interested. They would organize a committee, they would give out interviews to the newspapers, preach sermons on the subject, get some good bills introduced into the legislature—and make a great splash!

I sat back and listened to it with grim amusement. This was to be Oliver's debut in New York. In vulgar phrase it was a "press agent campaign." Oliver—the progressive, the fighting clergyman—was to get columns of free advertising. There would surely be a great mass meeting in one of the theaters and Oliver would get his chance to cast the spell of his oratory over fashionable New York. It was an admirable scheme. No attack on Tammany Hall, was not one of his deacons a director in the street car company? Did not the real owner of the gas company rent the most expensive pew in the church and did not complaisant Tammany Hall arrange to have the gas company's ashes removed by the city's street cleaning department? No support to the campaign for decent tenements, some of the congregation were landlords. And of course no playing with the dangerous subject of labor unions.

"J. H. Creet doesn't belong to your church, does he?" I asked.

"No," Mrs. Drake replied. "Why?"

"Well, he has a fat contract for manufacturing cloth for prison uniforms."

"J. H. Creet?" Oliver said, making a note. "A queer name. I never heard of it."

Their interest in the matter was evident, but where did I come in? Well—after all—publicity is a great thing. It must be the basis of every reform. I had very little faith in any real good coming from such a campaign, but at least it would call people's attention to the issue. It was not to be despised. So I fell in with the scheme.

Several outsiders have complimented me on the newspaper noise we made, supposing that I was the motive power of it. The praise belongs to Oliver—and his wife. It was remarkable the skill with which they handled it. It was amusing to watch the suave manoeuvres by which Oliver always secured the top line. For a month he worked hard, put in hours of real study. His great speech in Daly's was masterful. And then things fizzled out. None of the bills got past a second reading.

At one of the last conferences I had with Oliver, he asked me why I did not go to Tennessee and visit the Father.

"Why don't you have him come on here for a vacation?" I asked. "He hasn't been in New York since before the war."

Oliver shrugged his shoulders.

"I make a point of going out to see him every two years—but he'd be out of place here. The world has moved a lot since his day. He would not understand. He's the type of the old school. Progress is heresy. Why I'm sure he'd be shocked at my wearing a collar like this. He'd accuse me of papacy. I always put on mufti when I visit him."

It was the patronizing superiority of his tone that angered me. I realized suddenly how lonely the Father must be. I had always thought of him as quite happy in having a son who had followed in his footsteps. I am not sure but that with all my outspoken heresy, I was more of a true son to him than Oliver. I resolved to go out to Tennessee at my first opportunity.

I am half sorry I went. It was an unsuccessful visit. The barren little mountain village had changed not at all in the years I had been away. There were a few more battle monuments on the hillside and the people still talked of little beside the war. The big parsonage beside the barn-like church was just as I had left it. The Father's wants were looked after by the numerous progeny of Barnabas, the negro body servant who had followed him through the war.

I had been thrown out for my Godlessness and had been expected to go to the dogs. It was something of an affront to the traditions that I had not. To have written a book was a matter of fame in that little village. I found that the Father with childlike pride had boasted far and wide of my having been chosen as delegate to the prison congress at Rome. It was not to be accounted for that instead of coming back as the prodigal I should return as a "distinguished son." The minor prophets of the place were disappointed in me.

Even the Father was bewildered. He came down to the gateway to meet me—a fine old figure, leaning on his ebony cane, his undimmed eyes shining from under his shaggy white eyebrows. He put his arm over my shoulder as we walked back to the house, as though he was glad of someone to lean upon. And all through supper he talked to me about my father and mother. He told me again how my father had died bravely at the head of a dare-devil sortie out of Nashville. And he told me with great charm about the time when they had been children. We sat out on the porch for a while and he went on with his reminiscencing. Then suddenly he stopped.

"Oh," he said, "how I ramble. You will be wanting to go and call on Margot."

It was like visiting the ghosts. Margot had aged more than any of my generation. We were still under forty but her hair was quite gray. Her face had lost its beauty—pinched out by her narrow, empty life. And yet as she stood on the porch to greet me, as I came up the walk to her house, there was much of the old charm about her. There are few women like her nowadays. I knew many in my childhood—the real heroes of the great war. The women who in the bitter days of reconstruction, bound up the wounds of defeat, bore almost all the burdens and laid the foundations of the new South. They were gracious women, in spite of their arrogant pride in their breed. They knew how to suffer and smile.

We sat side by side on the porch—leagues and leagues apart. I found it strangely hard to talk with her. She told, in her quiet colorless voice, all her news. Her mother had died several years before. Al was married and established in Memphis and so forth. Just as the supply of news ran out, a rooster awoke from some bad dream and crowed sleepily.

"Margot," I said, "do you still steal eggs?"

"O Arnold," she laughed, "haven't you forgotten that? I have—almost. A long time ago I paid mother back and I saved fifteen dollars out of my allowance and sent it to the Presbyterian church."

I had always considered myself a fairly honest man, but it had never occurred to me to make restitution for these childish thefts.

"It was awful," she went on, "why did we do it?"

"Margot," I said, "haven't you ever committed a worse sin than that?"

She fell suddenly serious. It was several minutes before she replied.

"Yes, Arnold, I've been discontented and rebellious."

I looked out at the village street, at the uninteresting houses, at the glare of the "general store" where liquor was sold and where doubtless Col. Jennings, illumined by the moonshine whiskey of our mountains, was recounting to a bored audience of loafers some details of one of Stonewall Jackson's charges. It was needless to ask what it was that made her discontented, against what she had been rebellious. And the deadly torpor of that village life seemed to settle about me like a cloud of suffocating smoke. There sat beside me this fine spirited woman—useless. Her glorious potentiality of motherhood unused. Defrauded of her birth-right—wasted! I had an impulse to jump up and shake my fist at it all. I wanted to tell her that her greatest sin had been not to revolt more efficiently. But that would have been cruel now that her hair was so gray.

"Do you know who has helped me most?" she asked. "Your uncle. He is a saint, Arnold. We are great friends now. He came here one time when father was sick. He has been a wonderful comfort to me. Sometimes I go and call on him. He's very lonely. And he's such a gallant old gentleman. When I see him drive by in his buckboard I always wave to him and as soon as he's out of sight I go over to the house and scold the niggers. They would never do any work if somebody did not fuss them. And you know it makes me more contented to watch him. I say to myself that if such a wonderful man, so wise and learned can find plenty to do to serve the Master in this little village there must be quite enough for just a woman like me. There's a heap of comfort in that thought. But sometimes I read some story or think about you all out in the big world and it seems very small here—and lonely."

There was nothing I could think to say, so again we were silent.

"Arnold," she said suddenly. "Do you ever read King Arthur stories any more?"

"Whenever I get five minutes," I replied. "The people I live with have a little girl—Marie. I'm teaching them to her."

"I'm so glad—and Froissart?"

She went into the house and brought out the old soiled volume. We looked through it together and then she said that perhaps I would want to take it East for Marie. But I had a feeling that she wished to keep it. So I said Marie was too young for Froissart yet. Once more we fell silent. I remember the open book on her thin knees, her thin aristocratic hand between the pages, the profile of her face. Lamp-light shone out through the window upon her and she looked almost beautiful again.

I am never sure of what is in a woman's heart. But I could not explain the constraint upon us except that perhaps she had always been waiting for my homecoming, still nourishing in her heart our childish love—still hoping. But there was nothing to hope. It was not in her power to conceive what I was. I was battered and scarred by fights she had never imagined, disillusioned of dreams she had never dreamed. I had left the village years ago—irrevocably. She would have been utterly lost in my world. At last, rather mournfully, I said "good night."

The next day the Father was on the porch when I came down. He greeted me with a sort of wistful expectancy in his eyes. And my cordial "good morning" did not seem to satisfy him. I did not understand until at breakfast.

"My son," he said, "I have often wished—it would have made me very happy—if you had married Margot." So he at least had hoped that this would be the result of my home-coming.

"She's a rare girl," he said, "a fine spirit. A good wife is a great help to a man in leading an upright life. A pillar of strength."

"The fates have denied me that help," I said. And I did not realize till too late the pagan form I had given my words.

But the match had been lighted. The Father did not believe that any good could come to a man except from the religion of Christ. Try as hard as I might I could not prevent the conversation from taking that turn. If he had loved me less we might have been better friends. But the only thing which mattered to him was the salvation of souls. And in proportion to his love for me he must needs seek my conversion. On the one point where we could not agree, his very affection made him insistent.

We both tried very hard to be sweet tempered about it. But I was in a difficult position. If I did not try to answer his arguments he thought I was convinced but unwilling to admit it. If I argued, it angered him. He would lose his temper and then be very apologetic about it. For an hour or so we would talk pleasantly of other things. Then inevitably the conversation would swing back to the subject he cared most about. After supper he at last brought things to a pass from which there was but one escape.

"My son," he said, "the day after to-morrow is the first Sunday in the month—Communion Sunday. You are still a member of my church, you have never asked to be relieved of the solemn responsibilities you took when you united with us. Will you join the rest of the members at the communion table?"

"I'm sorry, Father," I said, my heart suddenly hardening at the memory of the way I had been pushed into church membership. "I'll have to leave tomorrow night. I must be back at work early next week."

I had expected to stay longer. But for me to have gone to church and refused communion, would have been almost an insult to him. To have pretended to a faith I did not have, seemed to me a worse sort of a lie than the one I used. And so—having been home but two nights—I returned to the city and work.

# IX

Except for my vacations, I have missed very few working days in the Tombs since. And as the months have slipped along I have added steadily to my writings on criminology. To some it might seem a dreary life. It has not been so. There have been compensations.

The chief one has been the pleasant home in the Teepee. It would be easy to fill pages about it. But those who have been part of a loving family will know what I mean without my writing it. And it is past my power to paint it for those who have not shared it.

I recall especially the Christmas Eve when Marie was nine years old. Norman was at work at the table. Marie sat on my knee telling me some wonderful story. Nina came in from the kitchen where she and Guiseppe were concocting the morrow's feast. She sat down on the arm of my chair and said she had a secret to whisper in my ear. Norman looked up from his work and smiled.

"It's the one thing which has troubled her," he said. "Not having done her duty by the birth-rate but once."

The startled wonder came back again to Nina's eyes in those days. Even little Marie felt the "presence" among us and was awed.

But the fates had one more blow reserved for me. The year was just turning into spring when it fell. One morning at the Tombs, a court attendant called me to the telephone. It was Nina. Norman, she said in a frightened voice, was very sick. He had complained the day before of a cold and had gone to bed in the afternoon. I had not seen him that morning. When I reached the Teepee, he was delirious, in a high fever. We had no regular doctor, so I called up Ann on the telephone.

"It looks to me like pneumonia," I told her. "Can you send us a good doctor and a nurse?"

Within half an hour Ann had come herself with one of the city's most famous doctors.

Nina would not leave the bed-side. I waited for news in the library. It reminded me of the time, years before, when I had waited for a verdict on my eyes. I do not suppose that there are many friendships as ours had been. It is hard to believe that such relationships can be anything but permanent. It seemed impossible that I could lose Norman. But Ann made no pretense of hope. There was almost no chance she said. She telephoned out to her mother that she would be kept in town, and went back to the sickroom.

All the afternoon and all night long they fought it out. Sometimes when the suspense was too great I would go to the door. Nina sat with staring eyes at the head of the bed. Ann and the doctor were busy with ice-presses. At night-fall I gave Marie her supper and put her to bed in my room. She had become suddenly frightened and I sat beside her a long time, comforting her with stories of the Round Table, until at last she fell asleep.

Norman slept a little, but most of the time, tossed about deliriously—calling out to someone who was not there. "Oh Louise!" he would moan, "How can you believe that about me? I'm not spotless—but that isn't true. Don't think that of me. It's too cruel." But he got no comfort. The woman of his delirium was obdurate.

The dawn was just breaking when Ann came and told me he was

conscious. It was the end. Nina was kneeling beside him weeping silently. He smiled at me and tried to hold out his hand, but he was too weak.

"It's as though they had let me come back to say 'goodbye,'" he whispered. "Be good to them, Arnold—to Nina and Marie and the one that's coming. She's a good girl...." A look of wonder came into his eyes, with his last strength he stroked her hair.

"It's funny. I thought she was—just a toy—but she's got a soul, Arnold. Don't forget that, old man. Promise me"—I gripped his hand—"Oh yes. I know you'll be good to her. I know—that's all right. Poor little girl. I wish she wouldn't cry so.—I'd like to kiss her once more"—Ann lifted her up so that he might kiss her. "There! There! Little one. You mustn't cry. It's not so bad as all that. Arnold'll take care of you. Good luck—all of you. Don't be afraid.... I'm...."

It was a queer funeral. Some of his relatives, who had cut him since his marriage, came. It was on a Sunday so the Studenten Verein could turn out. Mrs. O'Hara, whose coal he had bought for seven years, came with her eight children. So did our washerwoman, Frau Zimmer, with her epileptic son. Guiseppe rode in the front carriage with Nina, Marie and I, and cried more than any of us. The Studenten Männer Chor sang a dirge. In the motley crowd I saw a man in the costume of an Episcopalian clergyman. As they were dispersing, he came up to me.

"I am unknown to you, sir," he said, "I want to tell you that I believe in immortality—and that I am sure your friend is sitting on the right-hand of our Heavenly Father. I hope to be worthy to meet him again. He was so good that I am surprised that he escaped crucifixion. I am only one of many whom he pulled out of hell. I can not...."

He burst into tears and disappeared into the crowd. Somehow, out of all the tributes to Norman which poured in on me in those days, the incoherent words of this unknown clergyman touched me most. What his story was, how Norman had helped him, I have no idea.

When we got back to the Teepee, we found Ann there, she had put things in order for us. She took Nina to bed and gave her something to make her sleep. Then she joined me in the library. She picked up her hat to go away, but I detained her. And so we sat together through the afternoon. As I remember we talked very little—except for some directions she gave me about Nina's health. At twilight Guiseppe came in with Marie, whom he had taken for a walk in the park. We all had supper together. Ann helped me put Marie to bed and then she went away.

It was very comforting, having just lost one friend, to refind another. There has been no ripple of estrangement between us since. Our love relation has been the anchor—the steadfast thing—of my later life.

Norman's will left a comfortable annuity to Nina and the children, the rest went into his educational endowment. I am a trustee of both sums. I think they have both been administered as he would have wished.

The baby was a boy. Nina told me that long before its father died, they had arranged, if it was a boy, to name it after me. I would have preferred to have called it Norman. One evening, as I was writing in the library, I glanced up from my paper. Nina was nursing the youngster, there were tears on her cheeks.

"What's wrong?" I asked.

"Oh! I wish he could have lived to see the man-child. Sometimes I was afraid he might grow tired of me. But he would have loved his son—always. I wish he could have seen him."

But I wish that Norman could have lived to see Nina. I had always a feeling that he did not entirely appreciate her. She has developed greatly since his death. Not long afterwards I began to notice long and serious Italian conversations between her and Guiseppe. And I asked him one day, jokingly, what they found to talk about so earnestly.

"I am teaching her, Mister Arnold, how to be a lady. Now that their father, who was a gentleman, is dead, it is necessary that the mother of the children should be a lady."

Guiseppe is too much of a Republican and Nina too little of a snob for these words to have anything but the noblest meanings.

"It is difficult for a simple man like me," he went on. "But have I not been a soldier of liberty on two continents? I have seen many fine ladies and I tell her about them. And also I have read books."

Nina as well has taken to reading. Painfully she has recalled the lessons of her brief school days. Of course I have helped her all I could. She has taken the responsibilities of motherhood in a way she would scarcely have done if Norman had lived.

It was perhaps a year after his death, that I came home one evening and found Nina in a great flurry. On tiptoe, her finger on her lips, she led me into the library and closed the door.

"Oh! my friend," she said, "you will not be angry? There's a woman in my room. Such a sad old woman. She is very drunk. I found her downstairs— in the hallway. There were boys teasing her. At first I was frightened and ran upstairs. Then I remembered how he would never leave anyone so. I brought her up to my room. You will not be angry?"

She has turned the Teepee into an informal sort of a rescue mission. I never know whom I will find in my favorite chair. Sometimes they have delirium tremens and shriek all night. At first I was worried about the effect on the children. But Nina and Ann said it would do them no harm. I cannot see that it has. One thing about it has impressed me immensely. It has often happened in my work that I have brought home a boy or a man from the Tombs and let them sleep on the divan till some better place was found for them. Not infrequently these guests have departed without formalities, taking as mementoes any silver spoons they found at hand. Not one of Nina's women have stolen anything. It passes my understanding.

Nina has a great admiration for Ann, but does not understand her at all. She cannot conceive of the reasons why Ann refuses to get married. It is a thing to philosophize about, the attitude of these two women towards matrimony. They are both good women, yet to one marriage seems a degradation and serfdom, to the other marriage meant escape from the mire, emancipation from the most abysmal slavery the world has ever known. Watching them has helped me understand many of life's endless paradoxes.

The only new thing which has come into my life since Norman's death has been the children. I am legal guardian for Nina's two. And several years ago, when Billy—Ann's nephew—grew to high school age, she turned him over to me, fearing that all-woman household might not be the best place for a growing boy. So he came to the Teepee, going to school in the city, spending only his week-ends at Cromley.

My work in the Tombs goes on as ever. A new prison has been built, with cleaner corridors, roomier cells, sanitary plumbing and so forth. But the old tragedy goes on just the same. My title has been changed from county detective to probation officer, and I have been given some assistants. Certainly there has been improvement. The rougher edges of justice have been worn off. But the bandage is still over the eyes of the goddess. The names of the judges have changed, but the inherent viciousness of their situation is unaltered. There is now, just as when I started, ten times as much work as I can do to even alleviate the manifold cruelties of the place. It is still —in spite of the new building—called the Tombs.

And Suzanne? If anyone should ask me what has become of her, I would have to reply by a question—"Which Suzanne?" I have seen very little of the one who came back to America. Once or twice I have encountered her in public meetings. Three years after I came back from Europe, I received her wedding cards—an architect named Stone. I knew him slightly. He seems to be very much in love with his wife. One comes across their names in the papers quite frequently. They are active socialists. But Mrs. Stone is a strange and rather unreal personality to me.

But there is the other Suzanne, her of the slim, boyish form, who tried to learn to throw stones like a man and was vexed when I laughed at her, the

Suzanne who loved the poppies, the Suzanne of our earnest discussions, the Suzanne who was a prophetess, the enthusiastic apostle of the new faith, who like Deborah of old, sang songs of the great awakening to come, and the Suzanne of Moret—whom I loved. She still lives. I cannot see that the passing years have in any way dimmed the vision. Mrs. Stone is getting matronly, her hair is losing its luster. Suzanne is still straight and slender. There are moments when she comes to me out of the mystery of dreams and, sitting on the floor, rests her head—her fearless head—on my knees. I run my fingers through her amazing hair and try to capture the fitful light of the fire, which glows there, now so golden, now so red.... And as the dream is sweet, so is the awakening bitter.

# BOOK VII

I come now to the last section of my book. There can be no doubt that it must be about the children.

As I get older, in spite of my best intentions, the work in the Tombs grows mechanical. Each new prisoner has of course his individual peculiarities, but I find myself frequently saying: "It's like a case I had back in 1900." And it is the same with my writing. It is mostly a re-statement—I hope a continually better and more forceful statement—of conclusions I have held for many years.

The light of these later yeans has been my vicarious parentage—these three young adventurers who call me, "Daddy." I suppose I look at them with an indulgent eye, magnifying their virtues, ignoring their limitations. But they seem very wonderful to me. Thinking of them, watching them, make me sympathize with Moses on Nebo's lonely mountain. Through them I catch glimpses of a fairer land than I have known, which I win neverenter.

On his eighteenth birthday, Billy asked me why I was not a socialist. I knew he was leaning that way. He is an artist. Ann wanted him to go to college, but he broke away to the classes at Cooper Union. Now at twenty-four he is bringing home prizes and gold medals which he pretends to despise. Many of his artist chums are socialists. I tried to get him into an argument on the subject, but, as is his way, he would not argue. He would only ask me questions. What did I think about this? What did I think about that?

About a week later at breakfast; he handed me a little red card, which was his certificate of membership in the party.

"You can't join till you're eighteen," he said. "You see, Daddy, I don't think a chap can ever paint anything, do anything worth while in art, unless he believes in something besides himself—something bigger. I don't know anything bigger than this faith in the people."

He had a pretty bad time of it the next Sunday at Cromley. His grandmother is such a seasoned warrior for anarchism, that she has as little tolerance for socialists as our "best people" would have for her. Ann was neutral, for she holds that what one believes matters not half so much as the way one believes it. And I would do nothing to dampen the youngster's ardor. It is amazing to me. He has the faith to look at our state legislature and believe in democracy, to look at the Tombs and believe in justice.

In fact I have sometimes thought of joining his party. I would like to enter as closely into his life as possible. But all this talk of revolution repulses me. It is the impatience of youth. The world does not move fast enough for them—they forget that it moves at all. But it has spun a long, long way even in my life.

I recall our fight for a reformatory. It ended in fiasco. But it was only the beginning of a movement. Baldwin was a man who held on. Before long he had persuaded a western state to try his scheme. To-day there are more than thirty of our states with reformatories for boys. The later ones, better than Baldwin's dream. And then this probation system. It is the biggest blow ever dealt to the old idea of the Tombs. Of course it is having growing pains. The special advocates of the system are distressed because of the hundreds of probation officers only a few are efficient. Give it time.

And of broader import is the awakening of democracy in the land. It will take a generation or more before historians can properly adjudge this movement. To-day we see only sporadic demonstrations of it, speeches here and there, in favor of referendum and so forth. The real issue often veiled by the personalities of candidates. The noise is only the effervescence of a great idea, a great aspiration, which is taking form in the mind of the nation.

The country is ten times as thoughtful about social problems as it was when my generation began. Recently the legislature made an appropriation to give me a new assistant in the Tombs. I wrote to several colleges and a dozen men applied for the job. I could take my pick. Twelve men out of one year's college crop! I was a pioneer.

And young Fletcher, the man I chose, asked me the other day, what I thought of Devine's book, "The Causes of Misery." He is beginning work on the basis of that book. And Devine speaks of "The Abolition of Poverty" as if it was a commonplace. No one dared to dream that poverty could be abolished when I was a young man. We thought it was an indivisible part of civilization. I remember when I first heard Jacob Riis talk of abolishing the slums! I thought he was a dreamer. The tenement house department reports that a million new homes have been built in the city—under the new law—with no dark rooms. And the abolition of tuberculosis! Why I can remember a cholera epidemic! These young socialists do not realize what we have done.

Last summer I took Nina and Marie and young Arnold, he is ten now, down on the Maine coast to an island where Billy and some of his artist friends have a camp. As I mingled with this colony of ardent young people, in spite of the sympathy, which real friendship with Billy has given me for them, I felt like a stranger. I am sure they think I am an old fogey. My mind kept jumping back to my own youth, comparing them with what I had been at their age. In so many ways they were better men than I was, better equipped for life.

I remember especially one conversation with Billy. He had just finished a canvas as the twilight was falling. I think it is the finest thing he has done yet. There is a stretch of surf in the foreground and beyond the islands rise higher and higher to the peak of Mount Desert. I cannot describe it beyond these barren details. Somehow he has accentuated the rising upward lines, by some magic of his color he has infused the thing with immense emotion.

"What are you going to call it?" I asked as he was putting up his tubes.

"It hasn't any name," he said. "It's just a feeling I get sometimes—up here with the sea and the mountains." He pondered it a moment, seeking words. He is not a ready talker. "I think it's one of the psalms," he said at last, "you know the one that begins: 'I will lift up mine eyes unto the hills, from whence cometh my help.' It's sort of religious—being all by one's self and looking up."

"What is your religion, Billy?" I asked.

He sat silent, stopped arranging his brushes and looked off at the last of the sunlight on the summit of the mountain.

"Have you got one?" I persisted.

"Oh, yes," he said quickly. "Yes—at least sometimes it comes to me. There are days on end when it doesn't come—barren days. And then again it comes very strong. I haven't any name for it. I think the trouble with most religions is that people try to define them. It doesn't seem to fit into words."

Again he was busy with his kit. But when everything was ready, instead of starting home, he sat down again.

"It's funny," he said, "I'm quite sure you can't talk about religion satisfactorily. But we all want to. And as soon as you try to put it into words some of it escapes—the best part of it. I think that's why painting appeals to me. You can say things with colors you can't with words.

"You remember those reproductions, I showed you, of Felicien Rops, the

Belgium etcher. You didn't like them. I don't either. He's wonderfully clever —My God! I wish I could draw like that man—but I don't think it's art. I don't think he ever looked upward—lifted up his eyes to the hills. I guess my religion is just that indescribable something which changes craftsmanship into art. I want to draw well, I want my color to be right, I want technique—all I can get of it. But even if I was perfect in all these, I would have to lift up my eyes unto the hills for help before I could do the real thing—the thing I want to do."

"And when you lift up your eyes, Billy," I asked, "who is it that gives you help?"

He spoke rather reluctantly after a moment's pause.

"That's the trouble with talking religion. You get mixed up between the figurative and the literal. Does it really matter Who—or Where? I don't think of any person up there in the afterglow on the mountain top. There doesn't have to be any hills even. Sometimes I get 'help' in my studio—with nothing to look up to but the white-washed lights and the rafters.

"We all need 'help' and when we get it—we've 'got religion.' It's all so vague that we have to use symbols. One person has associated 'help' with high mass and choir boys and tawdry images. Another gets his connection by listening to a village quartet murder 'Nearer my God to Thee.' When Nelson was over illustrating that book on Egypt he learned the Mohammedan 'Call to Prayer.' It's a weird sing-song thing. There are millions of people who, when they hear that, get the feeling that they need 'help' and chase round to the Mosque. I haven't found anything more suggestive than those words of King David.

"Sometimes my pictures are rotten and I sign them 'William Barton.' Once in a long while I paint one that is better,—better than my brush tricks, better than my technique, better than just me—and I always put a little star after my name. It means 'this picture was painted by William Barton and God.' That's my religion."

"It's all summed up in that old Jewish song—'I will lift up mine eyes unto the hills, from whence cometh my help.' Do you know it?"

Yes. I knew it. I sat in the Father's study, all one fine afternoon, when the other boys were playing ball, and learned that song by rote, in punishment for upsetting his inkwell. It seems very wonderful to me that the Bible should seem a thing of beauty to a youngster. It was at best an unpleasant piece of drudgery for me—more often a form of chastisement. What stirs the deepest emotions in Billy's heart, only reminds me of a blot of ink on the Father's desk and the shouts of the boys out in the street whom I might not join.

I had been suspecting for some time that although Billy and Marie both call me "Daddy," they were coming to realize that they are not brother and sister. My suspicions were confirmed the other day by Nina. She asked me solemnly what I thought of Billy. And when I declared that he was the straightest, cleanest, finest youngster I knew, she said.

"Perhaps. But he is not as fine as Norman was."

I said that God had apparently mislaid the mold in which He had cast Norman.

"I wish that Marie could have as good a husband as I did—she's a better girl."

Nina has immense respect for her daughter. And Marie deserves it. A habit of philosophizing forces me to realize that the greatest part of the world has failed to appreciate, has in fact utterly ignored the existence of, this marvelous foster daughter of mine. There are, doubtless, many parents who even if they had had the good fortune to know Marie would stubbornly prefer their own daughters. But if I were twenty years younger, I would certainly enter the race against Billy. She gets her looks from her mother—pure Lombard—but she has inherited Norman's irreverent, incisive vision and his tricks of speech. She decided to follow her father's chief interest and now, at nineteen, is attending a kindergarten normal school.

But the thing, for which I give Marie my highest reverence is her attitude to her mother. She knows the truth. I found that they had talked this over before Norman died. It was his wish that she should not be told by strangers. And so nothing was hidden from her, no questions were evaded and she grew into the knowledge of her mother's story, with as little shock as she learned the multiplication table. It is very sweet to watch them together, this quiet, sad eyed old woman, who can write with difficulty and this superbly modern girl, who has had every advantage of education. Marie has sense enough to know that very, very few people have been blest with finer mothers.

A few nights after this talk with Nina, I found Marie alone in the library reading a red paper covered book by Earl Krautsky—"The Road to Power." Across the corner, in his big, boyish handwriting, was scrawled, "William Barton."

"Marionette," I said, thinking of what her mother had said, "Do you believe in free love?"

"Not for a minute," she snapped, "it's just another of your man tricks to get the better of your superiors."

Marie is a suffragette. But her jibe at me did not satisfy her. The thing was evidently on her mind. She came over and sat on the arm of my chair.

"Don't laugh at me, Daddy. It's so serious. I think it's all wrapped up in the big woman question. How can there be any real freedom except among equals? In the bottom of my heart I think it is a beautiful ideal. If I were in love with a man, I'd just want to be with him. It seems a little degrading to take a justice of the peace into one's confidence in so private a matter. I would feel ashamed to tell a stranger I was going to love my sweetheart. And in a sense I like the idea of freedom. It would be horrible to have my husband kiss me because it was the law; because he'd promised to—if he didn't really want to.

"But that's only a private personal view of it. It doesn't seem to me the important thing, what the politicians call 'the main issue.' This trying to be individually free, this fussing over individual rights, seems sort of early

Victorian...."

"What," I interrupted, "you wouldn't call Ann—one of the first women to win distinction in a profession—you wouldn't call her Early Victorian?"

"Well. I don't mean Ann. She's an exception. No, she isn't either. I mean her, too. Nowadays we think of things socially. It doesn't matter so much whether I'm free, whether I get justice, it's the others—the race—we must work for. Ann's wonderful. You know how much I love her. But she don't look at things the way we do.

"We must think not only of the few women, here and there, the giants like Ann, who are strong enough to stand alone, but of all the women—and the children. That's just the point. We're trying to learn how not to stand alone —how to stand together. We've got to ignore our own preferences and rights and learn to fight for woman's rights.

"Doesn't most of the prostitution come from the free love of weak girls? Even when the cadets go after them just to make money, isn't it love on the girl's part? What they think is love? We must fight and fight and fight to make women realize that they mustn't love just for themselves. That it isn't right towards the race for them to love blindly—that it's a sin, a social sin, for us to love until we're sure of ourselves, sure of the man, sure for the children. It's a sin for a woman to sacrifice herself to a man just because she loves him—a sin even to take risks.

"Somehow, until we've won freedom and equality and independence, we've got to insist on guarantees. I don't see how we can get them except through laws, through old-fashioned marriages. We women who are stronger, and better educated and able to support ourselves and children, we must always think of the others who are less fortunate. And as long as you men take advantage of any of our sisters, we won't listen to your free love talk. So there!"

"Daddy," she said after she had rested her cheek against mine for a while. "I'll tell you a secret. Ssh! Don't you ever breathe it! Do you know whom we suffragists have to fight? It's women! If it was only you men, we'd have won long ago. It isn't the men who enslave us. It's tradition and habit. Long training had made us selfish—divided—weak.

"Just take the worst case. It's mother's story all over again—all the time. She tried to get away. Half a dozen men, instinctively, acted together, for their common interest—and were strong. They didn't reason it out. Blackie did not have to say to them, you help me beat my girl, and I'll help you beat yours and so we'll keep them all scared. It's a long inherited tradition with men to act together like that, second nature—almost an instinct. But when a cadet beats a girl, do the other girls rush together like that and fight for their common interest? No. Each one for herself sneaks off and tries to placate her man. It's just the same with 'respectable' people. If a woman tries to be free, the men are all against her with their legislatures and courts and all that. Do the other women stand together to help her? Oh, no. They cut her. Just like the prostitutes, they try to ingratiate themselves with their husbands by spitting at the one who tried to be free.

"If we women were only civilized enough really to co-operate, to stick together, shoulder to shoulder—oh, we'd put you men in your place quick enough. Individualism, trying to stand alone, is the worst enemy women can have to-day. We've got to learn how to use our united strength.

"And we are learning—too. Remember that big shirtwaist strike? It was wonderful the way the girls stuck together. I don't believe that any time before in the history of this old world women have stood by each other like that—with such loyalty. A lot of your stupid men-papers, had editorials wondering why up-town society women took so much interest in the strike. Why, even the rich suffragists have sense enough to know that solidarity is ten times more important than the vote. If you men only give us a long, hard fight for it, make us throw stones and slap policemen and go to jail and all that, we'll learn this lesson of standing together and then we'll know how to use the franchise when we get it. Oh! The time is coming, Daddy. Watch out."

"I'm not frightened." I said, "If I was as near to thirty as I am to fifty, I guess I would be an enthusiastic suffragetter. Anything you wanted would look good to me. Do you think I would have had any chance if I had encountered you when I was young enough to be your lover?"

"I wonder what you were like, Daddy, twenty years ago—just when I WAS beginning. Oh, I guess I would have liked you. But even if I did, I would have sent a lawyer to you with a long contract, specifying my various and sundry privileges and your corresponding duties. Then I would have led you down to the City Hall and made you sign each and every article with a big oath. How would you have liked that?"

"I'd have submitted joyfully."

Her arm tightened about my neck.

"And do you know what I would have done then, Daddy?" she asked after a moment's silence. "I guess—just as soon as we were alone—I'd have torn up that contract into little pieces. And I'd have said, 'Oh, My Lord and Master, be humble to me in public, for the sake of all my poor sisters who are afraid—but here in private, please, trample on me some. And oh! if you love me—make me darn your socks.'

"Oh Daddy, that's the heart-break of it all"—there was a catch in her voice—"That's what's hard. We know that we must fight for our freedom and equality—for the other women's sake. And all the while—if we are in love—what our heart cries out for is a ruler. We want to serve."

I think when I get a chance I will tell Billy to show his muscle now and then.

So this is where I am today. My experiment in ethics? It has failed. I can no more surely distinguish right from wrong today, than when I was a boy in school.

My best efforts landed Jerry—innocent—in prison. The one time when I violated every rule I had laid down for my guidance in the Tombs, when I lied profusely, played dirty politics, compounded a felony, and went on a man-hunt, with hate in my heart, I disposed of the pimp Blackie, freed Nina, gave happiness to Norman. Marie is the result.

Certainly one of the best things in my life has been Ann's love. It came to me without any striving on my part, it has been in no way a reward for effort or aspiration. Step by step it has seemed to me wrong. I do not believe in free love. I cannot justify it any more than I could stealing eggs when I was a boy. It was something I wanted and which I took. Yet I am quite sure it has been good.

On the other hand, the time when I strove hardest to reach a higher plane, when I was most anxious to be upright and honorable, those days I spent in France with Suzanne, resulted in the most bitter pain, the most dismal failure of my life. This is not a little thing to me, even after all these years. The days come when I must open my trunk, take out her rucksac and the map —the only mementos I have of her—they are days of anguish. Why should it not have been? My life seems bitter and of small worth when I think of what it might have been with her.

I am as much at a loss today in regard to moral values as I ever was. I have little hope left of succeeding in my experiment. This is the sad thing. The good fight has been a long one. From the continued campaigning, I am prematurely spent. Under fifty, I am prematurely old. The *élan* of youth is gone.

At the Hotel des Invalides in Paris they tell the story of a war-scarred crippled veteran of the Napoleonic wars. His breast was covered with service medals. At one of the annual inspections a young commander complimented on his many decorations. "My General," the old soldier replied, "I can no longer carry a musket, it would have been better to have died gloriously at Austerlitz."

I am far from the sad pass of this decrepit veteran, yet his story touches me nearly. The best days have flown. I have lived intensely. Into each combat whether the insignificant skirmish of my daily work, or the more decisive battles—I have thrown myself with spendthrift energy. I do not regret this attitude towards life. I am glad I met its problems face to face—with passionate endeavor. But the price must be paid. Nowadays I have little ardor left. The youthful questing spirit is gone—and I have not found the Holy Grail.

Perhaps these young people are right. I may have started wrong—in trying to find the truth for myself alone. Perhaps there are no individualistic ethics. They may find the answer expressed in social terms. Perhaps. But I have no energy left to begin the experiment again.

But once more I must repeat, I do not regret my manner of life. We are offered but two choices; to accept things as they are or to strive passionately for new and better forms. Defeat is not shameful. But supine complaisance surely is.

Out of the lives of all my generation a little increment of wisdom has come to the race. Neither the renaissance, nor the reformation seem to me as fundamental changes as we have wrought. We have made the nation suddenly conscious of itself. We have not cured its ills, but at least we have made great strides in diagnosis. And my experiment—in its tiny, coral-insect way—has been an integral part in this increment of wisdom.

I am more optimistic today than ever before. And if I wish to live on—as I surely do—it is to watch these youngsters in their struggle for the better form. How much better equipped they are than we were, how much clearer they see!

I think of myself as I left college—so afraid of life that I was glad to find shelter among old books. I recall how strange seemed that first dinner in the Children's House with Norman. And then I think of Billy. Why! The knowledge of life those pioneer settlement workers were just beginning to discover are conversational commonplaces among Billy's friends. The abolition of poverty!

The vision comes to me of Margot, delicate, fragile, ignorant—too ignorant to be afraid. All the wisdom of the ages—past and future—seemed to her to be bound up in the King James version. I compare her with Marie. She is as strong as a peasant girl. I have given up playing tennis with her, she beats me too easily. And the certain, fearless way she looks out at life takes my breath, leaves me panting just as her dashing net play does. She speaks of Ann as early Victorian, she would I fear place Margot as Elizabethan.

Most wonderful of all, these youngsters have never had to fight with God, never had to tear themselves to pieces escaping from the deadly formalism and tyranny of Church Dogma. They never had to call themselves Atheists.

And then I think of how Billy and Marie are facing this biggest problem of all—this business of love. They will have their squalls no doubt and run into shoal water perhaps. But they are not blindfolded as I was, as Norman was—as all my generation was. Pure luck was all that could save us. They are steering—not drifting.

Yes. My story is ended. The old troupe has been crowded off the stage. There would be little interest in writing of the work left me—brushing the wigs of the leading man, packing the star's trunk,—pushing the swan for Lohengrin, currying the horses of the Walkyrie—it will all be behind the scene.

And how I envy them their faith! Ave—

Juventas—morituri salutamus!

\*    \*    \*    \*    \*    \*    \*    \*